AF428160

Praise for *Unwrapping*

Others have shared the techniques and theory of the art of care; Gura is the only one that I know of who has brought that carefully honed practice into proper focus with the dramatic perspective it deserves. What could be more amazing, surprising or compelling than people helping each other along their way through life?

– Gary Gunderson, M.Div., D.Min., D.Div.
Professor, Faith and the Health of the Public,
School of Divinity,
Wake Forest University
Winston-Salem, NC

It's difficult to find a book that is teaching vital information while absorbing the reader simultaneously into a story, allowing our imagination to take us there. Gura found the middle world between reading enjoyment, learning about hard and triggering topics, and tools that can be utilized for learning.

– Laneita Williamson, R.N., B.S.N.
Trauma-informed Care Manager,
Winston-Salem, NC

More Praise for *Unwrapping*

I absolutely loved this novel! So many different storylines. The characters are real and their stories are true. I feel for them.

– Maria Teresa Jones, M.Div., B.C.C.
Spiritual Director and Dreamwork Facilitator
Ceiba, Puerto Rico

Take intriguing plot twists, romantic angst and generational trauma, and you get *Unwrapping*. I came away with deep empathy for Gura's well-developed characters. An informed, touching read.

– Sherry L. Allen, L.P.C., N.C.C.
Owner and Principal Therapist, GrowSteady
Nashville, TN

Unwrapping

a novel about generational trauma

Leslie Gura

Paths to Peace Publishing
Winston-Salem, North Carolina

Winston-Salem, NC

Copyright © 2026 by Leslie Gura
Library of Congress Control Number 2024934230
Gura, Leslie
Unwrapping
cover illustration by Richard Boyd

Print ISBN: 9798994279120

Ebook ISBN: 9798994279113

Printed in the United States of America

FIRST EDITION

All rights reserved. No part of this book
may be reproduced in any manner whatsoever
without written permission from the author.

www.lesliegura.com

Dedication

To my wife, Terrie, whose unwavering encouragement
and support means everything.
To my children, Alex and Sydney, for making me proud
in their independence.
To my dog, Nilla, who blessed our family with fourteen years
of unconditional love before going to the
Rainbow Bridge.
And, finally, to my clients—past, present and future—
for the bravery it takes to pick up the phone,
walk into the office and sit in that chair.

Contents

Foreword

I've had the privilege of serving as a behavioral health clinical provider and executive leader for the last quarter century in North Carolina and now in Washington state and have seen the evolution of clinical theory during that time. From psychoanalysis to family systems, from behavioral analysis to cognitive approaches, different theories have had their day in the sun, and each has left an indelible mark on the world of counseling and psychotherapy. All have their own camps of solidarity and loyal followers. Many eclectic therapists, like myself, find value from all of these theoretical approaches, and we seek to blend the best practices from the collective whole to deal with the specific problem presented by the person in treatment sitting in front of us.

Today, behavioral health is in a metamorphosis. We are recognized as a key healthcare priority for addressing chronic medical conditions and improving impacts of social drivers of health. And there is new emphasis on trauma, derived from a 1990s study on "adverse childhood experiences," which concluded that such experiences in childhood lead to an increased potential of facing chronic medical conditions such as obesity, diabetes and chronic heart failure. Follow-up studies continue to confirm this truth for a variety of mental health conditions, too, such as depression, anxiety, bipolar disorder, substance use, and victim or perpetrator of physical, sexual and psychological abuse.

Intuitively, counselors and therapists have known this for decades. As one supervisor in my world has said, "We are all a result of our collective traumas." That's not necessarily a bad thing, as we can also build resiliency skills through difficult experiences when there is appropriate support and the right tools are made available and practiced.

As you read the following pages, becoming increasingly interested in the ongoing iteration of the life narratives that Les Gura paints, you will see many facets of the trauma influence on our life. You will see reference to "Big T" and "little t" traumas, which, regardless of their differences, can have ongoing and similar impacts.

Les Gura has done a fantastic job of imagining the intricate details of the trauma histories and current life realities of the characters in *Unwrapping*. Read it and know that you will reflect on your own history, present and future— and that can be a good thing!

– Bryan Hatcher, M.S.W., Dr.P.H.,
Chief Behavioral Health Innovations Officer,
Blue Ridge Health,
Hendersonville, NC

Author's Note

The developing brain has an amazing capacity to absorb information, but there were moments in school growing up when I felt overwhelmed. When this occurred, although I don't recall the exact process, I do know that I usually turned to writing. I would take notes from a textbook using my own language, to break down the confusing parts in a way I could understand.

This might have been the start of my writing life. I grew to value words and language and was blessed by speed—from taking notes to typing to conceptualizing stories. These skills served me well through nearly thirty years as a journalist, followed by eight years of communications and marketing. In the latter field, I often found myself bored, becoming disconnected from "purpose." It's what led me to my new, and hopefully final, (though I would never say never) career.

It was the fall of 2021. I had obtained my graduate degree in clinical mental health counseling (three years), completed a residency program in psychotherapy and spirituality (two years) and embarked on a fellowship program (one year) focused on trauma, during which time I would also, separately, receive training in Eye Movement Desensitization and Reprocessing (EMDR). I began to feel overwhelmed, just like when I was a kid attending P.S. 69 in Jackson Heights, Queens.

And so I turned to writing again to help me regain a sense of control of the information flooding my system. This time, however, rather than simply take notes, I had a different idea. Why couldn't I use the information, especially relating to trauma, which was so evident in many of my clients, to tell a story of counselor and client. I was inspired by Dr. Irving Yalom, a psychiatrist whose therapy-based fiction was required reading in Wake Forest University's master's program for counseling, as well as the television show *In Treatment*, which depicted the relationship between a therapist and several clients.

My thought was to focus a story on the therapeutic relationship and the growth that occurs between client and clinician when the process works well. I could apply the modern concepts I'd been learning about trauma treatment—including elements of sensorimotor psychotherapy, internal family systems theory and my own base system of narrative therapy.

I did not know what to expect when I began writing. I'd written two novels previously, neither of which had been published. I only wanted to untangle the concepts in my head. But as the story continued to develop, I realized I was making the very connections with my characters that I make in my office with clients.

All this being said, *Unwrapping* is a work of fiction, and the characters and their stories were created solely from my imagination. I have seen clients with many different and difficult traumas, but none of their stories in any way matches those of the characters in this book, which I set in the city of Durham, North Carolina, ninety minutes away from Winston-Salem, where I live and practice.

The story weaves together the components of generational trauma that have affected the dual protagonists of the story, often using flashbacks, seen in italics mode. The same technique is used at times with other characters. Because a therapeutic relationship works best when it benefits client and therapist, I also wrote the therapy sessions in third person to give each protagonist equal weight, then turned to first person for each in their individual "post-session" thoughts.

One of my secondary goals in writing the book beyond helping me conceptualize trauma is to further destigmatize talk therapy in general. I envision readers enjoying this story and also becoming informed at least a little about the therapeutic process.

Prologue: Before

Lilah was walking to the subway from her job as a seamstress in one of the few remaining factories in Manhattan's garment district the day she met Patrick Hanrahan. She was earning minimum wage and lived with her mother, just the two of them the past sixteen years, since Kevin Flynn walked out. Her green print dress was worn but her embarrassment about being seen in it was eased by the fact that it hid her knobby knees and accentuated her nicely shaped chest. A black kerchief kept most of her red hair hidden except for the wisps escaping behind her ears.

Lilah didn't look forward to squeezing into the filthy, graffiti-laden D train and hoped no one would grope her. Almost on cue to her subway worries, a group of men across the street chirped at her and at another young woman walking briskly just behind her dressed more stylishly in blue jeans and a faux satin white blouse. Lilah kept her head down, but her peripheral vision caused her heart to skip a beat.

A wiry six-footer with a mop of brownish red curls atop a sweat and dirt-streaked gray t-shirt was approaching. Lilah realized she was the object of this guy's attention, not the girl in blue jeans. She inspected him more closely.

"Hey!" He looked back at his work buddies and winked.

"Hi." She swallowed the word and barely looked at him. Clearly, neither of them was silver-tongued.

A sudden thought intruded for Lilah. She desperately wanted to break her cycle of boredom. Up and out the apartment by 7, downtown by 8, working by 8:30, calling it a day at 5:30 (or 6:30 or 7:30 if production quota wasn't made), back down into the subway and home. Scrounge something out of nothing from the fridge and share a worn sofa with Mom listening to her bitch about either her father or Mr. Skudera, the skeevy building superintendent with bad breath who Mom believed had the hots for her.

Lilah hadn't been out in weeks. Mom wouldn't let her go anywhere by herself. And they didn't have a car. Could spending time with someone nearer her age be any worse than becoming a bitter, lonely woman like Mom?

"Name's Patrick. You work around here?"

"Yes I do." Lilah pointed to a brown brick structure across the street. "Meyer's. I sew. I'm Lilah."

"What are you, 18?"

She nodded.

"Ha! Nailed it. Listen, I gotta get back with my team. Edison crew. And lunch is almost up. Wanna share a phone number, Lilah?"

Lilah was confused. "Lunch?"

"Yeah. Swing shift. Won't get off til near midnight. But Friday's a half day."

Something about that twinkly smile. And the fact that once he was talking with her, he didn't look back to his buddies anymore. She reached into her purse for a pen, grabbed his hand and impulsively scrawled the number on his palm. Something in her hoped he thought that was sexy.

When the phone rang that night, Lilah flew off the couch to get it before Mom could, and even stretched the cord as far as it would go around the corner into the kitchen, because she sensed Mom listening. Lilah heard the slur in Patrick's voice and instinctively recognized it. Mom had complained constantly that her father left because he loved alcohol more than he loved them. Patrick, though, readily acknowledged he'd been drinking with his buddies. He said she should come out with them Friday and she'd see drinking was fun. "It'll lighten you up after a long day of work."

She lied to her mom that first night, telling her she was meeting a friend to look at a possible new apartment. Patrick took her to O'Reilly's Pub by Herald Square. Everyone knew him there; he said he and his crew had been on a long-term job involving upgrades around Macy's and Gimbel's. She tried a beer and did a shot. It was her first alcohol since coming of legal age. When she told Patrick she had to get home because her mother would call the cops if she wasn't back by 11, he winked at his friends, and they all serenaded her goodbye. Then he hailed a cab and gave her a $20 bill.

"Take this beautiful lass home, squire," he said to the cabbie.

Lilah giggled. Until that moment, she'd never had a cab ride in her life. He leaned into her as she stepped in, put his strong arm around her waist and planted a wet kiss on her lips, running a rough hand through her red locks. "You're a keeper," he whispered. "I'll call you and we'll really do it up next week."

***

Lilah spent the next Friday night playing gin rummy and listening to Mom's incessant coughing as her cigarette smoke plumed around them. She took a couple of cigarettes herself, a habit she hated but couldn't drift from between Mom and the girls at work.

It was Sunday afternoon when the phone rang, and Patrick sheepishly told her that he and the boys had gone bowling Thursday night and they had Friday off that week and the weekend had gotten away from him. He apologized. She accepted it.

He showed up at her job and treated her to a hotdog lunch on Tuesday, and they made plans for that Friday. She would meet him at the apartment he shared with three of his coworkers in Alphabet City.

She wore a royal blue dress that accentuated her hair and a matching blue beret. When she rang the buzzer and walked up, she was struck by the grime along the stairway. She knew that it was no different than her own, and she felt embarrassed at judging Patrick for where he lived. He might be a few years older, but everyone had their issues. He gestured her to sit down at the wooden dinette table. He was wearing a white tank undershirt and jeans. Lilah had overdressed.

"Lemme pour you a shot. Catch you up."

Lilah didn't know what to do. She didn't particularly like the whiskey she'd tried the first night with Patrick, but he wanted her to join him. She noticed his muscular arms. She decided to sip the shot slowly.

"Are you okay, Patrick? You're quiet."

"Lost my job today."

"Oh, Patrick, I'm so sorry. What happened?"

"They laid off the whole team. Said the job was finished and they had no more work. My roommates are drinking at Clancy's, but I knew you were coming and didn't want to disappoint you."

"That's terrible. We don't have to go out. Save your money. What do you have in the pantry?"

She rolled up the sleeves of her dress and put the beret in her purse while taking out a banana clip to hold back her hair.

Quick as could be, Patrick jumped from his chair, grabbed her by the arm and pulled her up, kissing her hard. She'd only kissed a couple of boys before, and it was clumsy and tentative. That was not Patrick Hanrahan's style.

She enjoyed the kisses despite his physicality. But she gasped when he sharply pulled up the hem of her dress and put his hand inside, feeling a chill as his rough palm grazed her side and stomach on the way to her breast, where he went right underneath the wire of her bra to feel her. She wasn't prepared and she didn't want this.

"No, Patrick."

"Come on, I can feel you. You want it. I do, too. Let's not kid each other."

Before she could even respond, he broke the catch of her bra and picked her up, one hand on her back inside the dress and the other outside, and carried her back to his bedroom. She glanced around and saw clothes strewn everywhere. She also noticed three empty Dewar's bottles lined up on a dresser. It was the last thing she saw before he overwhelmed and took her. She never thought about screaming. She simply endured.

***

If there was a tender side to Patrick Hanrahan, it came after the rape, when he told her she was his girl and he'd do right by her.

"Red, I'm just gonna call you that; you don't mind, do you? Better than Lilah. Anyway, I'm gonna head to North Carolina. One of the former crew guys went there to do some work for Duke. That's a big power company. Figure I can do that or maybe work for one of the tobacco companies."

Lilah was too sore to hear much, a dull ache that she found surprisingly tolerable. A few minutes later, he was snoring, and as she looked at him beside her, she didn't feel the hatred she thought she would. The hatred Mom had for her father.

Lilah left soon after, slipping out so as not to wake him and doing what she could with the bra straps to keep it in place under her dress for the subway ride back to the Bronx. Her mother was waiting to lay on some Catholic guilt but Lilah wasn't having it.

"Mom, I'm tired. I'm just going to bed."

"Did you not learn anything in church?"

Lilah had been drifting from the Catholic church the past few years, tolerating it on Sundays only to keep her mother at bay. Sarcasm was her only tool as she turned her back.

"God didn't have anything to do with what happened tonight, Mom."

She slammed her bedroom door, flopped on her bed and ruminated. How was Patrick any worse than anything that awaited her here? He was kind to her. He seemed to like her. And even though she'd told him "no," she'd only said it once, and he'd been drinking.

Her final thought before sleep was that she could do worse than Patrick Hanrahan.

***

With her mother giving her the silent treatment, she continued to see Patrick, who was now drinking all the time since he didn't have a job to worry about. Then, about a month later, Patrick called to tell her the Duke job had come through and it was time to head south. He wanted her to go with him.

It didn't take Lilah long to decide. She left her mother a note saying she was heading to a new life, and even if they didn't see each other again, she loved her. They bought Greyhound tickets, pooling their money. Except Lilah noticed she put in seventy dollars and Patrick ten bucks. He told her not to sweat it, that once he got working, they'd be riding high. He did find some extra cash in his pocket to dart into the liquor store and pick up a bottle for the trip. Lilah didn't take his offer of a swig; she had started getting sick.

Kiely was born nine months later, and Lilah found she loved motherhood, even if they had to scramble for every penny. It turned out Patrick's buddy had only come up with a minimum wage position for him to handle traffic when the power crews were working. Lilah also began to argue with Patrick because it seemed part of whatever income he earned was always dedicated to alcohol. She tolerated it while she was pregnant because he was surprisingly gentle with her, and even with Kiely once she was born.

Gentle Patrick, however, didn't last. As a couple they settled into a routine of job-and-town hopping, and Lilah into a pattern of confrontation and avoidance. She protected Kiely from Patrick's drunken rages, but couldn't avoid them herself. Patrick forced himself on her so often and so roughly that when she miscarried a second child, she secretly had doctors tie her tubes and managed to hide her scars and recovery by claiming she had the flu. She didn't want and didn't think she could handle another child with Patrick Hanrahan as the father.

Patrick drifted closer to Virginia and eventually managed to gain work in a small tobacco operation in King, North Carolina, being an all-hands worker. It was regular hours, and Lilah made sure his ass was up on time in the morning and out the door, regardless of his state. She also found herself cruelly cutting Patrick down to size, inviting his violence. She knew she'd taken on her mother's persona, but she was powerless to stop it. She also knew her impatience spilled onto her treatment of Kiely once her daughter started school.

Lilah worked a couple of cashier's jobs at local stores and began squirreling away her cash from it. Just in case. She took out a life insurance policy on Patrick, getting him to sign it when he was too drunk to notice one night. She didn't trust him to reach his 50th birthday given his drinking and the fights he found himself in at the bars he haunted 'til all hours.

The thought that kept her up at night for more than forty years was what might have happened if she hadn't written her phone number on Patrick's palm that day in 1981.

Maya

H E SAID HE WAS A TRUCKER WITH AN EMPTY RIG ON his way to Knoxville for a pickup, Don something or other. I didn't really hear; I was excited to learn he was on his way, not coming back. He'd be loaded.

I think about the pluses and minuses as he waits to pay his bill. Crowded Friday night at Rogue's Pub, a dive bar next to a Holiday Inn Express in Jackson, Tennessee, right off I-40. No one really saw me since I slipped into my corner booth. I'm dressed to disguise, wearing a low-brimmed, black Raiders cap and black-rimmed glasses with no prescription lens 'cause my eyesight is perfect. Black leather jacket over torn black jeans with a long slit on the right leg to show off some skin. My favorite Led Zeppelin tour t-shirt, worn and low cut. I'd gone to the bar for my one beer, a Bud Light, and was still sipping it an hour later; I'm pretty sure if the blonde tending bar was asked, she'd vaguely remember some chick in black. A blues-rock band is playing the back room, and the distorted blare is almost but not quite making Stevie Ray Vaughn's "The House is Rockin'" undecipherable. Strangely, it isn't awful. With tomorrow being the final day of the cross-country journey, I can just hang here and walk back to the Super 8 up the road.

But I watch Don, or was it Dan, pay his bill, and I have to make up my mind. He'd slow-walked past my booth on the way back from the john so I could feel his eyes. Maybe he'd glanced at me via the bar-length mirror as I caught him polishing off a pub burger. He was 40-ish, brown mustache and two-day stubble. When I gestured for him to sit, he'd volunteered his name and journey before I said a word. I was direct.

"I'm horny and not long for this town. Wanna fuck around?"

Now I have to decide whether to go through with it. I watch him chat with blondie and hand her some bills. I get up and walk quickly to the exit. I push through the door, feeling him right behind. He puts his hand on my shoulder outside, and I turn back to him. "How much?" he asks. I tell him $200, not including the room. In the end, it won't matter. Not to me, at least. He starts to turn toward the Holiday Inn entrance, and I point up the road to the Super 8. "Cheaper. Plus, I have an arrangement." He nods and says what I want to hear: "You need a ride?"

***

My mind had Jackson and this trucker so far in the rearview I'd barely heard his question. So he repeats it.

"I was wondering how long you've been hookin', darlin'. That was some good fun."

"I'm not a hooker. Just lonely."

"And what did you say your name was?"

Small talk is not my bag. Plus, I don't really know what the fuck I am. Just that I'm not a hooker. I reach down for the vape in my purse and light it quickly. I pull my body up so my back hits the headboard and Mr. Trucker—Dan, I'm quite sure—is still prone below me. I stroke his head gently, easing him into where I hope he goes. To sleep.

"I'm just me," I finally answer. "A wanderer, I guess you could say. Call me Deena."

"Huh."

He doesn't offer more, and I know he's drifting. Guys are predictable after sex. Dan takes three minutes. I wait until the deep breath of sleep is steady and he produces a light snore. I consider just taking his money and running, but his car is right next to my Mazda. That would be a risk, and I like control. That much I know.

***

I touch my phone inside the purse to make the power come on, providing just enough light to leave the bed without disturbing him, use a tissue to grab his condom off the floor where he'd dropped it and slip into the bathroom. It's sparse, with a dirty feel, from the thin yellow towels to the uncovered fluorescent light over the sink, which I leave off, using only the light of my phone. I keep the door cracked so I can hear in case he stirs.

First, I drop the condom in the toilet. Then I wipe his sweat off me, enough that I feel clean. Then I wash my hands and up my arms with the cheap bar of generic motel soap. Finally, I flick the soft shower-fan light on and look in the mirror. Not too bad. I use a face wipe and clean up the black mascara that got smeared amid the sweat of sex. His sweat. As I put my bra on, I flex my arms. They're well toned, a far cry from when this journey began, long before the break with Deena. Before everything became crystal clear for me. I'd used Deena, tonight, though. Thoughts of her and me in bed help make this sex more tolerable. As I slip on my torn jeans, I glance back to the mirror and check my calf muscles. I reach down and feel them to make sure there are no knots. I need them strong in the next couple of minutes. Yes, all the work has been paying off. I straighten up and observe myself. Twenty-five years old, pale complexion of the Irish, my beautiful dark eyes, short black hair with bangs, compact body with small boobs that work with the rest. I am not fucking embarrassed by this part of me anymore. Plus, I can probably kick Dan's ass flat out if I have to. But that wouldn't make much sense, and I know I won't need to. I reach past the ASP baton in my purse, my danger zone tool, and instead get out my go-to, the homemade GHB, and grab one of the cheap washcloths from the bathroom.

He's still lightly snoring. I put my bag next to the motel room door and unlock it. He really isn't a bad-looking guy, and the sex wasn't particularly rough, as it can be with some of these assholes. *FOCUS, Maya.* God, I hate getting distracted. Come all the way across the country to do a job. Just fucking focus.

I hop lightly on the bed and in one fell swoop plunge the washcloth over Dan's nose and mouth, pinning him powerfully down with my legs. His eyes open wide with a comical, "What the fuck," that I've seen before. But he's got no fight in him. The whole thing takes less than 15 seconds and he's knocked out, I'm betting 'til morning when I'm hours away. I hop off the bed and grab his pants from the floor. An overstuffed brown wallet falls out, and I catch it mid-air. Good sign. He has another $700 inside. Hot damn.

What was it I'd told the trucker when he asked what I was? Wanderer. Nice word. Not the right word. Definitely not wanderer. Thief, I guess. Avenger soon. Next stop, North Carolina. Home.

Steve

"I CAN'T BELIEVE I'M BACK HERE AGAIN. WHY IS THIS STILL happening to me?"

Jill looks at me plaintively. She's an attractive woman. Forty-three, light brown hair. Beige silk blouse over light brown skirt. Professional.

I watch her from my perch on my brown leather straight-back chair. As usual, she has eschewed the beige leather loveseat for my red side chair, on which she sits cross-legged, head hanging in shame. One of her tan stiletto-heeled shoes, which had been dangling from her foot, drops quietly to the carpet. She lets it be.

"I really don't get it, Steve. We've been working together for nearly a year, right? Been through the whole 'Daddy's girl caretaker' thing. I'm not supposed to be codependent to these guys. I'm really not. I wasn't to Al. But he's doing the same thing to me as my father."

I pause to give her venting time to hang. I don't want to say it. And I wince inside knowing I have to. "But here we are again."

As I expect, it sets her off. I gently nudge the Kleenex on the oak coffee table between us closer and she takes one. After she wipes, a bit of black eyeliner breaks away from the underside of her eyelid and lands just below her left eye. I gesture to her, and she dabs it clean.

"I guess we have more work to do," she says, sniffling.

"You have the tools. But it is up to you to use them. What is it you need to do most?"

"Recognize physical signs of anxiety."

"And?"

"And use a skill to regulate my emotions before acting. Be in my thinking brain."

"Right. Remember, your tears here aren't just because you're in the codependent role, which is our longer-term fix. It's because you exploded in your old manner, fight-or-flight, when Al pulled you in today, right?"

Jill nods, head down. "What am I going to do, Steve?"

"What do you want to do, Jill?"

"Kick Al in his goddamn nuts!"

I burst out laughing, and after a second, so does Jill.

***

I'm leaned over the wireless keyboard on the big oak desk and pause in mid-sentence to reflect as I jot my progress note on the session with Jill. It was nearly all venting, as she raged about the injustice of being terminated by the man she had slept with and who'd been her champion over the previous four years, a married man. And therein was Jill's issue with this cheating lawyer. A single child raised in a strict Catholic home by an alcoholic father who'd beaten and threatened her until she left at 17, Jill had wound up marrying another alcoholic. When their child went to college five years ago, she filed for divorce, and Al, her boss, had been there for her—the man of sympathy. He promoted her to top administrator and came on to her. Jill, starving for the affection of a "good" man with no addiction issues, fell for his lines of an unhappy marriage and promises to make her a new life.

But when, after recognizing he wasn't going to leave his family, she tried to break it off, she quickly felt his wrath in terms of a bad review and sudden misery at work, a ninety-day termination process that devastated her. And led to her profanity-laced outburst at him today—albeit behind closed doors.

I'd been working with Jill to understand when her "lizard" brain was active, the instinctive part of the brain responsible for the fight, flight or freeze response to protect from danger. I explained to her that the appearance of physical symptoms of anxiety in her body—sensations, pains, nerves—are a tipoff to her lizard brain trying to come out and play, and that by using certain techniques, she could divert back to her thinking brain, the part that's supposed to be doing the heavy lifting when a person isn't being directly threatened.

Of course, Jill's primitive brain response was building during the evaluation state, not unexpectedly. She's like a cat cornered by a dog; she's trapped in her situation. Her "fight" response, given her childhood traumas with her alcoholic father, is not surprising. Further trapping her, Jill knows that in the legal community, trying to act legally against an unfair termination would make it extremely difficult for her to find work at another firm.

Al has done a job on her. And she is helpless.

Aha! I wasn't able during the session to conceptualize the common thread between Jill's two alcoholic male relationships and the situation with Al. But there it is. Powerlessness. The difference for Jill, though, is that this one is workplace vs. home, and in this one, she chose to become involved with the married boss vs. having no choice in picking her father. Nor could she have anticipated that her husband would turn out to be an alcoholic.

I'm going to have to do some work with Jill on grief—the grieving of lost relationships, the grieving over her own ability to see the warning signs when it came to Al. But Jill wants to be in therapy and is committed to personal growth. She's a great client.

I save the file, take a swig of no-longer ice water from my Yeti and lean back in my office chair, locking my hands behind my head. I love the insights I gain from this work. It gives me the J-U-ICE, as my old teammates used to say. I look at my black At-a-Glance appointment book. My bible.

I pull out my folder to grab the paperwork I need for a first session and turn back to the computer. I have to complete the progress note on Jill and plug her appointment next week into the computer.

But I have a sudden thought about the new client and addiction. I walk over to the built-ins between the eight-foot-tall arched windows that look out on the stadium and quickly find *Dear Old Man* on the second shelf from the top, where I keep books about family relationships. A total guess, but my instincts are usually pretty good. If this client is 25 and an addict, there's a good chance of shame or guilt that she's let her parents down. I want Charles Wells' essay available. The one that says, "My children owe me nothing." While I'm at it, I grab an info sheet on local NA meetings; she may already have it, but it shows I'm already thinking about her to have it handy. First impressions with mandatory clients are so important. I finally turn back to the computer and Jill's note. I'll have just enough time after finishing it for a quick mindfulness exercise to clear my head before the new client.

Session One – Diagnostic

S HE TOOK A DEEP BREATH AS SHE APPROACHED THE CONVERTED brownstone a block off downtown. She'd parked her gray Mazda 3 hatchback a couple of blocks away, right by the minor league ballpark. "Get Your Bulls Season Tickets," the huge sign attached to the red brick facing said. In early December, though, baseball was still months away. Maya was glad she'd not used the parking lot behind the brownstone, as the woman on the phone at "Gloves Off Counseling" had suggested. She needed time to get her head right.

This dance was just starting and it was for a reason, she reminded herself. This was the guy who had fucked her life by fucking with her mother's mind. Everything that had happened to her in the past dozen years could be linked to her mother's time with this guy. On the Gloves Off website, which she'd been studying in the three months since she'd arrived, Steve Prescott's face wasn't what she had imagined. He didn't look like he was 47, as his bio said, and he didn't fit the image Maya had of him, the smug professor type. But looks are nothing.

Maya climbed the six steps up to the heavy double door and opened it. The brownstone held four different offices, with the suite for Gloves Off at the back of the first floor. She pushed through the practice's interior glass door and was pleasantly surprised. It smelled like fresh bread. A young woman sat at a cubicle behind a half wall. There were tracks on top of the wall, Maya noticed, but no sliding glass. Either they were about to put in the security or had decided it wasn't needed.

"Hi. You must be Maya," the woman said. "I'm Kenzie. We talked on the phone. It's good to see you here. I think I promised we have some forms, right?"

Maya took the clipboard Kenzie offered. Before she could ask, Kenzie held out a pen. "We use black. Has to be black. All forms in black ink. And you're probably wondering about the bread. Isn't it amazing? It's the micro-factory over yonder."

Maya looked out the window where Kenzie pointed to a huge complex of renovated factories and lofts, but she didn't offer any cheerful response. Kenzie was probably about her age. But so very different. She must be happy as a clam in her first "real-life job." She was wearing jeans and a deep blue, patterned blouse that accentuated her short, sandy hair. She was pretty. No ring.

FOCUS, Maya! You don't care about anything right now but this session with Steve Prescott.

She turned to the honey leather loveseat-chair combo and sat down to do the paperwork. No one else was waiting, which Maya thought was odd, considering it was 11 on a Monday. And there were three other counselors with the practice, according to the website.

"We time appointments every 15 minutes to limit overlap in the outer office," Kenzie volunteered in a sing-song voice, like she was mind-reading. "Steve will come out to get you in a few minutes. I think the timing will be just right for you finishing up the paperwork!"

***

Steve watched the young woman's eyes go around his office, and he was amused and surprised. Amused because he liked to see how his clients reacted to his baseball memorabilia—the pictures of him pitching in his high school uniform; the glad-handing at his contract signing with the Tampa Bay Rays; the eerie image of him leaving a mound at twilight in the Durham Bulls minor league park, the setting sun creating a shadow across the field, his head down and face obscured. His clients frequently asked about that particular image, and he told them it came near the end of his career, when he was aware he was facing surgery that would likely keep him from ever reaching the big leagues. In fact, though, he loved the image because it captured him in a moment of vulnerability, rather than triumph. Just a little something unexpected.

Steve liked throwing a curveball to clients and didn't mind one thrown right back at him; when a client fooled him—in a good way or bad—it was a lesson. By sharing a vulnerable side of himself, the story of his failed efforts to reach the majors, he hoped in an understated way to encourage clients to recognize and consider vulnerability. He wondered if the woman casing his office even as she read his Professional Disclosure Statement would have a vulnerable side. She finished it and looked up, her eyes piercing, accusing.

"So what, I'm like supposed to be impressed you *almost* made the big leagues?"

Not yet even thinking vulnerable, apparently. He laughed out loud at both her directness and his misdirected hope. He also made note of her anger.

"No, Ms. Andino. I'm just sharing information. It's mostly a conversation starter because the work of therapy is about connection. Two people able to have conversation where maybe that's been a problem elsewhere in a person's life. I don't know your story yet, and we'll take some time to get to it."

He watched her slide back into the couch, moving from the edge where she'd been perched since coming inside five minutes earlier. She wore torn blue jeans and a maroon T-shirt with a simple Nike swoosh over the breast. She had three brow piercings on her left eyebrow and one under her lower lip. The flower of a black rose tattoo poked from underneath the left T-shirt sleeve, and her lower left arm was covered with flower tattoos. A large "Live Free or Die" and snake ran along most of the inside of her right arm.

"Nice tat. Are you from New Hampshire?"

"I don't know what the fuck you're talking about."

"Live free or die. It's the state slogan in New Hampshire. Doesn't matter. I like the tattoo."

She shook her head slightly but didn't say anything back. This one might be tough to put at ease.

"Let me run through some of the basic stuff about counseling for you, Ms. Andino. Do you mind if I call you Maya? You can call me Steve."

"Yeah, whatever."

He did his basic pitch about privacy and how what was said in the room would be strictly between them, unless he believed she was suicidal or homicidal. He repeated the line that counseling was about connection, and that, even though she'd been told she had to come here, what they accomplished would largely be about their ability to open up to each other. And that there were no miracle cures in counseling for anything.

All through his pitch, her eyes were on him, and he found it a bit unsettling. Most of his clients were reserved in the first few sessions, especially those mandated to come; they didn't make direct eye contact frequently. This one's almost unnaturally dark eyes were like steel bores.

"So, Maya, we're done with the preliminaries. Now it's your turn. I know you have an order to be here, but tell me how you got here. Whatever you want that helps me understand not just why you're here, but what you'd like to get from our time together."

She sighed, but before she could say anything, Steve jumped back in.

"What you'd like from our time together in addition to having a signed slip of paper that says you were here."

That got a little smile. At least Steve thought so—maybe more smirky, but lip definitely curled up.

"I did some drugs, got caught, here I am. What else?"

She continued to challenge Steve with her stare. He caught the anger, but sensed an inner pain.

"Not fun getting caught, I imagine. Can you tell me some more?"

She told him she was at a club with three friends, and they were doing coke in the bathroom when cops showed up. She had the rest of their stash for the night in her purse. Originally charged with possession, the count was upgraded to intent to sell because the cops were trying to squeeze her to give up their supplier. Her friends bailed on her, and Maya took the weight. She was released on her own recognizance and was told by her court-appointed attorney to get therapy—which would be paid for by Social Services—before her next court date, to show she was getting help. So here she was.

She relayed the story with little emotion, almost like she had it memorized, Steve thought. The anger she'd flashed in comments to him and in her stare was gone in the retelling. He wondered if she was reciting this tale to keep her emotions in check.

"Guess it sucked to be ghosted by the women you were with. But you were loyal. To your drug supplier, anyway. What about the friends?"

Maya shook her head. "Screw them. Weren't really friends anyway."

"I see."

"I'm not going to tell you anything more. Look, I was told to come here. I'm here."

Back to the intensity. Steve sighed. They stared at each other for a full minute. Steve had a hunch.

"Maya, I know you see this as something you have to do. I'm fine with you just sitting here for forty-five minutes at a time for however many sessions you're mandated to be here."

"Eight."

"Eight, okay. That's a lot of sitting-around time. I'm not going to judge you on whether you have a drug problem. It's not my role. Your urine test will determine that."

She was smiling, once again a sardonic little insider smile.

"What, you have that test beat?"

She shrugged. "Maybe."

"Okay, then why not do something else with this time? I mean, your background says you spent most of the past seven years in California. And here I thought you'd been in New Hampshire. Anyway, I can give you an idea that I think might be interesting for us to explore that has nothing to do with drugs or rehab, and it might just make our time together go in a different direction. What do you think? Wanna hear it?"

Another shrug. Steve plowed on.

"One of the things I like to do with my clients is ask them what they want. Not necessarily what they want out of therapy, although that can be important."

He paused and put emphasis on each word of his question: "*What do you want?*"

She sighed. Dove into her black handbag and took out some lip balm. Checked her nails, which were bare but trim. She might be a wild child or playing one, but from the nails to the minor makeup that enhanced the natural, rough beauty of her eyes, hair and pale skin, he sensed she cared about the look she put out to the world.

"I want to know about you," she finally said.

Me? I'm an open book. You know some of my story, the whole failed major leaguer part. I didn't think you were interested."

He watched her carefully. This was one of those curveballs.

Well, you want me to tell you all about me and what I want, but how and why the fuck should I trust you? I don't know who you are. Baseball doesn't mean shit to me. Why are you doing this?"

The movie *Silence of the Lambs* flashed in Steve's head, and Hannibal Lecter's deal with Clarice Starling for a *quid pro quo* before he would talk to her about the murderer Buffalo Bill. Steve decided this young woman wouldn't get the reference. Judgmental for sure, but better to not introduce a cultural factor that emphasized their age difference. If these sessions were going to go anywhere, they had to start with some level of trust; maybe by sharing a little bit, he could get his *quid pro quo* naturally.

"Why am I doing what, Maya?"

She shrugged. "This, counseling. Why do you bother?"

"The short answer is when I got drafted by the Rays, I was in high school. And it kind of came about unexpectedly, after I'd been planning for months to go to college. So I promised my parents I'd go to college during the offseason. It took six years, but I did it. I was a psych major.

"Once I knew my baseball career was over, I did the simple thing and went back for my master's in counseling, essentially the same field as psychology. I like talking with people, love working with them. Pretty simple, really. I take it you haven't latched onto that something for yourself yet?"

She gave Steve a look that screamed *duh.*

"Okay, then. Any thoughts on 'What do you want?'"

She looked at him again, then dropped her head, tugged at her shirt sleeve.

"I'm not looking for any sympathy. I don't even know why . . ."

Steve waited. Sometimes the best tactic in counseling was silence. Kind of like Vin Scully, the famed Dodgers announcer, letting the audience tell the story by keeping his mouth shut at a big moment.

"My father died when I was 10. And my mom killed herself three years later. Okay? So yeah, maybe I have a little chip on my fucking shoulder and I'm tired of talking about this shit. Counselors at school, fucking foster parents who think they know everything. I'm just tired. *What I want*, Steve, is to be done with all the fucking talk."

Post-session: Maya

MY MIND IS GOING A THOUSAND MILES A MINUTE AS I half-walk, half-run back to my car. I throw myself in, turn it on and crank the volume on the classic rock channel I'd been listening to on the way over. Just about the only thing Mom gave me that I actually value—the music she played incessantly.

The chords of "Free Bird" come up. Fine, yeah, I'm free all right. Except for all my fucking baggage, which just about started to give away the whole game a few minutes ago. What the hell was I thinking, mentioning my fucked-up family already? What if he puts it together? All because he seemed like he actually cared? And wasn't this the guy who amped up Mom and put me on the path to foster hell?

The song ends and I put the car in gear. Plenty of time to chill at my little pad, a rooming house I'd found on Craigslist, perfectly fine and plenty cheap, not even a week's rent in advance. I'd hardly touched the $6,000 I'd stolen during the trip. A quick bite, maybe some Greek yogurt, some core strengthening, then a quick run and off to the diner. Funny how I look forward to the diner, a gathering spot for people of all shapes and sizes at all hours of the night. I love the gleam of it, the bar stool counter, the service/waiting area bar and the jibing between the front crew and the back. I really don't need the money, but working there cuts down on the boredom and takes my mind off the task at hand. Plus, Billie is a pretty awesome boss.

On the other hand, I always enjoyed school, and it's been the same for work. I have talent and smarts. I know that. Except for the people I allow to get too close. *FOCUS, Maya! You didn't allow the assholes into your life. You didn't have a choice.*

The opening chords of The Who's "Who Are You" blast through the speakers, and I have a sudden flash to Don the trucker asking what I was. Or was it Dan? Interesting coincidence on the song. I remember one of the counselors I saw so long ago telling me she didn't believe in coincidences. It's taken awhile, but I've come around to her point of view on that.

I'm going to need to be more cautious with Steve. Make sure I'm more in control of how much I tell him and in what order. It's weird how much he was already willing right in the first session to share about himself. My other counselors never did that. Could he be trying to trip me up? Does he have any clue?

No, no way. I absentmindedly punch my 8-ball rearview mirror toy at a traffic light. I only picked it up because it reminded me of the rare occasion when Mom let me into a bar she tended, and I got to watch the pool players. Some of them were cool as hell. Especially the women who played in high heels.

Well, the dance has begun. Now I just have to see it through.

Post-session: Steve

I COMPLETE THE BASIC PARTS OF THE DIAGNOSTIC REPORT ON Maya Andino, but the narrative portion is more elusive. Conceptualizing a client after the first session is usually one of the fun parts of the job, but Maya is a challenge. I think again about her final statement: wanting to be done with talk. Definitely anger and attitude, and yet . . . and yet what? Something about her little diatribe doesn't ring true. Just like the story about her drug arrest. There might be truth within it, but not the whole truth. No wonder I can't finish this narrative.

I stare at the "reason client is in counseling" question on my report. Easy enough. Drug referral, with eight mandated sessions, theoretically paid for by the state, just like any other referral. But the drug referral created another weird moment. When I offered Maya the list of NA meetings, she pooh-poohed it, dripping with sarcasm. *Do I look high?* Something about the way she said it had made me pause. It was a sharp line, an angry line. It didn't have any of the chronic user's waffle.

Before I could even challenge her, almost as if she knew I was going to challenge her, she'd retreated into further explanation, saying she'd been clean since the arrest and wasn't going back. She had a job as a night waitress at a local 24/7 diner, so she didn't even have time to get into trouble. Why would this tough young woman be embarrassed at dropping a sarcastic line in sync with the rest of the persona she'd displayed during the session? And for that matter, her sarcasm didn't match her hint later about being able to beat a drug test. Could she be playing some type of game? Wouldn't be the first time a client tested my ability to figure out what was real and what wasn't.

The one thing I'm quite sure of after one session is that Maya Andino's issues are not about drugs. In fact, drugs are the least of it for her. Of that I have no doubt.

I have only about twenty minutes before my next appointment, though, so I jot down a tentative diagnostic code, F43.20, adjustment disorder. It's the most benign code in the entire *Diagnostic and Statistical Manual of Mental Disorders*, or *DSM*, the book that rules all for therapists and insurance companies. Maya clearly has something going on in life that caused her dysfunctional response of using drugs—the adjustment in adjustment disorder. I don't see enough despite the arrest to consider a diagnosis of some type of substance use disorder. I take a deep breath. I'll have to finish the rest of her note later. I have to admit, Maya is likely going to be one of those clients I don't get in too deeply with. She's here for only seven more sessions, and that's just the way it goes. I hate it when that happens.

I bullet point the topics I need to raise with her next session:

• Born and raised in North Carolina, but then to California and now back. What's that about?

• Inferred problems with foster care after mother's suicide. Go slowly, but will she share?

• Father's death. She only said he died, nothing more. What does she remember about it? Bond with mom?

One thing I know. This young woman has had a world of pain in her life. Many adverse childhood experiences, and I know those mean potential physical and mental health problems throughout her life. She is fortunate to have been caught now and ordered to therapy, and I need to do everything I can in my time to reach her. She has resilience, that's for sure. Might just help her release the anger within. If I win her trust. A fourth bullet point occurs to me.

• Check out her lower arm tattoos. Cutting scars?

And then another thought intrudes.

Maya's tone asking why I got into counseling was raw. She *needed* to know. Her intensity says she's looking for something, maybe something she didn't get during an adolescence in which trauma was taking root. I think about the same period in my life, one where I found potential. I grab my baseball from its little metal holder on my desk. It's the one I collected after my final game in Durham.

***

First pickup game of the year and my buddy Charlie Palmer is digging in at the plate and ragging me already. "You suck, Steve. Toss me more of your soft shit. Love that." He'd already hit two sharp shots up the middle. I'm not really a pitcher, though I do feel a little more powerful. Part of me wants to really let loose, and as Charlie keeps up a string of insults, I feel my heart start to race. I should just let it go. It's not like I'm gonna kill him.

I toe the mound of dirt in the middle of a largely ragged field in central Evanston, Illinois, where the gang, eight of us, love to get together. It was once a Little League field but had long since been abandoned for tonier digs in the south part of town. Even though it's filled with rocks and very little green, it's still recognizable as a baseball diamond, so it works for us.

It was a balmy 55 degrees on a March Saturday of my sophomore year and we were bored as hell, when one of us, I think Joey, said "baseball," and we ran back to our houses, grabbed balls, gloves and a couple of bats. Baseball's always been part of my love. My dad is a Cubs diehard, which meant I was, too. He came to every Little League game, and I know he was disappointed that I never made any of the All-Star teams that got to travel.

I touch my faded Cubs cap and stomp around the mound. I'm only pitching because Josh said he was beat. He'd been out with his older cousin the night before and gotten smashed on screwdrivers. He's having a tough go of it.

Josh is the one who can snap a curve; he'd been pitching since Little League and had always made the All-Star teams. I usually played outfield, but with Josh under the weather …

My friends have been giving me shit about my growth spurt for weeks. There's a bucket of balls next to me on the mound because we don't waste a player catching. The cage includes a plywood backstop and we let balls go there and just collect them every few minutes and start again.

The ball feels smaller in my hand.

"You gonna keep feeling it like it's Mary Jane?"

Low blow. Mary Jane was my first girlfriend. Lasted about three weeks and ended on Valentine's Day last month when I didn't get her anything. Live and learn.

But the barb makes up my mind. I smile and do a little rocking motion on my windup, twisting back on my left leg against the worn rubber for extra leverage and, almost without trying, I explode forward as my weight shifts, my left arm letting fly. Charlie is a righty and the pitch is way outside, but it flies by so fast that he jumps back anyway. The sound the ball makes as it explodes into the plywood is unlike any of us have heard before.

"What the fuck was that?" Josh says from behind me, where he's playing short.

"Jesus, Steve," Charlie says from the plate. "You lookin' to kill me?"

Even though my head is saying "what the fuck?" my arm is telling me "thank you," that it was waiting for me to finally let loose. And, come to think of it, I had been lifting weights over the winter, a carryover from my stint on the freshman wrestling squad at Evanston Township High School.

I pick a new ball from the bucket and smile. "Shit, Charlie, don't be a pussy. Get back in there."

I let loose another with my newfound might and it's closer to the plate and Charlie swings about a full second after the ball has crashed the backstop again. Two more misses after that and I call out: "Next?"

I continue with this a while, a mix of crazy wild balls and pitches close enough for the others to swing at and miss until we switch sides. Josh comes up to me.

"Dude, you throwin' some smoke. You ask me, you may not have liked wrestling that much, but you've got to go out for the baseball team."

"Ya think so?"

Josh shakes his head. "I know so."

***

One year later.

"Dad, do you have to do this?"

"Steven, we've talked about this. You have a talent. Your high school coach is simply ignoring you. It's wrong. I'm only going to say that to the school board."

"I know, but …"

"There are no buts, Steven. Listen, when someone is treated wrongly, you advocate for them. It's really that simple. I try to do that for my employees and I hope they'd do the same for me."

"I just don't see how this is going to end well. My teammates are going to hate me. It's gonna divide the team. Coach is a jerk like that."

Dad's been all over this ever since I told him about Coach freezing me out as a starter. Yes, my first year was wild as hell, but the camp Dad sent me to over the summer made a huge difference, and most everyone on the team believes in me heading into junior season. Except Coach.

Dad's been a manager at Ace Hardware all his life, and people look up to him; he's always involved with our church doing ushering or hosting new families. He's really enthusiastic, sometimes more than people need, I think. Including me. But compared to the fathers of my friends, he's great. I know he wants me to succeed.

As I look at him now, I notice the gray on the sides of his temples. It's really the only sign of him getting close to 40. Well, maybe that and the crow's feet by the corners of his eyes. Somehow, they only make Dad more intense.

"I think you need to trust me, Steven. I am only going to state the case to the board; I'm not going to trash the coach. But our taxes pay his salary. And if he's not doing right by kids with a God-given talent like you have, then he's not doing the job I'm paying him to do."

"But you're not paying him, Dad!"

Dad smiles at me.

"Do you know how much I made last year, son?"

"No."

"A little over $52K. Not as much as some of your teammates' fathers, I'm sure. And some $12K of that went to taxes. God willing, son, the job I'm up for at corporate will give me a chance to earn a little more. But I'll be damned if a coach who earns even one dime of my taxpayer dollars is going to deny an opportunity to you based on some prejudice or favoritism or whatever bug is up his ass telling him to keep you on the bench."

I know I'm not moving him on this issue. When he uses even a modest curse like "ass" he is seriously ticked off. It's a fire I don't know if I'll ever develop. I just hope I can manage my teammates after it goes down. But I'm afraid it's going to get ugly.

***

Another year later.

A bead of sweat hangs from the brim of my cap as I stare at Jonesy. I know he's calling fastball and I'm in the same groove I've been in for nearly all of senior year. I shake my head to get the sweat off more than anything else and Jonesy laughs. He saw it from way back there. He knows it was the sweat, not that I was shaking him off.

I have to focus, though. After all the craziness—Dad fighting to get me a chance, Coach hating my guts and getting his guys to freeze me out, the school board firing Coach after junior year—well, I want this thing to end perfectly. Final game of the year. No playoffs, but it's been pretty drama free. Last out of the seventh and there's a runner on second, but I don't pay him any mind. We're up 4–0. I rock back and fire, and the Eagles batter surprises me, disappoints me, actually, by making contact. It's a harmless foul pop behind first, where Tommy grabs it easy. Jonesy runs over to me on the mound, as do my teammates, and we all high-five and bounce before lining up to shake hands with the Eagles.

Just like that, my high school areer is over. I'm looking forward to college. Staying close to home for the full athletic ride at Northwestern, but Mom and Dad are happy. And I do get to live on campus with the jocks. Four teams scouted me during the season, but I haven't heard from them in a couple months. The new team coach, Coach Jim, told me not to sweat it; the scouts would be back by my sophomore year of college.

***

The phone rings so rarely now that it doesn't even register until Mom calls me to come downstairs. She's holding the black house phone and looking at me weird and trying to catch my father's attention in the den at the same time. I answer and watch as she hustles into the den and whispers to Dad, hearing her say the word "Rays" at the same time I say "Hello?"

"Good evening, Steven. And congratulations. This is Thomas Perkinson of the Tampa Bay Rays, and I'm delighted to let you know that we have selected you in the 17th round of the amateur draft. Welcome to the Rays organization."

My first thought is it's one of my teammates playing a joke. My second is that no one calls me Steven other than my parents. Dad walks in and I cover the phone's mouthpiece and give him the news of who's on the other line. Mr. Perkinson continues.

"Now I know this might come as a surprise, being as we didn't even scout you during your high school season, but we've been reading reports and watching video and you may be aware the Rays are all about developing pitching. And before you say a word, I know you've accepted a scholarship from Northwestern and it's totally your prerogative to go with that ... "

Dad takes the phone from me before I can even say a word.

"Hello there. This is Steven's father, Hal Prescott."

"Well congratulations to you, too, Mr. Prescott. We're a family-oriented organization and we like speaking with not only the players we select but of course their parents as well."

"Can you tell me what this means for my boy?"

Dad is listening, and my mind is racing. It's only a month until I'm starting at Northwestern, and the baseball team's training staff has already reached out and wants me to stop by next week to get me prepped for my pre-season regimen.

As Dad continues to talk with Mr. Perkinson, the vision I've had of wearing the purple jersey of the Northwestern Wildcats dances and changes. Now I'm seeing the clean white lines of the Rays.

*****

Mom and Dad sit on one side of our kitchen island and I'm on the other. I've laid out my case, and it basically comes down to impatience. "I don't want to waste time in college when I can play pro ball now. I can always go back to college. Guys, it's the BIG leagues."

Mom is nervously playing with her brown hair all the while, repeating the same thing over and over. "You've agreed to go to college. You've won a scholarship. You'll be playing ball there, and you can be drafted again. Every year. And you yourself say you're only going to get better."

I repeat my stock answer. "I also can get injured, Mom. And then I won't have anything."

"Of course you will. You'll be in college. You'll have a degree and a career."

Dad has largely been quiet during the discussion. When I told my parents we needed to talk, he knew why. And after 20 minutes of back and forth between Mom and me, he's ready to pass judgment.

"Son, I believe you're making a mistake. But I understand your thinking. What about this: You do baseball for a year or two and promise to do college in the off-season, and even maybe some during the season."

Mom starts, "Hal . . ."

Dad holds up his hand. "Your mom and I have talked, and we have agreed this is the only circumstance we will accept."

I look at Mom and I understand Dad just made a unilateral decision. It feels like they've been arguing more in the past few months and it occurs to me that this is more of the same, Dad not supporting Mom. On the other hand, he's willing to let me play ball. I feel like that first time pitching to Charlie three years ago. I'm all powerful.

***

I put the baseball back in its holder. What was it my mentor Jim used to say? *"A good therapist always tries to relate from within his own experiences."* Maya is at a threshold moment of her life, just as I was at the end of high school: What happens next?

Her future for now is being shaped by her traumas—and that's got to be the target of my work with her. My background doesn't include "big T" trauma, and although I consider the Dad/school board/team fallout issue to be "little t" trauma, it's trivial compared to Maya's life events. More crucially, though Dad and I had our issues, I had an intact, supportive family, a kind of trauma cushion.

Today was only a first session, but I like Maya. That's important. Easier to work with clients we enjoy working with, and when we get ones we don't, we fight hard, or at least I do, to find some part of the client to like.

I glance at the clock and realize I have just enough time to begin my box breathing exercise to regulate my system, easing the transition to my next client, a journalist with a drinking problem that's been getting worse in the four months since his wife took their two kids and left him.

I lean backward in my office chair and tilt my head toward the ceiling, then slowly begin tossing the ball above me with my left hand and catching it with my right, getting the tosses in sync with my breathing.

Toss on the inhale. Catch on the exhale.

Toss on the inhale. Catch on the exhale.

Toss on the inhale. Catch on the exhale.

Session Two – Delving

THEY STARTED THEIR SECOND SESSION WITH A SIMPLE enough question from Steve: "How'd you wind up in California from North Carolina, and what brought you back?" It led to a meandering story in which Maya talked about needing to get away from her third foster home in four years as soon as she could and hitching her way west, settling in Southern California with a vague dream of being discovered and a reality of needing money to survive.

She'd run away from her last foster home at 17, saving $400 from working at McDonald's, buying a bus ticket to Nashville to get away quickly and then slowly hitching her way west. It was dangerous for a 17-year-old, and Steve had lots of questions for her (not the least of which was why she was running), but he held back, deciding to just observe and give her the feeling of driving the dialogue. He felt she was being more truthful about this part of her life than the story of her arrest at the first session. He also noted the tattoos and their placement down to the wrists and believed she might have at one time been cutting herself. But that would be for another time. He still needed to get more under the surface of Maya's life, the "heart-of-the-matter issues," as Jim used to call it when he was supervising Steve's early days as a counselor.

"I got to L.A. in late August, stopped in a Ralph's, which is a supermarket there, to get a snack and saw a HELP WANTED sign and applied. I mean, I had a job within two hours of being dropped off, and they have this bulletin board there and I was looking at the listings for roommates, and one of the cashiers saw me looking and asked if I needed a place, and next thing you know she invited me to join her and two other girls who were sharing a two-bedroom. They'd just lost one of their roommates and they needed a fourth to make the numbers work."

"Sounds like you got off to a nice start there."

"Yeah, I mean, it wasn't like anything that great, having four of us sharing one bathroom, but we could swing it."

"I see."

"You don't exactly sound interested, Steve."

Warning sign.

"I'm sorry, Maya. I am interested. I appreciate your sharing it with me, and I feel like you really accomplished something in getting yourself all the way across the country, finding a job and a place to live just like that." Steve snapped his fingers for emphasis. "But I am curious about something, and I think that's probably what you saw in my hesitation."

"What's that?"

Steve was glad she bit. He felt like this inquiry might make or break any chance of success with her.

"I'm wondering what it was like for you as a teenager to hitchhike cross-country, especially—and I'm going to take a guess here, Maya, so please don't hold it against me if I'm wrong because I mean well—for someone who probably faced some personal dangers while in foster care?"

There. Trauma was on the table. *Let's see if she bites again.*

She had been looking at him while she asked, but broke eye contact and Steve knew immediately he had struck a nerve. Would she be vulnerable or would her tough-girl persona come out?

He could feel her internal struggle. Her face had gotten even more pale, she'd balled up her fists and he watched her, head down, take two deliberate slow breaths. *That's interesting.* She was practicing mindfulness to restore calm, even if she wasn't aware of it. He thought he saw the tiniest of tears in the outside of her right eye as she looked up at him again. He knew she would not give him the answer he wanted. But she did surprise him a little.

"You know I'm not going to answer you. But I think you're just trying to do your job and you're not nearly as obnoxious as the counselors I had to see after my mother died and during foster care. Yeah, I had some issues in those years. They weren't easy and I handled them in my own way and I don't really want to think about them right now. okay? It's taking me a lot of work not to just get up and leave now. But I will answer your question about coming cross-country. After my mom killed herself, I wound up being raped just three months into foster care by a fucking asshole when I couldn't—I mean didn't—know how to fight back. He was the foster father, Steve. Later on, I got beaten up in foster care. And then I was fucking raped again, by goddamn twins. So, no, going cross-country by myself was not that big a deal. I had a knife and I had my wits. That's all."

She sat back and pulled her legs up under her crosswise in the wing chair. Steve continued to watch her, and this time she didn't break eye contact. The steel bores were back, righteous and defiant.

"Thank you for sharing that, Maya. I'll respect your willingness with what you want to share, when you want to share it. But I do want to know your full story, even if it means beyond the eight mandated sessions if you're willing."

No harm in putting that idea out there, though she was already shaking her head.

"But that's not something you have to decide yet, Maya," Steve continued, before she could give a flat no. "I'm glad you made it there safely, and I'm impressed that you were able to create a new life for yourself. Are you willing to share more about what California was like? Did you stay with the market or find something else? Stay with the same roommates? How'd you make your way there for what, almost seven years was it? Take your time and start wherever you want."

***

Maya considered what to talk about next. She knew she had to give to get what she wanted. She thought Deena would be a good topic since it kept her in California. And she'd never really talked about Deena with anyone. She just had to spin it so he didn't start connecting too many dots.

She told Steve how Deena Pullman had popped up in Ralph's one day and flirted with her while paying for some beer. Deena had light brown hair in a buzz-cut with colorful tattoos on every inch of her body from the neck down. As she was wearing a bikini and flip-flops, that was a lot of visible territory. Maya couldn't help but stare. "Too bad you're not old enough to drink with me, Maya," Deena had said, reading her name tag. "You are cute, though. I'm Deena. Catch ya later."

Maya recalled being embarrassingly tongue-tied, but dreaming that night of what it would be like to trace Deena's artwork with her finger, to kiss her tanned neck and be in her embrace. Maya considered herself bi; she was attracted to guys and girls and that was nobody's business but hers. But she gravitated toward women. At that point, it had barely been a year since the twins and she held that anger toward men in particular, despite having met some cool dudes in North Carolina, on the road and here in Southern Cal. She hadn't been with any guys in her life but had an honest-to-God girlfriend for a hot minute in North Carolina. She always thought of that girlfriend, kindly Val, the first person to be gentle with her, as having broken her true virginity.

"Two days later, Deena came back and chose my line to check out. Did the same thing each of the couple of days after that, too. She asked when I had a break. We wound up at one of the boardwalk coffee places in Venice; she worked at a tattoo parlor. She shared a two-bedroom on a back street. Her room was like a closet."

She saw him watching her intently and was suddenly self-conscious sharing how she fell for a woman. But his eyes were soft and sympathetic. He wasn't judging. And he wasn't lusting.

"Anyway, I don't know if it was because she was older—she was 27—but she took me to bed that first night and I guess it was, you know, love. A couple months later, Jenna moved out of my place, and two days later Michelle left. Deena suggested she move in with me and Suzie; she made enough money that we didn't need to find a fourth roommate; she paid for two people."

"What was it like to live with someone ten years older? Someone so, I don't know, secure?"

"It was great. I mean, for a couple of years. She always had cash. She paid for everything. Bought me clothes, earrings, did my tattoos for free. I stopped cutting."

There was that curveball. Steve simply nodded.

"Yeah, I saw you staring at my tattoos before. I knew what you were looking for. Scars. Yes, it's true. I cut myself. All the shrinks I've talked with tell me all about how it's because of the rape and other abuse. How cutting gives me control. Whatever. I don't really buy all that psycho crap. It was just something to do."

He nodded again.

***

Slowly, Maya painted a picture of a woman she was allowing to take complete charge of her life. Although Deena brought out Maya's sexual passion during loud, emphatic sex—with Deena calling all the shots—she also pushed out the last roommate, Suzie, who felt uncomfortable being a heterosexual third wheel. Deena told Maya to quit the supermarket and a friend of hers hired Maya as a bartender at a restaurant right down the boardwalk from the tattoo place. Deena knew a guy who made fake IDs and got Maya one that said she was 21—legal to serve alcohol. Deena would hang in her corner seat on the bar for hours, which, conveniently, also was a place where she could easily store and sell pot, a little side business.

Maya said she loved the rush of life with Deena initially, the way she would grab her hand to introduce her to her beach buddies, caress her face, show her off. Deena taught her how to become a young woman, too, from grooming herself more neatly for the beach to picking out appropriately tight, suggestive shorts.

But as the second year with Deena began, Maya also noticed more negatives. For one thing, she found herself, like Deena, mocking people behind their backs, at the bar or to their mutual friends. Maya also thought nothing of asking simple favors from people like Suzie but she rarely returned the favor.

On the day Suzie told her she was moving out, she waited until Deena had left before pulling Maya aside. Suzie told her Deena was turning her into a "beach cunt," a phrase for women who'd use their looks and their body to get what they wanted. As if to prove her right, the day she actually left, Deena accused Suzie of stealing a bag of pot. The pot later turned up in a nightstand drawer. Maya began to realize that her life revolved around Deena's schedule—and that she didn't ever see the women she'd made friends with in the first few months in L.A. One day, when Maya didn't make it home until 3 a.m. on a night Deena got home at midnight, she wound up being accused of trying to hook up with one of the muscle boys from the beachfront gym. The "fight" ended with Deena pinning her to the bed and telling her she'd do anything for Maya, then making her scream in pleasure as if to prove it.

Steve interjected. "Sounds like Deena had some control issues. Or perhaps you were mostly unaware. She was a source of love and money; for the most part she kept you safe. What else did you notice as you got more involved with this woman?"

Maya paused. This was a strange game, giving in hopes of receiving. Truth, but not the whole truth. When she was playing the road game, there was the fear of having unwittingly picked up a psycho. With the counselor, it was a game of wits, even if Steve didn't know it. In a way, she found it intoxicating. She decided to give a little more because she wanted more, needed more, from him.

***

"Deena was strong, probably forty pounds heavier than me, but muscle pounds, you know? She worked out at the Gold's Gym on the beach. She told me the owner let her work out for free because she showed him the time of his life and even though it was years earlier he was still willing to pay."

"Did she ever abuse you?"

"No. No way."

"Well, did she ever intimidate you, you know, imply she could hurt you or frighten you? I'm not talking about what happened the night you came home late from the bar kind of stuff. I mean really threaten. Especially if you were to leave."

"No, Steve. She wanted me to get strong, like her."

He looked puzzled, and Maya liked that look. Steve's sandy hair and light brown eyes gave him a soft look, but he was smart. He was cuter than Dan the trucker for sure. She could understand what her mom might have seen in Steve back when . . . *FOCUS, Maya!*

She looked up to continue and knew Steve had caught her in her little thought bubble. He raised an eyebrow. She certainly wasn't giving that away yet. It would have to be the robberies.

***

"I know what you're really trying to find out is when it all ended. And it did."

Steve nodded, both indicating his awareness and for her to continue.

"Well, it took another three years. A lot happened in that time. Deena taught me how to pump iron and take care of my diet and my body, at least better than I had been. One day, she told me she had another side business that she wanted me to be involved with. I pretty much did what she said at that point. I was kind of like a mini-Deena.

"That night while I was working the bar I noticed her checking her cell phone, a second cell she used, which I always thought was for her pot deals. Turns out it wasn't. I got off at 10 and she asked me to come with her on a journey. She smiled when she said it, kind of her teasing smile, and I could not resist when she used it on me, so off we went. We drove a couple miles to Santa Monica, and she pulled up to a hotel, kind of a dumpy joint, and I follow her out to a room. 'We're here,' she announced through the door and we walked into a room that proved the place was a dump. I mean, peeling paint, ancient TV, that kind of thing. Deena took my hand and said to the guy, 'Just remember. You don't stick it in this one. You only get to watch.' Then she turned to me and said, 'It's OK, baby. Just be with me.'"

Steve looked concerned. But Maya was into the story and didn't want him to interrupt.

"It's not that she was selling me, Okay? What it was is she had been telling me she used to be into the swing scene, and she still liked a dick once in a while, even though she was with me. But she only did it to get something else out of it. Like money or drugs, right? She sold this guy on the idea of a threesome in which she would be the mistress, 'cause she always led and she'd bring a disciple who he couldn't touch. She got really physical with him, made him watch us and then did him. I mean, she was in complete command of him. He obeyed everything she said. I remember she wore a black negligee under her clothes, and she had a whip, you know, one of those sex whip things with a hard metal piece on one end and some rubbery straps on the other, and she used it on him, both ends. I got hot watching her tease him and I was ready for her. It felt like playing this role, sex in front of a stranger, was something I did every day. The whole thing took all of fifteen minutes, you know, 'cause guys."

Maya thought and kind of hoped Steve would be disturbed or at least surprised by the story, but he wore the same empathetic expression.

"But then came the surprise part."

That finally got a reaction from Steve. "Okay."

Maya was annoyed by his total acceptance of what she was sure would be shocking, but she continued.

"So I hadn't said a single word since we entered the room, and Deena said when she's done she had to use the bathroom and left me with the dude, who's just dozing the way guys do after sex. I totally ignored him 'cause I was trying to figure out if I should be furious at Deena, but I saw the money he'd given her at the start and figured some would be for me so I couldn't be that worried. Next thing I know she's back and said to him, 'Hey, lover, that was great, wasn't it?' And he was saying something and all of a sudden she jumped on him while he was still lying on the bed and smacked something over his nose and mouth and he couldn't even fight. I thought she killed him. But she just looked and me and winked. 'Check his wallet, take the cash and let's go.' There was like a grand inside. On top of what he'd already paid her."

She paused to give Steve a chance to respond. "That's quite a story. So you robbed the guy. That wasn't the end for you and Deena, though, because you said it was three years before you broke up."

"I'll get to that. But don't you want to know what happened? We get back to our place and Deena was sky high. We smoked some pot, then she took the fifteen hundred bucks we'd gotten and gave me four hundred. She looked at me a little guilty about it, said 'I set it up and I had his dick in me.' I didn't really care, though, because I was still high enough on the act itself. You know, I'd been raped and I'd been assaulted. This was kind of like revenge with a payoff. Deena had given me a gift. And I was grateful. I felt like I'd never had so much power in my life. Crazy love, right?

"But over the next year or so, things changed. We wound up doing one or two of these robbery gigs a month. She had an ad in some online thing that attracted guys who wanted two women. She screened pretty well to make sure it was likely the guys would have cash. She also started to get me involved sexually; she said the men were more likely to stay in line if they got to fuck us both. I went along 'cause she upped my share to just under half; she always kept extra because she was in charge and made the arrangements. I also learned over time she didn't just have the GHB that she used on the first guy.

Steve didn't want to disrupt the story, but he couldn't resist. "GHB?"

Maya looked at him with a frown.

"Yeah, you know, like knockout stuff."

"Oh, like chloroform."

"Yeah, but this stuff works much quicker. Anyway, Deena also had a blackjack in case something went wrong, and she taught me how to use it, you know, since she was the one who tried to do the GHB. "Make sure you hit him at the base of his head, so he doesn't bleed." And sure enough, one night this slob, a guy you never would have thought would be strong, surprised her. I mean, he was maybe 50 and not in shape at all, but he grabbed hold of her arm and lifted it off his face before she could really clamp down. I didn't even have time to panic because this all happened in like two seconds flat. I grabbed the blackjack and whacked him hard, right in the back of the head near the neck like she told me and he crumpled. I knew I didn't kill him, but I was scared shitless. We made crazy love that night, too. Deena said she was so proud of me for saving her, saving us.

"But it wasn't the same. I'd started to get pretty strong from the gym. I mean not as strong as Deena, but strong enough and smart enough to find my voice, you know? I told her I wanted the split to be 50–50 and I'd be happy to make the arrangements. I could tell she was pissed, but she agreed. Then I discovered running. I was getting out early on the beach in the early mornings because it's a rush, and running's something Deena didn't do and didn't want to do, even when I asked her. Though I was kind of glad she didn't want to, and I think she knew that. Instead, she became jealous of my time, I guess. Maybe she thought I was showing off for the early morning jocks. We started arguing more. But I couldn't break away from her. We loved each other."

Maya stopped for a breath and noticed Steve leaning back in his chair and looking skyward.

"What are you thinking? I'm talking to you, right? You wanted me to talk."

Steve smiled at her, that easy smile again. Maya wondered if he used it to hit on women. Guy like that, former ballplayer and a brain? He could have made out great with the chicks at Venice.

"Remember last session, Maya, when I asked you what you want out of counseling? And you said—"

"—I said I wanted to be done with all the fucking talk."

"Right. Or maybe you want to be done listening to others talk?" Steve's gut was telling him Maya's story was more truthful, but not yet complete. She was shielding parts of her story, which of course wasn't surprising. This was the story that she could control, and it demonstrated her strength. He wanted to get her to talk about when she was not in control in her life, because those moments would be where they could do their best work to change traumatic memories to bad memories, trauma-driven negative self-cognitions to cognitions based in the present. Perhaps even give her a sense of hope and a better direction.

She watched him guardedly, eyes down but sneaking looks at him; Steve never dropped his gaze from her. He wanted her to understand nothing she said scared him or made him think less of her.

When Maya ran her hand through her hair, Steve noticed how dark it was, so close to her eyes. Her eyebrows were not quite as dark. He glanced back to her tattoos and thought about the scars underneath. His instinct told him to throw another curveball.

"Hey, what's your natural hair color?"

"What?" Her slight rise in pitch, a nearly two-syllable pronunciation of the word, gave away her momentary panic. It was the first time he'd heard a wobble from the tough girl she took such pains to project. Steve knew he'd scored. Maya was not a brunette. Another disguise, not unlike the tattoos. But Steve didn't want to shut her down.

"Just a sudden thought. You were saying about your tattoos earlier, and I just realized your hair is so dark it's probably not the natural color, especially after those years at the beach. But that's neither here nor there." Actually, it was very here and there, but he didn't want to press. He needed her to regain her confidence. "Let's get back to the Deena story and what led you away from her in the end."

Maya didn't pass up the opportunity to grab back the narrative.

"I'll tell you about Deena, but I want something, too. I want to know about you. I don't really understand counseling, but it seems it's going to be part of my life. How can I be sure to trust you? "

"Fair enough. Tell you what. You finish your story about Deena and then fire away at me, Okay? Bottom line is I want to be able to help you, and I'm open to your needs."

***

"A couple of years ago, we were hanging at home and Deena was online and laughing. She said her new ad was gonna bring us a bunch more clients. I realized I'd socked away maybe five grand by then, and just like that, I was done. I'm not sure why. The rush wasn't a rush anymore, I guess. I told her that and we had a big fight. She was screaming at me, then she was crying to me. I didn't budge, and that night she slept on the couch. Next few days she tried to be nice, she tried to guilt me, she tried to reason. But I stuck to my guns. She did the next job by herself. I knew she was going to, and I just went to work that day and when I got home, she wasn't there yet. She rolled in about 2 in the morning drunk.

"A few hours later when I came in from my run, she was just hating on me. She threw a ten-dollar bill bill at me. 'Here's your share. Fuck you.' I told her I was done with her, and as soon as I could find a new place, I was outta there. When I got home that night, she was gone. And so was my five grand. She'd trashed the place to find where I kept my money. I still had a few hundred in my checking account, but that whole thing got me thinking about leaving L.A. I did not want to see her face again, but we were both still around that beach scene. Then she started coming into the bar picking up, or trying to pick up, other women whenever I was working. I wasn't sure if she was trying to win me back or make me jealous, but I also realized I didn't give a fuck. I didn't have any feelings for her anymore.

"I also knew I was as strong as she was by then. So one day I walked into her tattoo parlor and told her if she ever showed her face in the bar again unless it was to return my money I'd kick her goddamn ass. And I punched her in the gut and didn't hold anything back."

"Did it work?"

"She didn't ever come back while I was there. I look at it now and we had something nice in the physical department, but the whole time, she was using me. And it wasn't like the robberies, the sex, prostitution, whatever you want to call what we did was rape, but it was, ya know? Except she was the rapist. When she took my money, she raped me no different than my fucking foster father, and no better than what we were doing to those johns."

Steve took a swig from his water bottle. "Thank you. I'm sorry about what happened. Tough lesson. You sound like you learned a lot."

Maya shrugged. "Whatever. Your turn."

"What do you want to know?"

***

Steve didn't have to think long to respond to Maya's question.

"Worst thing that's happened to me as a counselor is easy. It was twelve years ago, and I'd been counseling for a couple of years when a young woman came to see me. She was struggling with self-esteem and substance issues, and I didn't read her right. She wound up dying by suicide."

Maya wasn't impressed. "You know, I shared a lot more about me than you just did. You're gonna have to do better."

Kiely Hanrahan wasn't ever far from Steve's thoughts, a stark reminder of the sacred bond counselors have with their clients and the pain of failure. But though Kiely had been gone for more than a decade, Steve still had to be careful from an ethics standpoint of not pointing to who his client was even now. He decided in the moment that in the interest of his work with this client, he could use his discretion and share something of what happened with Kiely.

Steve opened the middle drawer of his heavy antique oak desk and withdrew an Indian head nickel.

"Check this out."

He perceived a quick, short intake of breath. But if he was correct about her reaction, it was quickly gone.

"Yeah, so?"

"It tells the story."

***

I enjoy observing Kiely, her bright red hair occasionally flopping down onto her forehead, especially when she becomes animated, inevitably prompting a casual, yet almost dramatic brush and sigh of annoyance. An Indian head nickel dangles on a chain around her neck. She says she wears it in memory of her partner. It makes her remember his human side. He liked to collect unique but inexpensive things, which she says was stupid. But this thing was about all he'd left her. Her contradictions are one of the aspects I'm still trying to figure out.

Kiely's little girl voice tries but never quite succeeds in hiding the wounds of the 29-year-old woman inside, the person who'd fatally stabbed her partner when he tried to choke her to death in an alcohol- and cocaine-fueled rage three years earlier. Her voice has a lilt, which I'm pretty sure is intentional, done to lure men (and maybe me, too), but also a tiny quiver that belies her pain. Kiely is the first client I've seen to prove Jim's warning correct that all counselors fall in love with a client at some point in their careers. He didn't necessarily mean romantic love but rather some form of physical attraction or empathic need to nurture or strong desire to protect. Jim's also told me if I recognize it, I need to address it with him in supervision.

I've seen Kiely a dozen times now, and believe we're making progress addressing what I've diagnosed as depression, even though I've also heard some disturbing thoughts about self-harm, ideations that she quickly laughs about and says she'd never act upon. "I have a daughter to raise, after all, Steve." Kiely is struggling with alcohol in addition to her depression, or perhaps because of it, and that is resulting in her losing hours at the restaurant where she bartends. She calls in at least once a week claiming her daughter is sick, but in reality it is Kiely. She knows it and her bosses know it. She can't get out of her funk. She admits she occasionally takes it out on her 13-year-old, smacking her for no particular reason. I'm not ready to notify Social Services, but it's a troublesome part of her story. I'd spent part of our previous session doing psychoeducation with her on child welfare.

I'm not much older than Kiely, and I feel like my years striving for the big leagues but falling short helps me in my connection with her on her own sense of loss in not achieving her dreams in life. I've been working to help her understand her desires and to try to confront her aggressive nature by doing mindfulness-based breathing exercises whenever she feels a tingling in her arms, a physical sign that her temper is flaring. Kiely has a wonderful throaty laugh, which, along with her wicked, deadpan humor gives me hope for her. She likes to kick off her shoes and tuck her bare feet underneath her. It makes her look like the teenager I imagine she still wants to be. In the past two sessions, she'd brought me first some brownies and then a jar of homemade salsa, little "thank you"s that prove she knows her way around a kitchen. But she admits she only cooks when she feels like it. Which is becoming rarer. If she's not working, she says, she tends to stay in bed or on the sofa. She'd gotten a food stamp card a few months earlier and says she's too embarrassed to use it when she goes to shop. So she sends her daughter instead.

I'd been using a therapy model called Internal Family Systems to help her identify parts of herself that tended to be dysfunctional. Today, I decide to talk with her about using her talent in the kitchen to more positive ends.

"Kiely, I'm going to do something I don't often do with clients. We're supposed to let you do work for yourselves, but I enjoyed the food you've brought me and so I took the liberty of looking up this training program someone told me about at a local food pantry."

"Wow, you did that for me, Steve?"

I think she's being sincere and not sarcastic, so I continue.

"Yes, I did. You may not realize it; maybe no one's ever told you this, but you have talent. Anyway, in the program, they teach you kitchen skills like cutting vegetables and other prep work with the goal of getting you placed at local restaurants. It's a way to get people hired. Turnover in restaurants is crazy. It will be a chance for you to finally find full-time work."

I hand her a printout with the information.

"Do you really think I can do this?"

"Not only do I think that, but if you put in the work, I can see you one day owning your own restaurant. You have a personality that draws people in. It's the dark parts of that personality that you have to be able to recognize when they want to come out. If we can work on some coping skills, we can push down the dark parts and allow your true self to shine."

"Thank you, Steve. This really means something to me. Did I tell you I make a crazy good grilled cheese sandwich?"

As she discusses the way she browns her bread in a pan by buttering the outside, I find my mind wondering if my approach is the smart one. Part of me knows I'm pushing a solution more so than with my regular clients. Why is that? Do I want her to succeed so much that I'm overlooking the darker parts of her personality? Am I trying to rescue her? I scribble a note to speak with Jim about Kiely. It's time.

***

Steve paused after telling Maya a little more about Kiely when he noticed her shaking her head at him.

"Look, I'd like to tell you more, Maya, but as I said ..."

"You don't have to treat me like a child. I know you can't tell me that much. What I want to know is about the nickel. You said it 'tells the story.' But then you didn't say anything about it."

"Ah the Indian head nickel, yes, sorry about that. She wore it, and after she died, it arrived in the mail. I guess I hold onto it as a reminder."

"A reminder? Of something so awful?"

"No, Maya. A reminder to myself that I'm not perfect. Can't save everyone. In fact, let me rephrase because honestly, I'm really not trying to save anyone. I'm hoping to assist people find what they need to get to a better place. Make sense?"

She nodded.

"I'll buy that. I'm sorry for you."

"Thank you, Maya. I appreciate that."

She leapt from her seat so suddenly Steve flinched.

"Sorry. Time's up, right? I have stuff to do."

"Yes it is. See you next week."

Post-session: Maya

I WINCE WITH THE CUT. IT'S JUST ABOVE THE RIGHT KNEE, the point of my Swiss army knife piercing the skin and drawing a bead of bright red. I start to pull it slowly back toward myself but hesitate. Instead, I touch my finger to the blood and lick it. I haven't done this in six years. I suddenly hear a firm, authoritative woman's voice in my head. *Do you really want to start? Do you need to?*

That's what the woman shrink at the Social Services agency said to me about cutting when I saw her a few months after my first foster father raped me. The asshole had gotten off because I wouldn't press charges and they promised to get me out of that place, which they were happy to do and not have to deal with the publicity that charges could bring. I fucked that up big time. Fourteen years old, though. What was I supposed to do? The shrink had deep red hair, probably dyed, wore gold-wire glasses and had a severe look about her. It's what I imagine my mom might have looked like if she'd ever gotten her act together and gone straight. The shrink was a cold bitch. But she did get me to thinking about cutting. She made it less fun. Maybe that's why I stopped.

I take a tissue out of the glove compartment and wipe the knife down, then fold it and return it to my purse. Why had I just cut myself? Was it really as simple as hearing Steve's edited version of his work with Mom? Was it all the Deena shit? The little bit of blood has already caked. Won't even leave a scab.

It's good to finally start getting to what I need to know. But the story is weird. He seems to have liked her. Next session I'm not going to blab so much. I have to make him tell me more. Like how he got to pushing her so far over the edge. I take a couple of slow breaths in and out, the technique taught to me by the social worker I saw after the fuck-me twins did their thing. At least that one taught me the ability to calm down quickly. She also planted the idea that I could get the fuck out of dodge by talking so much about choices and controlling what I could. Steve's actually the fourth shrink I've seen, come to think of it. There was that guy, the school counselor, after Dad's death. Did I get anything from him?

I pull into a parking space outside the house and take the steps quickly. Just enough time to get cleaned up and run to work. As I put the key in the lock, I get a flash image of the Indian head nickel. I open the door and charge inside, fighting back tears. Fuck me.

Post-session: Steve

THE BIG PURPLE DSM IS OPEN IN FRONT OF ME. Maya's story today was a big "uh-oh." Participating in a string of sex fantasy violent robberies, with prostitution thrown in, all under the tutelage of an older woman lover, calls to mind something stronger than adjustment disorder. I turn to post-traumatic stress disorder. Maya's had multiple traumas in her life, but we haven't gone deep enough yet to know if she has intrusion symptoms, avoidance, or negative alteration of cognitions or mood, all hallmarks of PTSD. My money's on all three. But is PTSD a likely primary diagnosis for Maya?

And do I need to report her to authorities? She confessed to some heavy criminal acts today. But I also know there's no proof of any of those acts, and my duty to work with this client who is seeking help probably requires me to know a lot more before I consider whether there is anything to report to authorities. I don't see her as an immediate threat to others, which would be the main reason to report.

I turn back to Maya in session. She was spooked when I asked about her natural hair color. She's trying to cover up something, just like her cutting scars. Or is she? Cutting scars are like a badge of honor, and she was proud to admit that. The tattoos to cover them speak more to her relationship with Deena, and her desire for creativity and change. Hair color is something else. I need to know more.

I close Maya's chart and open my middle desk drawer, removing the nickel with the hole in the top. I'd gotten it in the mail soon after Kiely took her life. No note. It just showed up. I had no clue, but I tucked it in my drawer nonetheless. Kiely was a "miss," but she'd still haunts me after a dozen years. The only client I ever had who died by suicide. I simply hadn't seen her pain.

"Hey, boss."

Kenzie is hanging on the door frame, one arm on the post and her body leaning forward. She brings me back to reality.

"Jill canceled. Said something came up and asked if you'd forgive her the full fee. She's your last appointment, too. Why don't you get out of here? I can close."

***

Sam trots to me as I enter the condo and I scratch behind her ears the way she likes. She tilts her head and leans into me and I laugh. "You want your walk, don't you?" Of course she does. My 9-year-old black mutt with the white blaze on her chest needs her exercise. I still can't believe it's been so long since she came into my life, a kind of forced birthday present from Bobby Pru, my old Durham battery mate. He came to visit a few months after my wife, Sheila, had left me. Bobby brought me with him to the county animal shelter on the pretense he was thinking of getting a dog. Next thing I knew, this loving girl was twisting and turning every which way in her blanket to lick my face. I didn't think I was ready for a dog, being as I had no one at home anymore. But Pru noted my house was under contract to be sold, and he pointed me toward a condo development in the trending ballpark neighborhood with its own off-leash dog park. The only excuse I had was my own fear.

Sam isn't standing for my ruminating on her origin story. She bangs me in the thigh with her head. It hurts.

I leash her up, grab a couple of poop bags and head downstairs. It's brisk and I think I'm going to regret not grabbing one of my old Durham caps; my hair has been disturbingly thinner the past few years. Still, I let Sam play a good twenty minutes. There are only a couple of other dogs. One is a Pomeranian named Max who Sam occasionally puts in his place with her paw on top of his head. She has him by 40 pounds and doesn't feel like dealing with his jumping on her. The other is a pit mix who seems to have as little interest in Sam as she does in him. The pit's owner is a redhead, about 30. I'd seen her around, always when going out to our cars or in passing at the dog run, but we hadn't introduced ourselves. I nod to her and she waves, then walks over.

"Hi, I'm Jane. Jane Darwin. I live on the second floor. How are you doing? Your dog is so cute. I'm glad she puts up with Astro. Hope you don't mind."

"No, not at all. I'm Steve, by the way. Astro is very friendly."

As I'm speaking, Astro is putting his front paws on my leg getting ready to jump and I feel Sam getting ready to defend. I'm tensed, but Jane beats me to the punch by pulling on her harness leash sharply with a "No, Astro," and he immediately gets down, falling into place behind Jane with the slightest disappointed whimper.

"That's a good trick. You've done some training. Good for you."

"Thanks, Steve. If you don't mind my asking, what do you do?"

"I'm a counselor, a mental health counselor."

"Really?"

"Yup. Interesting work. What about you?"

"Admin at Brown and Meister; they're a local law firm. I'm actually in law school, though, so this is just to earn some cash."

"That's a tough road, law school and work. How do you make time for Astro?"

She smiles. "Oh, well, he gets all my spare time. And he helps me with studying."

"Nothing wrong with that."

"I love him to death, Steve, if you can't tell. Hey listen, it's good to meet someone interesting here, but—and this is not a line to get away—I left a soup on low on the stove. So I really do have to run. Maybe we can take our pups over to one of the big dog parks one day?"

Astro starts pulling her to the path hard, and Jane smacks her head.

"Should have known. Can't say the word 'dog park' in front of him."

"I know what you mean; Sam's vocabulary is amazing. By the way, the dog park sounds great. But I don't have your number."

"What's your last name, Steve?"

"Prescott."

"I'll find you and email. I'm good at that." She gives a "ta-ta" goodbye and I watch her go.

Was that flirting? It has been a while, but I like the idea of it, even if she seems a little young for me.

I watch her disappear toward her building, and notice her glance back toward the park. She can't see me because of her angle. But I like that she looked.

Maybe it was Jane's red hair, but the interaction makes me think of Kiely again, and the session with Maya today. I turn back to Sam. "Hey, girl, want to fetch your frisbee?" She does. Over and over and then some more. It's good relief from thinking. I don't like to have cases or memories rattling in my head when I'm home.

Sam usually eats at 6 and it's only 5:30 when we get back upstairs, but I make her food anyway, which she enthusiastically agrees is a good idea, slurping at some gravy from her can on my hand. After wiping off her slobber, I grab a bourbon glass and pour two shots from the minibar, then pile in ice from the fridge dispenser. I ease my way into my red leather recliner with its view of the ballpark and downtown; it's a higher, slightly farther vantage point, and it's from the other direction of my view of the stadium from the office.

I'm restless, though, so I step out on the balcony and pull out one of the tall boy resin seats, setting the drink down on the high-top table. It's not as comfy as the recliner, but the brisk late autumn air is good for the soul. I sip slowly, taking in the elm trees below and the way the wind sweeps up a handful of colorful leaves every time it kicks in.

I ponder the question that had been in my head for a dozen years. Two questions, actually. Had I fallen for Kiely? How did I not see evidence of suicide? Of course, they're unanswerable. Why do I do this to myself? Why is this one case so hard to let go? Misses are a way of life for counselors, and learning to let go of results over which you have no control has been, other than this case, easy for me. I credit my parents with helping me know there is always more to strive for; it's why I transitioned easily after the elbow. Would it have been nice to make the big leagues? Sure. Would it have been nice to be a millionaire? Probably. I'm not hooked on money, though, not like so many of my teammates—from high school to the minors.

Money doesn't save people from their own internal struggles. I once tried to tell that to Kiely, who was bitter about her poverty. I exhale loudly and long enough that Sam gets up and puts her snout on the other side of the door, fogging up a small round spot. I know there are dozens of clients among the hundreds I've seen that walked away thinking *this guy doesn't know jack.*

Kiely, though. I close my eyes and can see her face in the last session we had. She was hopeful when I spoke about the soup kitchen program and I looked it up online and slipped her the phone number. "I'm calling tomorrow, Steve." What was I missing there?

Maya's face suddenly comes back into view in my head. If there's one thing Kiely did for my trauma brain, she put me on high-alert mode for suicide in all of my clients since. Maya cuts herself, or she did for a period of time. And she's had so much trauma in her life. Mental note to self: Can't rule out suicide, even if her presentation doesn't speak directly to it.

I sit forward suddenly, pausing the bourbon glass at my lips. Why did Maya want to know about the worst thing that's happened to me? Is she asking something or is she trying to say something?

*****

I'd begun to pour a third shot but instead put the Elijah Craig bottle down midway. I pick up my cell and text my buddy Enrique Salazar. "You free? Grab a bite?"

I stick a plastic cup under the water dispenser in the fridge and sip while waiting for his response. It only takes a couple of minutes.

***

The Duke–N.C. State men's basketball game had brought a crowd to Tobacco Road, the restaurant just behind the ballpark, but we'd grabbed a high-top in the corner behind the long, modern bar that afforded us space to talk without straining our vocal cords. Enrique raised his Endless River Kolsch, a local beer that I'd gone ahead and ordered, too.

"To friends!"

Enrique waited for me; his nature was to defer. He reached for a platter of loaded pork nachos between us and stole glances at one of the big screens.

"I just need to talk something out, Enrique," I finally say. "You never judge. I've been thinking about a client from long ago."

"You've mentioned this client before to me, haven't you?"

I nod.

"What's got her on your mind?"

***

Enrique came to see me a few months after Kiely's death. The timing was perfect. After Kiely died, I'd referred most of my clients to other therapists and stopped taking new ones, limiting myself to the few clients I'd established a trusting relationship with. "Safe" clients. But five or six clients a week wasn't enough to pay my bills. One day over a burger and fries, Jim gave me a dose of reality. "Is losing a client going to drive you from the profession? If it is, maybe you weren't meant to be a counselor. I hope what happens here is you learn from this and keep going, keep testing yourself."

Enrique was then a shortstop with the Bulls, joining the team a couple of years after I retired. Team management, concerned about his erratic behavior and anger in the clubhouse and on the field, had suggested counseling. Enrique called the afternoon I got back from the lunch with Jim. I don't consider timing like that to be coincidence. Although I gave up the church of my upbringing long ago and don't believe in that kind of all-powerful God in heaven, I have come to believe there's too much I don't understand to simply call things like Enrique coming in as a client a coincidence. I see it as the will of a higher power.

During the initial diagnostic session, I'd found Enrique to be polite and shy, with no evidence of the anger that team management was worried about. He had a mop of curly black hair, combined with soft dark eyes and deep tan skin tone. I told him he looked pretty mild-mannered to me and asked how he acted out. Enrique, blushing and looking down, told me he'd been flinging his bat in the clubhouse after a poor game and cursing out opponents from the dugout. He'd also been angry with teammates, rejecting offers of help. He said he was frustrated over a slump. When I inquired how he was coping with the pressure, Enrique admitted that he was drinking a lot after games, usually by himself. He also had taken to using pot, which was fairly common among the players as a stress reliever. What concerned me was that Enrique had stopped going to the gym. In the cutthroat environment of the minor leagues, if you dream of advancing to the bigs, you have to work for it—mind and body.

Enrique had been signed as a slick fielding shortstop who might be taught to wield a good enough bat to get him to the majors, at least as a late-inning defensive sub. His first year in Triple-A the previous season had been promising; he'd batted .277 and whacked a surprising 10 home runs, not bad for a shortstop. His fielding was superb. But when he came to see me, his average was hovering at the Mendoza line (less than .200) and he led the league's shortstops in errors.

At our third session, I asked about Enrique's support system. Who could he talk to when he was struggling?

"My sister, Elena, I love her. But she just got married and I don't want to bother her. Plus, her husband can't stand me and I don't like him."

I felt that was significant, but Enrique started to talk about a cousin who he used to hang around with as a teenager. "But what's the point, Steve? You know, you were a player. I suck, and they're gonna ship me back down to Double-A, maybe even Single-A the way I'm playing. Just so mad. How did this happen?"

I watched him clenching his hands hard enough to make the veins on his arms stand out. I put him through a simple breathing exercise to calm himself, just as I'd suggested at our previous session, when I spoke about settling himself down as he stepped into the batter's box. But I had a hunch his batting slump wouldn't be cured by a resiliency exercise.

"Hey, Enrique. You said something a few minutes ago that I'm curious about. Your brother-in-law can't stand you. What's that about?"

Before I even finished the sentence, Enrique dropped his head and gently began to weep. I nudged the tissue box toward him.

"We went to the same high school in Miami. One day after school, he saw me in a stairway. It was during class. I'd arranged to meet a friend. He didn't like what he saw."

"Romantic?"

Enrique barely whispered. "Yes."

"A guy?"

He shot me a guilty look.

"And you're scared he's going to reveal your secret?"

"No. He's not going to do that. You see, Elena agreed to marry him after he told her I was 'a faggot.' She said if he wanted her to be with her, to marry her, he could never say anything to anyone about me unless I came out first. Steve, she married this asshole to protect me, not out of love."

"That's a heavy burden to carry, Enrique."

We sat in silence for the final ten minutes of the session and I asked Enrique to consider a question for discussion at our next session. Whose decisions can he control other than his own?

The next week, Enrique seemed more at ease. "It was her choice," he said. "Just as my I am what I am."

"So now what?"

"I'm not ready to come out, if that's what you mean. I can't. No way."

"Then why fret, Enrique? You control the ability to say what you want, act as you want, feel as you feel. That will always be there, right? And what if someone were to find out and that power and control were taken away from you?"

"I have no clue." Enrique's eyes started to tear up again.

"There's an old saying, Enrique. Life is hard by the yard, but a cinch by the inch."

Enrique stared blankly and I laughed. "You don't get it?"

Then Enrique surprised me. "Actually, I think I do. I just had to figure it out. It means live in the moment, right?"

"It sure gets easier when you do. I can tell you that. You know my dream ended on a torn elbow ligament, Enrique. Something I could not control. I learned to live by the inch and, well, here I am."

***

As far as Enrique knew, no one ever learned his secret while he was playing. He initially stopped seeing me at the end of that baseball season, which had gone better once he quit drinking and smoking pot. The next year, though healthier, Enrique still didn't return to the form he showed when he first joined the Bulls. That's the way it is for the majority of players; you only go as far as your talent takes you. When the team cut Enrique at season's end, he decided to quit baseball altogether. A cousin was starting a restaurant in Durham and wanted Enrique to be a manager, capitalizing on his local renown of three years on the team.

Enrique called me again a year later. He'd decided to come out to his family and needed to talk through his fears.

I was grateful for Enrique's willingness to let me along for the ride on his personal journey. And I realized my time with him had helped me rediscover the joy of counseling.

A few years later, long after the ethical limit on "dual" relationships between counselor and client had passed, I'd reached out to Enrique to say hello. I was curious about how he was doing, but I also wanted to share my gratitude over what being able to work with him had meant to me. Over beers that night at his cousin's Cuban restaurant, Havana Nights, in the American Tobacco Historic District, I told him how he'd helped me recover from a very bad experience with a client, one that he correctly guessed—and I did not deny—was suicide. Ethics didn't allow me to share further details, and Enrique innately sensed that and was simply present. A friendship was born. We shared a common love of baseball and sports, family and food. And we'd also both stayed in the Durham community when our baseball careers ended, another shared connection.

Enrique was one of the most balanced people I knew. In the past three years, he'd partnered with his cousin on a second restaurant, met and moved in with his boyfriend, a high school music teacher, made the cover of Out *magazine, and after a year of publicity as a former ballplayer willing to go public with his lifestyle, settled into a comfortable, secure adulthood.*

When I was troubled these days about things personal or professional, I often called Enrique. He helped me through my dating struggles, and though I couldn't share work details, being able to be present with him helped me to decompress.

***

Enrique is well aware of how little I can say anything specific about my work. He smiles, though, and asks what's bugging me.

"I have a new client who, as part of her therapy, wants me to share my past—specifically, the worst thing that ever happened to me as a counselor."

"And that's why your former client is occupying your mind."

"You got it, my friend. I can't really tell you more about the new client, but I keep thinking about my former client and I'm second-guessing myself about what I knew or didn't know about her. What I saw or assumed versus what I actually knew."

"You once told me you can't go back in time, Steve. You also reminded me—a lot—about what I could control."

"I did. But I feel like this new client is giving me an opportunity, and just like with the other one, there's something I'm not seeing."

"You think your new client could commit suicide?"

Interesting that Enrique picked up on the very question I'd thought about hours earlier. I think about it again. Nothing about Maya says "suicide." If anything, her background in robbing men, combined with the multiple adverse childhood events she endured, makes her more of a combustible personality with an antisocial and dangerous edge. I suddenly feel a lightbulb turn on, and Enrique sees my look.

"Okay, so time for the check, my friend?"

"Enrique, you're a mind reader. Yes. And thank you for listening to me babble."

My mind spins on the short ride home. Maya doesn't have an "adjustment disorder," the diagnosis I'd given her after the first session. But I'm positive that substance use is not her problem, either. In fact, drugs would be simply a disguise. I need to look more closely at Maya through the lens of antisocial personality disorder or borderline personality disorder. Enrique's suicide question had unlocked my thinking.

Maya isn't suicidal. But she might be homicidal.

Session Three ~ Eyes Open

KENZIE PUT DOWN HER HEADSET AND EXHALED. SHE HAD TO leave a message for Jill Travers, Steve's no-show from last week. She didn't like it when her boss's clients didn't even bother to call or cancel. She didn't understand why Steve didn't get as annoyed as she did. She made a note to check one more time, and then she was going to tell Steve she would bill for the missed session, though she knew he would tell her not to.

As she put the Travers chart back into the filing cabinet, her finger caught slightly under the handle and she took in a sharp breath. She'd nearly torn one of her nails, and she'd just had them done last night by her nail goddess, Emma, who created a midnight blue base with small sequins glued on. Doing her nails up was a treat she occasionally allowed herself once the bills were paid. She suddenly sensed a presence and realized she had a client at the window watching her admire her own nails. Flustered, she returned to the desk and smiled at Maya Andino, who smiled right back at her.

"I'm sorry, I didn't see you waiting."

The young woman shrugged. "Just checking in"

"Right. Steve's still with his 1 o'clock and, I guess . . ." Kenzie glanced at the clock, "oh, he's running a little late. So sorry. But actually, this is good. Quick question for you, Ms. Andino."

"Just call me Maya."

"Yes, of course. Maya." Kenzie felt that her face was still red after being caught admiring her own nails. Silly. Maya was probably about her age, but they were very different. She wondered how she got involved in drugs. Kenzie didn't know much about any of the clients, other than clients such as Maya, who'd been referred.

"I've been trying to get a line on your billing, Maya. But so far I haven't gotten anywhere with Social Services, which usually handles, um, you know, judicial referrals?"

"Oh, yeah, I have no clue."

"Well, do you have any contact info? They often give a card to the defendant, I mean the person, they're referring?" Kenzie immediately felt her face reddening again. Why was she so nervous?

*****

When Kenzie was a 16-year-old sophomore at Hillside High in Durham, she was a pep squad dancer, performing with 20 other girls and a handful of boys at football and basketball games. One handsome junior, Ryan Waddell, had been her boyfriend for a year, and everyone, even her mother, would comment on what a perfect couple they were. Ryan was 6 feet tall and athletic, dark hair that he wore long but neat. Some of the boys on the squad were mocked by kids at school, but no one made fun of Ryan. The consensus of their friends was that Kenzie and Ryan brought joy to any room they entered.

What she hadn't told her mom or her best friends, Danielle or Stephanie, was that Ryan was pushing for them to have sex. They regularly made out and she'd let Ryan feel her, but something wasn't right to her about it. She wanted her first to be someone who made her melt.

She also had a secret—she knew exactly what it would feel like.

The year before, she was studying for a Quinceñera as part of her religious school program at Immaculate Catholic School. Mom wasn't that religious, being raised Baptist, but Dad was Mexican-American and wanted the kids to be raised that way. So Mom got them into the school thanks to financial help from her own parents, who Kenzie who knew as loving and supportive despite the religious difference.

Catholicism became an anchor for Kenzie, even though it was kind of a pain. She said her prayers, but Sunday school and church had limited her ability to be as involved as she wanted to be in dance all those years. She was good, maybe even good enough to win a college scholarship. But that required time and practice, and Dad wouldn't let her drop anything church related for dance. She agreed on the condition they'd allow her to go to public high school, a point she reiterated throughout her middle school years, and she settled for working as hard as she could in weekly dance and dreaming of joining the pep squad when she made it to ninth grade.

At Immaculata, she struck up a church friendship with LuEllen, a 16-year-old who despised church. She was a Goth, not at all the kind of girl her parents would approve of, but whose questioning of nuns and even the priest at Immaculata secretly thrilled Kenzie. This little, dark-haired, shadowy girl dressed all in black got under the skin of every authority figure in the building. The other girls shunned LuEllen, but Kenzie would shyly smile at her when she challenged one of the nuns—"How do you know Jesus doesn't want me to wear black? He wanted people to be themselves."—and LuEllen approached her one day after the final bell, putting her hand on Kenzie's arm to let the other kids pass on the way to the stairway.

"You don't like this place either, do you?"

"It's not that I don't like it. I guess I just…"

"Just hate it, right?"

"I don't hate it. Why would you say that?"

"Something about it bothers you. I can tell. You know, if you keep that stuff locked up, you'll be slave to them all your life."

"Who's them?"

LuEllen looked at her like she was 4.

"Follow me."

LuEllen headed to the stairway. Kenzie followed.

In the stairway, LuEllen sat on one of the steps near a landing between floors. Kenzie sat down next to her.

Their faces were inches apart, and Kenzie realized LuEllen was wearing a make-up that accentuated her paleness.

"Them is the power, Kenzie. Our parents. Priests. Nuns. They all want to boss us around, make us do things their way."

"I guess. But they are adults."

"Do you think adults know best?"

"I mean…"

LuEllen put her hand on Kenzie's shoulder. She felt uncomfortable but also a tingle of excitement. More so than when Jimmy Parker had leaned in to kiss her on the cheek in the dark theater in seventh grade when she'd agreed go on a date with him. More so than when her first real boyfriend, Evan Alston, had kissed her on the lips and she'd opened up her lips in return, her first time making out.

Yet this wasn't romantic, Kenzie realized. LuEllen was fiercely passionate about this issue.

"Kenzie, adults, your parents, these church idiots, want to stop you from being you."

"I don't know what you mean."

She sighed in frustration.

"The Catholic church, Kenzie. They're trying to tell you what Jesus means. And they don't know that."

"Well, they probably know it better than we do. They've studied it for years, taught it for years."

"Not what I mean. Look, you're a good girl. I know you are. But you're also smart. Can't you see they would try to keep you from being you if they could?"

LuEllen took her hand off Kenzie's shoulder. And started to stand. "Screw it. I shouldn't have bothered."

Kenzie was confused. But she wanted to know more, and wanted more time with LuEllen.

She grabbed LuEllen's hand.

"No, tell me more. I want to know exactly what you mean."

LuEllen looked deeply into her eyes and brought the hand Kenzie had grabbed and was still holding up between them. She kissed Kenzie's fingers.

"You are a smart girl. I'm lesbian. What I'm trying to say is these people will never accept me for who I am, and I don't like hiding. Do you?"

Kenzie was processing what LuEllen had just said when she felt LuEllen's free hand and arm go around her waist and pull her in. Without hesitation, she responded as they kissed.

"GIRLS!"

Sister Mary stood at the top of the stairs.

***

"No, no card. Not that I can recall." Maya smiled, her dark eyes suddenly softening. "Hey, you know those nails are pretty nice. Can I see them?"

What a difference this girl's smile made, Kenzie thought. It was like she was a different person. She held out her hand to show off.

"Why yes, of course. I nearly just took one off. A woman I know does them. Have you ever had your nails done?

Maya looked at her and pursed her lips, suppressing a giggle. *It made her look even prettier.*

"Why, no, obviously you haven't. I'm sorry."

"What, you don't think I could have my nails done?"

"No, I mean I guess I didn't. But that's really bad of me. I shouldn't make assumptions about people."

Maya grinned back. "My turn to be sorry, Kenzie. I was just giving you a hard time. You take things very literally. And I sometimes get on people." Maya reached out and took a hold of Kenzie's palm, so she could bring it closer to her through the opening in the window. "These are really pretty. I like that deep blue. Goes nice with your hair. And by the way, you were right. I haven't ever had my nails done." Still holding Kenzie's left hand with her right, Maya showed Kenzie the nondescript nails of her left hand. She didn't chew her nails, but she kept them short.

Kenzie felt a shiver as Maya let her hand go. Had Maya slightly allowed her forefinger to stroke the top of Kenzie's hand when she released it? She felt a tingle as Maya turned away and headed to one of the seats. It was the same feeling she'd had eleven years earlier with LuEllen, who she'd never interacted with again. The nuns had LuEllen dismissed from the school and told Kenzie's parents. She was deeply embarrassed; she assured her parents that LuEllen had "jumped" her. Boys. Only boys, she'd resolved to herself that night.

The light blinking on her desk disrupted her memory and Kenzie stood up to look for Maya, who was watching her with raised eyebrows.

Kenzie paused before opening her mouth.

"He's ready for you."

"Thanks, girl. Everything okay?"

"Yeah, fine, Maya. Thank you."

Kenzie felt alive. She had buried the meaning of LuEllen's final words to her for years. *I don't like hiding. Do you?* LuEllen didn't believe Kenzie was lesbian. She *knew* it. How could she know that when Kenzie didn't know it herself?

The phone rang and Kenzie picked it up to make an appointment, responding mindlessly to that task as her mind raced over a newfound recognition. *I'm an adult. I don't need to please anyone else.* Maya had read her just then in a way not unlike LuEllen. She didn't want to bury the chills she felt inside. Dammit. She also realized she hadn't cleared up Maya's billing issue. She'd have to text her.

***

Maya appeared to be in a non-responsive mood. Steve was trying to learn more about the breakup with Deena but she kept pulling the conversation back to minor things, such as her job at the diner and how she found her apartment through a woman she met at the grocery store, just like what happened to her in California. She said she liked Kenzie, thought she was nice.

"You don't feel like talking about California anymore, Maya?"

She stared at him. "Well, clearly *you* do."

He felt himself starting to smile but he didn't break contact with those intense eyes.

"Here's the thing, Maya. Our time is meant to unlock some of the reasons behind your drug issue and show the court there is reason to believe this is not going to be a habitual thing, as you insist it won't be. But I can't do that without understanding more of your life. So these are things I need to know in filing my notes with the court. Make sense?"

"Not really."

She was so edgy. Steve decided to try again.

"Let's put it this way, Maya. You're not going to get a free pass on intent-to-sell charges unless the judge thinks you won't do it again. And he'll think that based on what I say in my reports."

This approach might be the only way she would cooperate, Steve thought. *Sometimes you have to kick a client in the teeth with reality.*

"Oh, is this *tough* Steve?"

He again felt himself starting to smile while keeping his eyes locked on her, and then he finally saw her come down from the tension, her shoulders sagging ever so slightly.

"I know, I know. I get this way once in a while. It's what you would call a defense mechanism, right?"

"Well, what way are you talking about, Maya?"

"Being a bitch. Always on my guard. It's 'cause of my mother. I told you she was a drunk and a user. But I didn't mean user like an addict. She fucking used people, like my dad and me. My dad died because of her, you know."

"No. I didn't know. Why don't you tell me a little about what happened?"

***

Maya had paused in the story of her crappy upbringing. She was sitting with her legs folded under, snuggled up in the chair, looking like a teenager rather than a 25-year-old. She took some slow breaths, seemingly regaining her composure, unfolded her legs and put them on the floor.

"I'm not crazy, you know."

"No. I don't think you are. But you've been told that?"

"My mother loved to manipulate people. I told you she drank, she used drugs. My dad did, too. But he wasn't mean. He was so nice."

"What was his name?"

"Tony. Tony Marino." Her voice noticeably softened and took on a higher register as she said his name. This was a side of her Steve hadn't seen before. He realized that in this moment, the young daughter of Tony Marino was present, not the hard-edged adult he'd seen so far.

"They got in fights all the time and when he went to work, she'd take it out on me. Whenever I got home from school she was on my case. 'Do the dishes. Clean the apartment. I know you're a slut.' This was like when I was 10. I didn't even know what a slut was. But she was drunk. My father was a writer for a marketing company. He didn't make a lot of money, I guess. As soon as he came home, she'd be on his case and he'd be pouring himself drink after drink. He was a good guy. He knew what she was doing to me."

"He stuck up for you?"

"Tried to. She was fucking relentless. You know she didn't take his last name. And she wouldn't let me take it, either."

"That bothers you?"

"It did when I was a kid. Just shows what a bitch she was."

Steve decided he needed to keep her in the past, so she could show him more than what her current-day pain allowed.

"Maya, do you remember a time, any time, when things weren't so bad at home? Think back. Some kind of memory that might bring a smile?"

She shook her head. "It was all shit, Steve. But your turn now. Tell me about that client you had. You left off right in the middle."

Steve saw Maya was leaning forward in her seat. She really wanted to hear from him, wanted the attention off herself. Interesting.

"Speaking of leaving off in the middle. You told me your father died because of her. How? You finish your story and then I'll finish mine."

***

"Whenever the screaming began, I just turned up the volume on the TV, right? I remember that night my father died, she got on him during dinner. I think Dad had picked up some Subway and we were just eating in silence, and they were both drinking. And she just suddenly started going to town, saying how this wasn't the life she signed up for, eating crappy sandwiches on a Friday night and when was he ever gonna pull his weight.

"My dad got this look on his face. It was sad. Comical. I was only 10, I think I told you. And I said something like, 'I like Subway.' And he smiled at me. But that really set off my mother. She literally just grabbed what was left of my sandwich—it was turkey, I can still see the meat hanging out of it when she snatched it. 'You like this?' I remember her voice was acid. 'You see, Tony? This is what you've made of our daughter. Pathetic.' And she turned and flung the sandwich, hard, behind her against the wall above the sink in the kitchen. All the shit inside? The lettuce? It went everywhere."

Steve heard the little girl again; he heard her breathing shorten. Good could come out of this, and though he didn't want her to get lost in reliving the trauma, he decided to hold his tongue and wait. In a near-whisper, Maya continued.

"I just ran to my bedroom, and I heard my dad asking her 'why?' He was so miserable. And she just poured it on, how useless he was and he was ruining her daughter, and that was it. And she's doing this at the top of her lungs. Why was she so mean? I hated her."

A single tear ran down the right side of Maya's face, and immediately she came back to 25. "Fucking cunt. That's what she was."

"So you said your dad died because of your mother?"

"I know he did, that's all."

Steve waited on her. There was more to this story, a lot more. But he quickly realized there would be no more young Maya in this session. She had shared what she wanted and now her guard was back up in full force. "How did he die, Maya?"

"Shit, Steve. That's a story for another day. I'm fucking exhausted. I hate even thinking about my mother. You talk. I'm done."

She shifted her position, refolding her legs Indian-style and crossing her arms over the blood red t-shirt she wore, looking down at her beat-up black Converse All-Stars.

"Before I tell you more, Maya, I'd like to ask you just one question about what you've shared. Is that okay?"

She pouted, but then nodded.

"As you were telling me that story, what was going on inside you?"

"Stomach was churning. I hate even thinking about my mother."

"So, deep in the stomach?" Steve pointed low in the belly.

"Kind of. Maybe a little higher. But it feels like when you swallow something cold really fast? It freezes your throat, but you also feel this weird stomach thing. I don't know. Sounds stupid."

"No, Maya. Not stupid at all."

"What difference does that make, anyway?"

Steve pounced on the chance to educate.

"Well, Maya, the body has a very specific reaction during trauma, or in this case, recalling a trauma. Your primitive brain, when triggered, tries to take over and protect with one of three methods: fight, flight or freeze."

Steve needed to help Maya see her responses as a function of a triggered brain if he was to even dream of helping her find long-term peace over the short-term time they would be working together. She seemed to get it.

"Can I control this trigger thing?"

"That's a very good question. We can work on that. You have endured a lot of different types of traumas, and at different ages. But awareness is the first key, Maya. Just being aware of your body's signals. Can you be mindful of those? And when you have one, for now just pay those signals some attention. Tune in to how they feel, breathe nice and easy as you do that, and then just try to soothe your mind, remembering that when you feel them most times now you are not in a circumstance that requires the fight, flight or freeze response."

Steve watched her fidget in her seat. Time for him to resume with his story. *Quid pro quo* was the name of the game with this one.

***

I'd arrived at work at nine, before anyone else that day, and buried myself in catching up on paperwork. It was just as I was putting client charts back in the gray metal filing cabinet when the phone rang. I remember as I picked up the phone, I tried to stretch with my arm to close the cabinet and couldn't make it. Then what Jim was saying penetrated my brain. "Wait, who's dead?"

I hardly heard him as he explained that Kiely Hanrahan had been found by her 13-year-old daughter, dead in her kitchen in what appeared to be a suicide. Everything after that was a blur. My then-admin Jessica came in when I called and she got out of me what had happened. I was sobbing, apparently, and hadn't even realized it. I remember she said she'd cancel my appointments for the day and backed out, closing the door. Jim arrived after that and just sat with me, not saying anything.

The police came by about midday, and of course a client's privacy does not end with their death, so I couldn't tell them anything other than nothing we had spoken about indicated that she was considering self-harm. And I was unaware of anything threatening in her life. I told them she'd talked enthusiastically about taking a cooking class. The police sergeant at the scene said she had apparently started the class at the food pantry. The knife in her stomach appeared to be a new one; three or four other new knives were still in their packaging on her kitchen counter.

***

Steve shrugged, keeping his eye on Maya. He hated retelling the story but the only reason he was sharing was to reach her. She couldn't be easily read.

"I get that she died, Steve, but why were you upset? 'Cause you screwed up?"

"That's a fair question, Maya. Every counselor I know fears having a client who kills themselves or, God forbid, murders someone else. It's a nightmare, especially because we're supposed to be trained to recognize the signs and respond. So if I had sensed my client was suicidal, I should have been taking proactive steps, such as alerting authorities or a family member."

"And you've carried this with you for so many years because you fucked up?"

Steve paused. He wanted to lash out at Maya, whose words seemed so cruel. But her eyes weren't angry. She was leaning forward. She seemed like she wanted to know what made him tick. Behind her own anger was curiosity, and curious clients have the ability to grow.

"Honestly, Maya, that's one aspect. I did screw up. And I do carry that burden and will carry it the rest of my life."

"But?"

"But there may be more. I shouldn't tell you this because it's going to come off wrong. There was never anything between my client and me. I liked her, probably too much, more than is safe for a counselor. That affection, and my belief I could help her succeed, probably blinded me to what was really going on inside her. She was playful in session, and as a result, I responded to her playfulness with blinders on."

"Sucks to be you."

"So now you know my worst story. And we can get back to you."

"Yeah, but, haha, time's up, Steve."

"Maybe so, but I won't forget that your story isn't finished. Next time, you get to finish your part. By the way, are you feeling okay about everything? You shared some heavy stuff today."

She waved her hand in the "no big deal" way.

"Okay, but Maya, I'd like you to remember those techniques we have discussed if you find yourself becoming anxious. Breathing, grounding."

"Yes, Dad."

Maya sprung up from her lotus position quickly. Steve thought she could have been an athlete with a different upbringing. He watched her take two steps toward the exit. Then she stopped and looked back at him without turning her body.

"Hey, what kind of client am I? Playful like that woman?"

Steve relaxed and smiled. "You know, you do have a playful side. You just showed it. But I was thinking to myself that what you are is very, very smart. And that's the part of you I want to cultivate in the next few sessions, because that's the part of you that will help you throughout your life if you are open to growing it."

As she left, Steve thought he heard her mutter, "We'll see."

Post-session: Maya

I PULL INTO A PARKING SPACE ON THE FAR SIDE OF THE diner, put the car in park and turn down the volume on Journey's "Don't Stop Believin'." After the session with Steve, I'd sped home, popped into shorts, driven to the high school track a couple of miles from the apartment and pounded gravel 'til my throat was raw from sucking in air. Back home, shower, get ready for work. Enough to keep down the spinning.

But now I'm fifteen minutes early to work and I don't feel like going in and I'm back in my head again. Either Steve is a really good liar or he actually liked Mom. Which makes him stupid but not the person who drove her over the edge. But what was her anger about? Why was she such a bitch, especially if Steve liked her or at least seemed to give a shit about her? She was so off-her-rocker crazy. A sudden memory at age 12, seventh grade, floods my brain.

***

I all but skipped home. My first report card as a seventh grader. A. A. A. A. A. B+. This after hours in my room cramming in everything, even Spanish, which I hated. I can't wait for Mom to get home from the store. I take my loafers off and let my toes rub into the gray shaggy bathroom mat. I'm all tingly. As soon as I hear Mom's key in the door, I run to open it, carrying my report card triumphantly in my right hand. I take two grocery bags from Mom.

"Guess what?"

"I don't have time to play your games. Just let me settle down."

"I got my report card, Mom. Here, read it."

Mom looks at the report, but her eyes are out of focus. She stumbles back, puts the report card down and grabs one of the bags back from me. Then she heads to the cabinet for a glass and removes a bottle from the bag she snatched. It's vodka. I run to the fridge and bring her a couple of ice cubes. Mom's plopped down on the sofa so I set her glass down on the end table. She seems unsteady.

"Here, Mom, I know you like it cold, right? So, sit down, here's the card. I really want you to read it."

She stares at the card, again without reading or even seeing it. I hear warning bells, feel the walking-on-eggshells nervousness, but I can't stop myself.

"It's all As, Mom. Well, technically not all As, 'cause I got a B+ in Spanish, but all my main subjects I got As."

Mom slooks right through me and my stomach starts churning. I'd totally misread how far gone she was. Her foggy look is that same look that's always accompanied by yelling and a smack. I back away toward the kitchen.

"Where are you going, you little punk bitch?"

In a flash, Mom is in my face.

"You think you're so fucking smart? You're no better than me and don't think some goddamn first report card is gonna change that. You're a loser, just like your father."

I want to run to my room, but Mom is blocking my path. I freeze, willing myself not to cry, but I feel a hot tear dripping down one cheek. Mom sees it, too.

"Baby, baby. That's just like you. You're so goddamn needy. 'Look at my report card. I have a great report card.' You know what? That report card isn't putting food on the table, is it? Where's my drink?"

I feel an opportunity. "Let me get it for you, Mom."

I sidestep to get around her, but not quickly enough. As I brush past, Mom puts her foot on my behind and shoves really hard. I'm flying through the living room, feet tripping and body pitching out of control. The last thing I see is the coffee table on the way down and I can't do a thing about it. My head smacks it flush on and I see stars.

***

Fuck her. Fuck this. I can't believe I'm crying over this shit. I grab a fast-food napkin shoved into the glove compartment and dab my eyes, trying to avoid smearing my black eyeliner. Ah, shit, that's a lost cause, too.

Maybe I will tell Steve the full story. He might not have driven her over the edge, but he sure as hell didn't know squat about her. He fucking failed her. Maybe he needs to know more than squat about me.

I feel myself raging inside. I take a deep breath. I slowly let it out. I do it again. And again. And just like that, I'm good. Time for work.

***

I'm only an hour into my shift when I feel my phone buzz in my back pocket, but I'm too busy to peek. Just as I'm clearing tables, Billie, the diner's manager and world's best boss, asks me to take the bar for the rest of the night. George had called in sick, and Billie knew I'd tended bar in California. It's a service bar, which means I don't get bartender-style tips. Billie reads my face. "Don't worry, beautiful, I'll make sure you get your tip distribution from everyone else, and who knows when, but our plan to go to a full-time bar is a go, and when it does, you're my barkeep, not George." Billie is a wiry, 30-something, sandy-haired woman who'd taken an instant liking to me. We flirt even though she has a girlfriend, but we both know it isn't going anywhere 'cause she is a straight shooter and not a cheater. I can tell. She's also kind of controlling. I can tell that, too. Though I guess you have to be controlling when you're running a restaurant and have a bunch of dipshits like George working for you. Billie's got my back, though, and that's really all that matters to make her okay with me.

As I slip a bar apron over my t-shirt, I pull out my phone to glance at the text.

Hi, Maya. This is Kenzie from Gloves Off Counseling. I wanted to touch base with you on something we kind of left hanging earlier today. It's about your billing. Can you get back in touch with me? You can either respond to this text or call me at the office. Thanks. And thanks for noticing my nails today! The text ends with a Bitmoji image of Kenzie, a cartoonish, more cherubic version of herself holding a string of balloons that say, *Thanks a bunch!*

I can't help but smile. Kenzie is earnest; I've never had anyone worried about billing so much. Of course, those other times there actually was insurance. I picture Kenzie making a couple of calls about my coverage and being confused. Poor kid. She is very different, a "good" girl, no doubt. I picture her and me together, me taking her to places she's never been. She didn't recoil when I gave her my little thumb test at the office. I just might make her an offer and see where it goes.

Post-session: Steve

I BLITZ THROUGH MY PROGRESS NOTES FROM TODAY'S sessions to move to the two things on my mind:

what's up with Jill Travers and giving more thought to Maya Andino.

I don't like to chase after clients; Jim told me long ago that a therapist shouldn't be working harder than the client. But Jill and I had been through her battles together and I hated the idea that she breaks from a bad influence only to believe she's free again from trouble in her life and doesn't need counseling. I know she won't truly heal until she confronts the foundational character traits that draw her to impossible relationships. I decide against calling, but dash off a quick email asking if she'd like to reschedule. It's all I can do. Now I'm the one who has to let it go.

I lean back in my gray mesh office chair, a slick, contoured number I splurged for, a rarity for me, at a going-out-of-business sale for one of the big-box office stores. Life really is okay, despite the ups and downs of clients. I take a sip from my now end-of-day-room-temp water (I guess the Yeti doesn't keep things cold forever) and smile as I recall how the session with Maya ended. Telling her I see her as smart was the right thing to do; she is, and she might never have had anyone recognize her for that. Even when she deployed those smarts in a dangerous way, the smarts are worth acknowledging. This young lady thinks on her feet, isn't afraid to act and is a survivor. I could see her wheels turning when I told her she was smart. Would that I could figure out the thoughts those wheels were turning.

I reconsider my thought of 24 hours ago. Could Maya Andino be homicidal? Could she be suicidal? This is where I failed Kiely, not correctly assessing for suicidality. I simply hadn't considered the full range of possibilities. Maya didn't have a problem knocking a guy out, and she'd admitted to robbing numerous men. She cut herself, so she could withstand pain. Yes, I'd say she's capable of killing someone. Now, could she also direct her anger at herself? Perhaps. But she seems to see others as flawed and displays a wisdom and even self-confidence that in this moment isn't speaking to me that she would turn her anger on herself. Might be worth a quick consult call to Jim, give him something to chew on in his retirement if I can reach him when he's not on a golf course.

A sudden thought occurs to me, and I grab my mouse and go to the screen. I type "Deena" and "Venice Beach tattoo parlor" into Google. Although counselors ethically are not supposed to "background" clients, the fact that Maya is a criminal referral allows me some latitude and actually makes sense given my hunches and the need to protect others, much less myself. Especially if I'm reading her wrong.

My jaw drops at the very first headline that comes back on Google: "Police Investigate Death of Venice Beach Tattoo Artist Found Strangled in Apartment." I click on the link of the newspaper article; staring back is a black-and-white image of a vibrant Deena Pullman laughing with friends at a beach volleyball match. Alongside her is a shorter woman with her back to the camera, turned sideways and whispering in Pullman's ear. Although the hair is longer, it is, without question, Maya Andino.

Session Four ~ Revealings

SITTING IN HER WORK STATION, KENZIE TRIED TO FOCUS on the day ahead. She fiddled with her fancy nails and hit the save button on the bill she had prepared for Jill Travers, then sent it to her "check later" file; as she had expected, Steve had nixed billing Jill for now. "Trust me," he'd told her. "She'll be back."

Kenzie's thoughts turned to Maya and the "new friends" get-together they had Monday night, arranged after Maya responded to Kenzie's text about her bill. "If you're game," Maya had texted back, "I have Monday off and would like to enjoy getting to know you outside of the office. Just friends. I'm seeking to meet new people now that I'm back in North Carolina."

Kenzie was secretly thrilled about that text. She took her time to respond, wanting to get the tone right. She wanted to let out that part of herself she'd denied for a while, but still wasn't quite convinced that part was real.

***

They'd met at Havana Nights, which Kenzie suggested, knowing the food was great and the bar offered a lively scene and some two-person booths. It had taken Kenzie nearly an hour to figure out what to wear. She chose a purple silk blouse over blue jeans and a minimum amount of make-up. She wasn't sure what to expect, and she prepared for the possibility they would be trying to flirt with men, but she believed in her heart they'd be flirting with each other. Maybe it was time for her to explore. While getting ready, she felt the way she had sitting in the stairwell with LuEllen.

Kenzie got there first and grabbed one of the booths on a raised platform in the back of the bar area where they could order food. She was able to see the entire bar and got up to wave as soon as she spotted Maya, who was dressed all in black—black cotton blouse over skintight black jeans with the black Converse All-Stars she often sported to her sessions with Steve. Her dark hair was gelled, and she wore small silver earrings. She looked like a high school girl, and sure enough, the waiter carded her as he took her order for an IPA. Of course, he then carded Kenzie, too, when she requested a margarita.

They barely talked while waiting for the drinks. Kenzie sensed Maya studying her and was working furiously hard to not blush every time she looked up at her.

"So, you know, I won't bite," Maya finally said as they clinked glasses.

"Yes, of course. I guess I didn't really think it would turn into drinks. Or maybe I did." Kenzie felt the blush come on strong again.

"It's okay, Kenzie." Maya reached out and rested her hand on top of Kenzie's free hand on the table. "I've been where you are. You're not sure. But you probably are."

Kenzie reached into her purse for a tissue as she felt a tear in her left eye. She took a deep breath and fought to regain a composed voice. Her initial instinct was defensive, to just get away. But that would be a lie.

Prince's 1999 began to play over the bar's speakers. "Great song," Maya said. "Want to dance?"

Kenzie started to get up but noticed Maya hadn't moved.

"That was a joke, Kenzie. My bad. This is really awkward for you, isn't it?"

Somehow, they got past that moment when Maya finally offered to just talk. She shared how she'd come back to North Carolina after living in Southern California for seven years, gotten a job at the diner and was trying to figure out what to do with the rest of her fucked-up life. Kenzie didn't feel comfortable asking her about the fucked-up parts, so she just listened. Maya was so self-assured. And so damn attractive.

When she asked how Kenzie came to work for Steve, Kenzie managed to finally put a few words together. She told her about growing up and being the first in her family to graduate college but deciding after just a couple of weeks of student teaching in a public school that she'd chosen the wrong profession. She managed to finish and get her degree, but post-graduation took a clerical job at a nonprofit, and two years ago applied at Gloves Off when she saw a job posted online. Something about working in a place where people were getting help for their problems, well, if she could be a part of that, it would be doing good. She loved working for Gloves Off, and Steve was a great boss.

"He ever try to hit on you?"

"Oh, no, Maya. Steve isn't like that at all. He wouldn't do that."

"You don't think he's ever been hot for a client? I think he's been staring at me a lot."

"Well, I don't know. I don't think so, though. He could get in trouble. And he could be your father."

"I know, I know. I was just testing you."

Maya flashed a dazzling smile and they spent the next hour talking about their jobs and their dreams. Maya told her she had no clue where her life was going but that it might be fun to own her own bar somewhere near the ocean, either coast. Kenzie hadn't thought too much about her own long-term plans either. She told Maya she felt she needed to be near her mom, so she couldn't see herself leaving Durham.

Their chat was interrupted when a man in a light blue cashmere sweater and jeans stopped by their table. Kenzie recognized him.

"Hello, Mr. Salazar. Maya, this is Enrique Salazar. He's one of the owners."

Maya looked at him briefly but was watching Kenzie seem to withdraw into herself.

"Hello, nice to meet you," she said. After he left, she reached out for Kenzie's hand, but Kenzie pulled it back. "What's wrong? You didn't date him, did you?"

"No," Kenzie replied. "But . . "

Maya waited.

"I just sometimes have to be careful because of my job. Enrique is one of Steve's friends; I've seen them leave the office together. And I suddenly realized I'm not sure I should be spending social time with a client."

"Really?" Maya said, a touch of anger in her voice. "You're not the therapist. And if Steve is half the guy you say, he wouldn't care. And we're just friends anyway, right?"

Kenzie reddened yet again. "Of course, Maya, you're right. I guess it just took me by surprise."

"By the way, Steve's not gay, is he?"

"Um, no, I don't think so. I mean, not that I know. Do you think . . ."

"No, Kenzie, I don't think so. But his friend is."

"Mr. Salazar? How do you know?"

"I have a good gay-dar."

Maya said it so matter-of-factly that it made Kenzie laugh.

"I'll take your word for it."

"Maybe I need to work with you on yours."

Kenzie tried to look away in embarrassment but Maya was watching her unashamed with those deep dark eyes, and Kenzie was struck by what should have been the ridiculous notion that she could fall deeply in love with this woman. Then Maya patted her hand and Kenzie felt a jolt of electricity and warmth ride right up her arm.

"It's cool, isn't it? Discovering new things."

Kenzie could only nod.

***

There was a woman in the waiting room when Maya walked in for her 3 p.m., but she strode past her and went straight to the counter and Kenzie.

"Hello, beautiful," Maya said.

Kenzie was secretly thrilled to hear Maya's husky voice, which she kept low enough that the woman behind her couldn't hear. "Thank you for the discretion," Kenzie told her back in a whisper. "I had so much fun the other night. Can't wait to do it again."

Their get-together had ended with a walk back to Kenzie's car on the street near Havana Nights, and Maya had given her the simplest kiss on the lips. But there'd been a lingering quality to it, a tease to more. Kenzie knew she wanted the more. And she knew Maya knew it. An orange light flickered on Kenzie's phone; it was Steve's signal that his client had left. During their date, Maya had asked her how Kenzie knew when it was time to send a new client since they didn't leave through the same door.

"Next Monday evening, Kenzie. I'll text ya." Maya blew her a kiss. "Steve's ready, looks like."

***

Her face was red, and her eyes had narrowed into slits. Tears were sitting at the corners, soon to roll. Maya was her 10-year-old self again, her voice soft and uncertain. Steve was mesmerized, but aware of her need to recognize that he was present and she was safe. He pushed the Kleenex box toward her to force his way into her recognition, hoping it wouldn't break the mood. She angrily snatched out a tissue, clenching it in her balled-up fist. Then she continued.

"So when she threw the sandwich I ran into my pathetic little bedroom and dove under the covers. My father didn't say anything, but my mom just kept screaming and yelling at him, how he was worthless. I heard the clink of ice, and I knew he was pouring himself another drink, and I peeked out, 'cause I could see a sliver of the living room with my door cracked. He downed an entire glass in like, two gulps. Then he poured another. It might have been whiskey, that's what he drank. I heard my mom say, 'You're a piece of shit. I fucked up big time thinking you could make anything of your life. And now my daughter is just like you. Isn't that great?'

"And I heard my dad say so sadly, almost a whisper, 'our daughter,' and you know what she said to that? 'Fuck you.'

"Then I remember she turned to the hallway and I kind of stumbled away from the door, hoping she didn't see me peeking, and I got back in bed. I had this dark blue blanket and I pulled it up over my head. I hated her so much."

Steve had been looking down, not making eye contact with Maya to give her space to share without feeling so self-conscious. Now he looked up to catch those dark, expressive eyes, and in that moment, felt her pain, even could imagine being in her shoes. It was one of those sacred moments in therapy, just being present.

After what he judged was a solid minute, as he heard Maya sniff and use the tissue, he used his soft voice.

"He didn't die that night from the booze, though, did he?"

It was instinctive on his part, but he needed Maya to share where this deep-seated pain came from, and the drunken arguments between her parents were not all. He knew it. The voice that came back this time was more Maya's current voice, with an underlying sense of pain and hatred.

"I fell asleep, eventually, just drifted away. You know, this was like every other day in our crappy apartment. I think it was so common the neighbors didn't even give a shit or think anything of it."

She sighed, a long, exaggerated exhale.

"You ready, Maya?"

She nodded. I waited.

"I woke up to my mom shrieking in my room. I'd been sleeping pretty deeply, and I saw my father stumbling around, fumbling with my blue blanket. She was calling him a pervert, and I realized he'd fallen asleep in my bed, drunk. And I also know he was naked. That's why he had the blanket around himself.

"They left the room and she continued yelling at him, but their voices weren't quite as loud, and my mom had shut my door and told me to stay the fuck in there. I did, for a while. But then I decided to peek. He'd turned away from her, and apparently grabbed his blue jeans but he was still not wearing a shirt. And she had a knife and he was mocking her. I think he said, 'Get real. I'm gonna get ready for work.' And when he turned away from her to go back down the hall, she said, 'Look at me, you fucker.' They were really close and I just heard a little gasp, like 'uhhhh.' Then she stepped back and I saw blood on her hand, and my dad sank to his knees. I think I let out a little shriek. I didn't even know what happened. But I closed the door, jumped back in bed and got under the sheet. I was cold as hell and shivering, but it wasn't that I didn't have the blanket, you know? A part of me knew what she did, and I was sure I was next."

Steve waited again. Maya had once again tucked her legs under herself lotus style on the couch and was rocking ever so slightly.

"She came in and told me to get up. She said the police were coming, that Daddy had had an accident, and I needed to be dressed. She wanted me to get ready for school and she told me to tell her when I was ready and she'd take me outside. When I did, she covered my eyes and hustled me past him. I knew he was dead and I didn't say or do anything. I just let her pack me up and off to school. I didn't tell a soul."

This time it was Steve with the long exhale.

"I'm so sorry for you, Maya. Your pain. Your loss. Your helplessness at that time."

She nodded, looking at him, and he thought he read guilt in her eyes.

"Do you blame yourself?"

"Fuck no. I mean, maybe back then a little bit, but I couldn't have done anything. She was crazy, Steve. I got pulled out of class and taken to the principal's office, and there was a social worker, I think, who brought me home. My dad was gone, I mean, you know, his body, and Mom was at the kitchen table with a detective, and he was talking all soft and warm to her. She had the fucking cops wrapped around her little finger.

"I can't imagine how difficult it was for you, ma'am.'"

Maya's voice had a mocking tone. "She told them he attacked her after she found him naked in bed with me, and she was so angry she grabbed a knife to defend herself, he tried to take it from her, and she stabbed him."

Steve could sense Maya's weariness of telling the story. Her eyes were puffy from rubbing and the steeliness and anger were coming back.

"That bitch put it on my dad, and I didn't do shit about it, Steve. They asked me if I had seen anything that morning and my mom looked at me and I said no."

Her voice dropped to the tiniest of little girl whispers. *They didn't even ask me if my dad did anything to me.* "So the social worker put us up in a hotel that night. She wanted me to see a counselor—hey, it was my first!—and by the next day we were back in the apartment, and it was like nothing had happened. That was when I just sort of clammed up for good, I guess. Stopped making friends at school. Stopped talking with my mother. Just realized I was on my own."

"And you were 10 years old."

Maya looked at Steve, and a tear rolled down her cheek. She dropped her head.

"You're brave for sharing that with me, Maya. Thank you."

Steve let the two of them sit and absorb the power of what had gone on between them: openness, listening, acceptance. He wanted to share about trauma with Maya, to help her understand the depth of her lived experiences.

"You know, Maya, suffering multiple traumas young in life, as you did, is awful. But it's actually *what happens after* that can lock a person into that fight-flight-freeze brain mentality of always being on high alert. You witnessed the most awful kind of violence imaginable, a murder. And the person a child would normally go to for support, a parent, was the perpetrator, while the other parent was the victim. I can't think of a worse way to experience trauma, because you had nobody. I'm so sorry for you.

"But in this space here?" He gestured with his arms to encircle the room. "You're safe, and there is no danger."

He waited another minute with her in silence.

"What do you feel inside now, having shared your story, Maya?"

"What do you think, Steve? I'm still angry."

"Rage and guilt, then?"

She shrugged. "I guess."

"Okay, I'd like to give you a little takeaway before we stop. I often share this with clients who've had trauma, and a lot of them find it pretty useful for easing that inner anxiety. May I continue?"

"Do I have to talk?"

Steve smiled. "No, Maya. Enough talk from you for the day. I want you to experience this on a sensory level. It's called the light stream technique. First, just think about this. If that anger inside you had a shape, what do you think it would be?"

"Just a blob."

"And if that blob had a color, what would it be?"

"Red. Blood fucking red."

"And if that blood red blob had a texture, what would it be?"

"What is this, Steve? Sounds stupid."

"Please trust me."

"Okay, it would be rough, like sandpaper."

"And if it made a sound, what would that be like?"

"A fucking scream."

"Okay, so now you have a blood red, sandpaper-like blob that screams. Where is it inside you?"

"My gut."

"Okay, Maya. I'm going to talk you right through this. Tell me, what color do you associate most with healing?"

She paused to consider. "Purple."

"Great. I want you to imagine there is a purple healing light in the center of the universe. It's a magic light, because you have the power to call on it and it does your bidding. It's an unending supply and you direct it to come to you and heal. So as you breathe nice and easy, call on that light. Feel it hurtling toward you. Now feel it enter your head, travel through your neck and surround that blood red blob in your gut. Feel the purple light pulsating all around it. Keep calling on it. More, more, more."

She wasn't saying anything, which Steve took as a good sign. He let her continue with her eyes closed and watched her breathing. After a couple of minutes, he softly asked, "What's going on right now, Maya?"

"It's fading."

"Then keep calling on your healing light. Let it blow that blob to bits. We can sit here as long as you like. When you're ready, count 1-2-3 and open your eyes."

She stayed with it another minute.

"That was actually pretty cool."

"Good."

"Might be the best thing any counselor has ever offered to me."

"I'm glad, Maya. Just remember, this is *your* healing light. When you feel that deep gut anxiety, call on it. Use it."

She sprang up from the sofa and whispered, "Thanks," as she left. Steve thought he heard her sniffle.

Post-session: Maya

MY SCREAM IS SWALLOWED WHOLE BY JAMMING MY hand against my mouth. So fucking exhausted and my head hurts. I think about the light stream thing Steve showed me and re-visualize the purple energy bolt coming from the sky right through my head and targeting that anger and frustration in my gut, which had returned. I give it a minute or two.

Not working.

What did he say? Breathing. Do it while breathing evenly. Okay, in and out. Close my eyes. On my back, I can see the purple light. I call it. It's flowing in. It's resonating around the fucking blob. I will the blob away, yield to its power. Holy shit.

It's working. Blob is shrinking. What did he say at the end to get out? 1-2-3. Open your eyes.

Whoa. The pounding's almost gone. I get a glass of water. I suddenly realize I ran out of there without going back to say goodbye to Kenzie. I look into my purse and can see the new text message before I get the phone unlocked.

Hi, Maya. Missed you leaving Steve's. Hope it went well. Just to let you know I am doing my job, lol, but I'm still not getting anywhere tracking down your billing info from the county. Forgot to ask you about it before. Hey, would you like to come over Monday instead of going out? I could cook us something fun.

I stare at the heart emoji.

I may have to start being a little more truthful with Kenzie. Especially if I want to get together with her. And I know I do.

Post-session: Steve

I'M COMPLETELY WINDED FROM THE RUN WITH SAM AS we take the elevator upstairs. Mental note to self: more exercise! I'm 47. I've been out of baseball more years than I spent trying to make it. "Samantha, can you believe that?" She looks at me, pleased to be recognized by her full name. I grab a handful of head behind the ear and scratch, letting us back in the condo and getting her a treat. Yup, this is my life. I laugh out loud.

Of course, everything I've done since leaving the office is a dodge. I'm a good enough therapist to know that. I'm also a failure, have always been, at leaving my thoughts behind when I shut the door at work. Deep down, that's why Sheila left. She knew she was second in my life and it wasn't good enough.

I've been wanting to focus on Maya since leaving the office. Such a heavy session today. I dared not introduce anything about the death of her former partner, Deena. Didn't need to spook her. She seemed to have a breakthrough today telling the story of her father's death, revealing her truth and her guilt about letting her mother get away with murder. Allowing her the chance to be raw, with the knowledge she was in a safe place while telling her story, was just the beginning. I know Maya needs to heal. Wants to heal. I hate that we have only four mandated sessions left. It's going to be a long shot to get her to keep coming after that. Today's session made me less worried about her immediate homicidal tendencies. I just want to keep her talking, keep processing the past through this present-day, safe lens.

I can't stay focused on Maya, though. Intruding into my thoughts about her is Mike Jones, the journalist who was my last client today. Alcoholic narcissist. I think he had a couple of drinks before seeing me. He had that minty smell of chewing gum to cover up the booze but denied it when I asked him right off the bat. I've faced that issue down a few times over the years, the therapeutic equivalent of worrying about being sued under dram law if I knew he'd been drinking but let him leave the office and he wound up getting in a crash.

***

"You sure you haven't had a quick drink, there, Mike?"

He looks at me with accusatory eyes. "You sound like my wife, Steve."

"That's not answering the question."

"Guess I'm used to asking questions, not answering them."

There's got to be another way to handle this.

"Let's forget it, Mike. What's going on in your world? Anything you want to put on the table today?" Standard line to kick off a session. But Mike throws me a curve.

"Steve, how'd you know it was time to hang it up as a player? I mean, you had the arm injury when the big leagues were in reach right? You had a shot, man, didn't you?"

I normally enjoy talking about my injury and the metamorphosis to counselor, but something in Mike's tone holds me back. I toss him a curve right back.

"How many sessions have we had, Mike? Gotta be twenty-five or thirty, right? I feel like maybe you're avoiding something."

Mike hangs his head. "I got served papers, Steve. Jen really wants out this time. But I can't let it go that easily. I can't not see my kids."

***

Mike's news wasn't exactly a shock. But I had a hard time understanding why he 'can't not' see his kids. Doesn't match the persona he puts out to the world. And to me throughout our time together.

Mike works for the Durham paper as a city hall reporter. He's a good-looking guy, 35, but with the careworn, reddish-hued face of someone whose drinking pushes his appearance older. His outfit of choice is blue jeans and sharp dress shirts. He's got bushy dark hair, sideburns with a hint of gray and a chin with a hint of double that he tries to hide with a perpetual three-day growth.

Mike's wife moved out on him with their two children three months earlier. It's what brought him to therapy. Although I've raised the issue of his drinking, Mike defends it as a necessary part of the journalism lifestyle. He sees his wife's lack of acceptance as the problem. In Mike's world, finishing a big story, hanging afterward with the crowd at the newspaper bar and getting home in time to kiss his 6-year-old son and 4-year-old daughter goodnight is being a good spouse. He grudgingly acknowledges that he frequently falls asleep with the kids and isn't present for Jen.

In that regard, his behavior matches his father's, who, a generation earlier, had tuned out his spouse. He left the family as Mike was entering high school. Mike insists he loves his father and doesn't see his father's actions as a problem for the family. My thinking is his father was his role model for his present-day behavior. We do tend to learn, for better or worse, from our attachment figures growing up.

Kenzie has mentioned that Mike likes to flirt with her, which tells me something about his ability to twist a story to his liking.

He says he loves his wife, but his attention seems more on others. He says he loves his kids, but barely spends time with them. In the same tone and breath, he tells me he's working on a book about the history of municipal corruption in Durham. He promises me a signed copy.

A few weeks back, I made at least one breakthrough with Mike. Rather than simply spinning tales of woe and lamenting his inability to get through to his wife with how much he loved her, that day he ducked his head when I challenged him about his constant drinking and need to be out with the crew. "It's not exactly all about hanging with the crowd. There was a girl."

It turned out Jen had caught wind of a rumor that Mike had gotten together with a college intern. She'd done some detective work of her own and tracked him to a new steak joint downtown, spotted him at a table for two with the girl and then waited for more than an hour to confront him outside. That's what caused her to leave with the kids.

But his admitting to the affair was not accompanied by what I thought would be a natural path toward personal growth and a potential family reunion. Recent sessions became more about him complaining. "Jen says I'm a drunk." "Jen won't switch the schedule and let me see the kids if I get a work assignment." "Jen won't even talk to me."

As far as I can tell, Mike hasn't slowed his drinking. He hasn't made progress on his book ("I can't focus on that while this is going on, Steve.") and he's worried about a future as his newspaper faces another round of layoffs. "I've been there 12 years, Steve. I make way more than most of the reporters. I've got a big target on my back, lemme tell ya."

***

I stare at the journalist before me; having read the paper regularly, I know he's a talented writer. Mike has a flair for phrases and pacing in his writing, and I've tried to encourage him to use that strength in creative new ways, finishing his book or pursuing other career opportunities.

"So how are you feeling about being served papers? Is it causing you any tension inside? Or are you just ticked?"

"Of course I'm ticked. I mean, this is it. She really doesn't care about us or family. She just wants to do her own thing. I called her Saturday night and she didn't answer. Texted her and she didn't respond. I think she had a date."

"Uh-huh. So if I'm hearing you right, Mike, you aren't necessarily feeling upset with the marriage, but more thinking about what she's doing?"

"No, no, no. You're twisting my words. I want her back. I want us back. I want the kids back."

"Why?"

"They're family, Steve. I mean, I know you don't have kids, but if you did, you'd know what it means. They're everything."

"I see."

We sit in silence for half a minute. I can see him stewing, so I set a bit of a trap. Kind of mean, but I want to open his eyes.

"You know my admin, Mike? Kenzie?"

He looks up, immediately interested. "Sure, I like her. She's smart. Gorgeous."

"She said something to me once about how you like to flirt with her when you come in."

"Well sure. I mean, who wouldn't? Do you think she's interested in me?"

"I don't think so, Mike. What I'm wondering, though, is why amid a marital crisis and your desire to fix things, you'd already be thinking about whether a 25-year-old likes you. Now, there's nothing wrong with that attitude—except if you're really trying to be committed to making your marriage work and getting back together. Which you just told me means everything *to you."*

I emphasize the word "everything." Mike's face reddens. "You don't like me, do you, Steve? I've been getting that feeling for a while."

"It interests me that you have that feeling, and have for a while. Tell me more."

"You keep trying to trap me. You're always criticizing me. I got nothing more to say."

"I hear you. I'm not trying to trap you, though. What I try to do is point out inconsistencies in the things clients say in here because that's where inner conflict often lies.

"Mike, what do you really want in your relational life? Whatever it is, I can tell you it takes hard work and commitment. You asked me before how I knew when it was time to hang it up. I knew because I thought really deeply about what I wanted, and that included what I didn't want. What I didn't want was to be forever chasing the baseball dream. I decided there were other dreams, more doable, for me. And I worked hard at it. I'll leave you with this question to think about for our next session. And, yes, I want you back for another session. Consider it homework. What do you want, and how hard are you really willing to work for it?"

***

I figure it's 50-50 whether Mike ever shows up again. I'm okay with that. Confront someone with a truth and you never know how they'll respond. Especially when they have a personality disorder. Or substance use. Or both.

The thought in my head as I absently continue to scratch behind Sam's ears is why Mike's story intruded when I was trying to focus on Maya. Something's not clicking for me. But I have got to stop thinking about work when I'm not at work. I grab a jacket and kiss Sam goodbye. I feel a plate of chorizo nachos calling me from Tobacco Road. A game, a beer or two. Clear the head. Tomorrow's a new day.

***

Not half a mile from where Steve Prescott was chowing down on nachos, Mike Jones had the end seat at Farley's, an Irish pub in the growing, gentrified area just off downtown. The barkeep, another Mike, ten years younger and notably thinner, slid him the Crown shot to go with his Yuengling. Jones nodded in thanks. He liked barkeep Mike because he didn't try to force conversation or talk sports when the bar was slow like this. Maybe Jen was right and he was a lush. Fuck that. He was a hard-drinkin' journalist and wasn't anything wrong with that. No DUIs and no D&Ds.

He glanced at his cell. Nothing yet from the office. He'd turned in a council preview piece early on a slow day with a note to metro editor Gina Palladino he'd be out and about working sources for the rest of the day. His choice that "out and about" was his seat at Farley's. He might just as likely run into a source here as anywhere else. Besides, Gina wouldn't get to his story for hours still, and even then, he was safe from a call. They were so fucking short-staffed no one had time to edit. *And who cares, anyway? No one gives a shit about typos anymore. Text society.*

He downed the shot and caught barkeep Mike's eye. All it took was a nod and he had his refill. He grabbed the beer first, downing half the bottle before turning his attention to the Crown. He couldn't get his mind off Steve Fucking Prescott. *Paying him God knows how much to be sarcastic and analyze me?* Gonna text him and tell him to fuck off. Done with that shit. He had a sudden flash, though. He didn't have Prescott's cell phone number. Asshole insisted people call him only on his office line. Like, what good would that do if you had a real crisis going on? A thought was bugging Jones, but he couldn't put his finger on it. His pal Mike slid on down from the two suits who'd walked in, holding the Crown.

"It's like you know me, Mike. Ya know, my name's Mike, too."

"Yeah, you mentioned it."

"Well, I like you, Mike."

"You might not in a bit."

"Whaddya mean, pal? I love you."

"Afraid I'm going to have to cut you off."

"No. You wouldn't do that to me, Mike. I'll take care of ya. C'mon, I'm not driving."

Too late. Barkeep Mike had already walked back to the suits. Fuck. *I should text Jen, apologize for everything. She's right.*

I'm a loser. He looked at his cell and called up his contacts, and . . . whoa, whoa, whoa. What do we have here? The contact listing said "Hot girl, shrink's office." How did he get that? He couldn't focus on it at first, but then he remembered. When he was flirting with her, he'd asked what she liked to do and she'd said she enjoyed live music, and he told her the paper had extra tickets to a Regina Spektor concert coming up at the Carolina Theater. She'd grabbed his arm over the desk in excitement. "Really? Could you get me in? I'll be your best friend." That's when she'd given him her phone number. When was that, last month? He wondered if the concert had happened yet. The thought of texting his wife vanished. He was on the chase. Crown gone, he sipped his beer slowly as he texted, unworried about the typos that autocorrect didn't catch.

"Hey there. Still looking for Spektor tix?"

Didn't take but a few seconds for the bubble to pop up indicating she was online and responding.

"Who is this?"

"Your friend at the *Gazette,* doll."

"Who?"

"Mike Jones."

"Oh, yeah. Well, I asked my boss and I can't really take a concert ticket from a client."

"I did not know that. Let me make it up to you. I can take you to dinner, or maybe a drink."

"I don't think so. Look, I'm busy. So, gotta go."

"I hear you. Don't want to keep you. Let's chat next time I'm in."

He turned off the phone, not wanting to deal with what he figured would be her next rejection. But he did have a reason to return to see Steve again. He thought he'd pop by to confirm an appointment.

Interlude: Between

*S*HE DOESN'T NEED A DOCTOR TO TELL HER WHAT SHE'S KNOWN FOR *three weeks, ever since the attack. The night she awoke to find him on top of her, naked down there, his face unseeing over his dirty t-shirt, pinning her down with his nicotine-stained, steely fingers, his hot whiskey breath gagging her even as she fought his weight 'til she was left drained, and then ripped raw, overtaken by his power, his hand over her mouth muffling her screams.*

She sensed him shudder while inside of her, and when he quickly pulled out felt liquid dripping. Disgusting. Painful. She sucked in her breath and held her nose, cringing as he put his head down so close to her face she could feel his stubble and raspy menace. "Now don't you be talking to your mama about this little get-together. All that crying you keep to yourself. You took it just fine, though. Gets easier after this. Make sure you clean up those sheets. You a smart girl, staying a virgin."

She wants to kill him, and considers the shotgun kept in his bedroom. But she hasn't ever learned to use it. Her thoughts turn to the chef's knife that her mother carefully washes after every use. She can stab him first in the gut to paralyze him, then yank his pants down and cut off his dick so he can't hurt her or anyone else again.

Just a matter of time.

And her mother. What a waste it was to risk another attack by telling her. "You have that child and then give it up. For the child's sake. You'll stay home. No one needs to know." She's as bad as him, staying through the beatings all these years. She had to know what he was capable of.

A thought nags at her brain, driven by the pain inside. She herself knew this was coming the past three years, every time he stared longer as her chest grew. Why didn't she leave? It's her own damn fault.

Suddenly, a different thought strikes, an idea more bold, more powerful, more uplifting than stabbing him.

Leave.

She can take what he's done and instead do what she's been wanting to forever.

Leave.

Could she really? Escape this crappy town where all she's ever encountered is cruelty. Classmates mocking her since she was little for her red hair, her shabby clothes. For being different. The hell with them. She'll leave. She and her baby girl. She doesn't know, but she knows. Of course it's a girl. And how else can she protect her baby than by leaving?

She'll make a life for her baby. One her mother cannot possibly imagine. One that leaves his rage, his alcohol breath, his painful fists, far behind.

Give up his child? No way. A better punishment is having his child. Loving it. Nurturing it. Letting her be the kind of child who does things with her life, who's not trapped. Who's far away.

She can head east, out of this godforsaken, hick mountain town. Get a job. Raise her right. Maybe even find a man, the right *man. After all, her mother told her they're not all like him. And she's seen the way the boys at school look at her. She'll get a different one. One who's weak, who needs her. Who does what she says.*

She must move quickly, though. Or be trapped here forever.

From this point forward, she'll have no mother or father. They're dead.

Her baby will have no grandparents.

She shoves aside the bedsheet that serves as a door of the closet in this awful room. The room where her mother absolutely, beyond doubt had to know what he did before she told her. She reaches deep inside for her navy peacoat, snakes her hand into the pocket and snatches the cash she's putting aside from the grocery, the money she's hid diligently for more than a year, giving her mother only half of her pay each week. She's not sure if her mother didn't realize she was squirreling some away or was too stupid to figure it out. Doesn't matter anymore.

Kiely slowly counts it out. Four hundred seventy dollars. More than enough for a fresh start.

She grabs her school backpack, removes the books and shoves them under the bed, then stuffs a couple days' clothing inside. With what's on her back tomorrow, it'll have to do.

Escape.

Maya

I'M FIFTEEN MINUTES EARLY FOR DINNER, AND KENZIE, somewhat flustered, lets me in while still holding a pasta fork in her hand, fleeing immediately for the stove in a state of frenzy.

"It's all coming together, Maya, I can't stop now."

Of course frenzy is the common state in the diner, so no biggie. I accompany her into the kitchen examining the surroundings. She's got three pots going; a big one with water near boil and a box of pasta next to it, a smaller stainless pot with sauce and an even smaller one with a nice smelling mix of mushroom, onion and garlic. A plate of freshly peeled shrimp sits next to that, along with some lemon slices, and I see the shrimp shells remain on a paper towel. Kenzie is stirring the small pot and checking the water. I lean in to kiss her neck but she feels my breath behind and jumps, whipping her head around and almost clocking me in the face.

"I'm sorry. Just, give me five minutes, okay? I'm not good with distractions."

"Can I help? Throw out the shrimp shells? Where's your garbage?"

"Thanks, but please don't worry about that. I really want to do it all for you tonight."

"Oh, I bet you do."

She hears me but has already turned to the stove and doesn't process my little joke. Amusing to see her in such a state, organized yet not quite under control. It's good to know it's not all perfect with her.

I drift toward the living room. She rents a simple two-bedroom in the city's Southpoint section off I-40. It's actually just down from my diner outside the mall.

It's a standard-enough-looking apartment, smallish kitchen with an alcove dining room opening to a full living room and a balcony overlooking the parking lot. My soon-to-be lover has put her touch on it with Ikea furnishings and pastel accent pieces and, on the wall above a soft beige leather couch, multiple framed images of family members of all ages. I inspect them as Kenzie inquires from the kitchen if I like chenin blanc.

"It's a light wine, so I like it more than a chardonnay. Be right there."

I don't have the heart to tell her I'm not a wine drinker and turn back to the pictures. I get so intent studying one of Kenzie in a softball uniform, circa age 14, that I jump a foot when she taps me on the shoulder to hand me a glass.

"Yes, it's me. I did have a brief jock period."

"I can see that. You hardly seem a jock, though."

"I think I wanted to prove that I could compete. My brother was a varsity football player, and my parents were so into his games. Maybe it was more jealousy."

"Or maybe that cute blond chick behind you on the first-base line?"

She says nothing, and I think I struck a chord, even though it was meant to be a joke. Gotta remember a good girl like Kenzie isn't going to just suddenly be comfortable with being out.

"Maybe, Maya. But she's not as cute as you." She leans forward and kisses my neck lightly. "Thank you for joining me for dinner. Cheers."

Wow. The newbie learns quickly.

I clink her glass and sip slowly, enjoying the wine and savoring the unspoken connection she's just made.

Strangely, the charge of that connection and the two of us together makes the pasta and shrimp more savory. We're deliberate in sharing our time and stories over dinner. I'm buzzed by the wine, which is really weird because I almost never drink wine. Maybe I'm just intoxicated by Kenzie's normalness. She truly loves her mother, big brother and baby sister, having lost her father to a heart attack seven years earlier, the day after her brother's last varsity game. She tells me that with her brother at the Air Force Academy in Colorado, she's drawn even closer to her mom and siblings, and to her maternal grandparents, who live in Mount Airy, the mountain community that I know was the setting for *The Andy Griffith Show.*

She notices how quiet I am as she speaks of her love for family, so she stops.

"What about you?"

I feel my tears too late to stop them; I know they're tears of grief for what I've never had. But I can't stop my shoulders from heaving. She moves closer, wrapping an arm around my shoulder and I just bury my head into her neck and cheek. Such a strange feeling to be held. Comforted. She smells like lemons.

I finally pull my head back, letting Kenzie continue to hold me.

"I think I may have given you more than you bargained for." I hate the way my voice wavers.

"I hope that's not possible."

"You wanted boogers on your blouse?"

We laugh together, still holding each other, and somehow my laugh morphs into a half-laugh, half-sob that doesn't sound like anything that's ever escaped my lips before. She's not bothered by it. Amazing.

"Thank you for not trying to solve me. I don't even know what this is about. Well, maybe I do."

"You can share anything you want with me. I trust you, Maya. Mama told me I have good instincts, and I think you're a good soul. I know Steve is trained and all, to understand and help when people are in pain, but sometimes we just need a hug, to know we're safe. And maybe to know we're not alone."

I nod and hug her tight, burying my head back in her shoulder. Then I lift up and lean in to give this woman—who's shown me more family in a few minutes than my entire lifetime—what I hope will be a sweet kiss. She doesn't hesitate a second. Sweet turns to soul.

We take our time, exploring each other's mouths and necks, seeking the sensitive spots that elicit soft moans and tingles, laughing delightedly. I notice the lavender scent of her hair, and drink it in.

By the time we get to the bedroom, my tears are gone and confidence back. I take my time with her, starting with soft kisses to her mouth, moving to her neck and slowly right down her body, eliciting moans with my tongue. She was shaking and then laughing, and I ask if she wants to learn. She does.

"Oh my God, you're actually really a redhead? You're so not a redhead."

"You don't think I'm fiery?" I whisper, enjoying feeling her insistent tongue. "Keep doing that and . . ."

"Keep doing what?" So she's a fast learner and a tease.

I don't answer her, though. I lie back feeling tears in my eyes again and hearing the moans of pleasure somehow coming from my own lips.

After, I dance my finger up Kenzie's back and venture a question. "What did you mean 'I'm so not a redhead?'"

She turns slightly to rest on her side, elbow digging into the bed and hand supporting her chin. She's really gorgeous. Not in a dangerous way, like Deena. Just very much alive.

"You're intense. Your eyes. Your demeanor. You have this 'I'm in control' air about you. And you are."

"But?"

"But I guess I think of redheads as more glamorous, maybe a little stuck up, even?"

"Really? Man, that wasn't me growing up. I was the tomboy. And kids hated me. They were mean, and I was small. But listen, let's keep the redhead thing a secret or I'll lose my air of invincibility."

She laughs.

"Who would I tell that to, anyway? Your secret is safe."

We kiss deeply again, and I shudder with pleasure.

Her whisper into my neck sends another spasm through me.

"Maybe we can do it again?"

I pull her close by way of response.

"I think that could be arranged."

***

Kenzie's amber clock shows 2:30 a.m. as I sit up against the bedpost. I can't remember a time in my life when my body felt like this, completely free of tension. I nod off with that thought in my head, right where I lay, half up against the pillow.

It's three hours later when I hear Kenzie talking softly as she kneels on the floor. I strain for ten seconds to hear what she's saying, thinking maybe she's sleepwalking. But she's not.

"Amen."

"You pray?"

"Good morning to you, too, lover. Yes, I pray. A vestige of my religious roots. I did go to Catholic school."

"Ugh, really?"

"Yeah, wasn't so bad. Dad was Catholic and he believed in religion more than Mom, and they were scared of us going to public schools, so Mom talked my grandparents, who are big-time Baptists, into paying the tuition."

"And you still pray. Wow. Church scares me. Bunch of phonies trying to tell you what to do with your life."

She jumps suddenly onto the bed, and pins me down. I instinctively start to protect myself, bringing both knees up before I realize she's being playful. I breathe slowly, so she can't see me calming myself. The room is still dark.

"That's why I don't go to church anymore, silly. But I can still pray. And feel good about my faith. I was praying for us, if you want to know the truth. That this real thing we seem to have will grow. Is that okay with you?"

My body releases the last of her tension, and I let her remain on top, chest to chest and accept her hug. I feel myself tearing up yet again.

"It. Is. Okay. No one ever prayed for me."

***

We fall back asleep, but I'm restless after fifteen minutes. I pull myself halfway up the bedpost again, prop the pillow behind and let my hand rest on Kenzie's hair, my fingers slowly drawing through the strands so as not to pull and wake her.

I linger in this glow, willing it to last. Laughs, food, stories, love, learning about each other. This is so different.

Steve

"Ow!" I'm startled when Sam butts my left kneecap, a quick reminder to pay her some attention. I turn from the computer screen and scratch behind her ears, prompting her to dig her head inward against me in a sort of doggie ecstasy. When I pause, she obediently trots over to her bed, a well-worn, red-and-black flannel shaped into the lump just the way she likes to lay, higher in the back and flattened on the front rim from where she puts her head on top of her paws.

I know I need to catch up on paperwork—and apply some critical thinking to my cases—but I don't want to rob Sam of pet time, so after a quick, ten-minute Friday afternoon dog park jaunt, I pile her into the car and it's off to the office. First, I stop to pick up an eggplant parm sub after calling Giuseppe's. They're so used to me by now—especially on Fridays when the office is closed but just about always go in anyway—that they have their delivery guy, Pete, come to my car out front. Sam is experiencing a new kind of doggie ecstasy, salivating on the passenger seat, knowing I've tucked something wonderful behind my legs where she can't get to it.

Sam bounds eagerly up the stairs and down the hallway; she loves being here. She runs around and around her bed here, a flannel one, then runs to the toy basket picking them up one at a time, bringing them back to me. I toss them around the office as I boot up.

I get Sam some treats to distract her while I open the eggplant parm, and then promptly spill tomato sauce onto the keyboard. *Damn.* I wipe absently with a napkin and ponder a new email from Kenzie. She's had no luck making contact with Social Services or the court system trying to confirm the referral so we can bill.

I open a new screen and type "Maya Andino North Carolina" into Google just to see. I don't expect much, and I get even less.

"What do you make of this, Sam?" She pads over expectantly.

"Why no, girl, I did not say 'Eggplant is served.' I said, 'What do you make of this?'"

Sam doesn't know, and walks back to her bed. I toss her another treat. "Catch!" She does. I love her to death.

I type Maya's name into a people finder search, which tells me there are three people named "Maya Andino" in all of the United States. One is the Maya here in Durham, though the only mention is a people finder service that notes a North Carolina driver's license. The second Maya Andino lives in Hawaii; she's 57. The other lives in Sherman Oaks, California, and is 27. An idea comes to me.

I type "distance from Sherman Oaks, California, to Venice Beach, California" into Google and learn the two cities are fifteeen miles apart, Sherman Oaks being in the famed "Valley" part of Los Angeles County.

I pause to think. No record of Maya Andino in North Carolina's legal system. She left California close to the time of Deena's death, which is less than a year ago. It makes sense there aren't that many references to North Carolina Maya, who would have been a juvenile before she left for California and therefore wouldn't have many reasons to be on the internet. I realize I'm doing a lot of "spinning" about her, the kind of thinking that takes up space in your head without resolution. The kind of thinking I often warn clients to avoid.

That is why I came here, though. Let's see. First I believed she could be homicidal. Then, after a session and instinctively believing she is honest and vulnerable, I rule it out.

Suddenly, I make a connection about why Mike Jones had intruded in my thoughts a few days ago when I'd been considering Maya's case. Mike was an alcoholic and had a personality disorder, narcissism. That's similar to what I was thinking; so did Maya, who had a drug arrest and, I felt, could be a borderline personality. Hers and Mike's presentations are very different, but the root insecurities and anger patterns bear similarities.

On a hunch I punched "Maya Andino" into the Facebook search bar. There's the "California" Maya Andino's page, and I open it despite the sudden sense of dread about what I might find. The Maya Andino looking back at me in a tiny, silhouetted image, despite a jet black, short haircut, does not appear to be "my" Maya. I squint to look more closely, but making out the detail is impossible. I save California Maya's profile image as a separate file and call up a photo editing tool to try to enlarge the image. Too grainy. But my guess is my first instinct was correct. It is not my Maya.

But who is my Maya Andino? Not on social media herself and no digital trail. I glance over at Sam. She's dead asleep. And I'm at a dead end. For now.

"You're still very, how would you say, 'pensive,' my friend?"

Enrique sits next to me at one of the high-tops in the bar of Havana Nights. It is 9:30, and the dinner crowd has thinned out. Only a couple of the high-tops are taken, though the bar itself, a rich mahogany that stretches forty feet, is still crowded with regulars who love to order pork nachos or plantains from the bar menu and catch a game. Enrique's baseball connections have morphed into community connections, and a diverse crowd in age and ethnicity are represented, though it is largely men. It's basketball doubleheader night on TNT, and the first game, Hornets–Heat, is neck-and-neck late in the 4th quarter. The boisterous crowd is decidedly pro-Hornets, rooting on North Carolina's own.

"I guess I am, Enrique. Good word. Still struggling to piece together the real stories behind a couple of clients. I hate that it occupies my headspace outside the office."

"Yes, I can see that. What would you like to talk about that has nothing to do with the office?"

I clap him on the shoulder. "Thank you, Enrique. This is why I stopped by tonight. Sometimes, I just need to speak with another human being. Face to face."

He's waiting for me, and I'm not sure what to say or how to say it.

"How's the restaurant biz? Things seems pretty busy around here for a cold December night."

Nothing like avoiding direct talk. If you want to talk, you have to talk. Enrique hadn't even answered. He knew I was stalling.

A roar from the bar disrupts me. LaMelo Ball has just split two Heat defenders, made a layup and been fouled. The Hornets might grab the lead with eight seconds left. We watch the replays. Enrique is still just waiting.

"Okay, my friend, non-work front."

"Yes?"

"I had a date this weekend."

"That's great news, Steve. Tell me more, I need details. Such a rare opportunity."

"Indeed, Enrique, indeed. But no, this all happened really quickly. It was a woman I met in the dog park outside of the condo. I'd seen her around, but we struck up a conversation one day, and we had a nice dinner Saturday at this Italian place over on Main, Cucciola."

"I know it. Fancy for a first date, no?"

I shrug. "She asked for Italian and it's a quiet enough spot. Anyway, it was nice getting to know someone. She's a law student, and maybe she was practicing, but she asked me lots of questions. She seems interested, you know?"

"Sounds promising. You going to see her again? Or maybe I should say, did it end well?"

"Sure did. Ended at her place. And mine on Sunday morning."

Enrique offers me a fist bump.

"Nice. You deserve a good woman, Steve. You've been alone for a while."

"Well, here's the thing, Enrique. You know how with my ex, Sheila, I think I mentioned the problem was my work took precedence. I could never devote that much time to her? So while I'm with this woman—her name is Jane, by the way—just lying there Sunday morning, what pops into my mind? Not the lovely dinner the night before. Not the lovemaking. And it was good, mind you. For both of us. I think, anyway. But it was work. I kept going back to work in my head."

He frowns at me.

"Have you ever tried some of the techniques you share with clients that you shared with me? I recall one in which you talked about using a grounding technique to be in the moment. I know if you were horizontal, maybe your mind wasn't on grounding. But you know what I mean."

"Thanks, Enrique. And yes, I worked very hard to focus. We wound up having a nice brunch out, said our goodbyes and hope to get together again. And she even let me off the hook. With her being in law school and working full time, she said she has no time for a major commitment. But she doesn't mind a friend with benefits. Ideal, right? And yet I'm hesitating. We're gonna take the dogs out this weekend and maybe do something after. I dunno. It's just odd is all."

"I hear you. Glad I'm out of that whole dating game." He punches my shoulder lightly. "Oh, two things I've been meaning to mention to you, how would you say, completely unrelated."

"Tell me, Enrique. I've been blathering on. Your turn."

"Well first, there's a ballplayer who stopped by one night here. He was pretty drunk. I got to talking with him after my bartender cut him off and got some coffee in him. He's feeling a lot of pressure from his family to succeed; they need the money. I passed him your card."

"Cool." I always enjoy working with ballplayers; it brings me back. Plus, there's probably no better training ground for counseling than being around jocks for years. All kinds of personalities and issues there for sure.

***

"Hey, Steve-o!"

I cringe hearing the boisterous bellow of Dylan Henderson, our second baseman, who's just come into the Bulls' clubhouse.

"Blue tossed me out, man. Can you believe that shit?"

I'd been sitting in peace on the short bench before my open locker, too tired to pull off my sweat-soaked jersey, too drained to drink from the blue Gatorade sitting next to me. I'd just been decompressing after getting the hook from Skip. Being yanked after giving up a couple of dingers sucks, but when it's your third straight awful outing, having a loud teammate in your face oblivious to your own pain was annoying at all get out. Still, I kind of like Dylan.

"What happened, Dyl?"

"He called me out on a pitch out here!" Dylan stretches his arms, waving the hands to indicate just how far outside strike three was.

"And you said?"

"I told him he missed the call."

"Told him."

"Well, I may have embellished it a bit."

"Uh-huh."

"Okay, look. I said he was a near-sighted piece of shit who should have settled nicely into retirement rather than try to make extra money and fuck over ballplayers."

He laughs as he says it, the bluster gone. I stand and clap him on the shoulder.

"Dylan, you've got a lot of talent. A lot more than I do. You're not gonna be in Durham long. In fact, I'm betting you'll be called up by the end of the year. Now you want to control your temper?"

"Sure.

"Can you ever feel your temperature rising inside?"

He thinks for a second, scrunching up his face in cartoon-like fashion. I can almost see his wheels turning, which makes me smile.

"Yeah, I sometimes do. I mean, I knew I was gonna pop off at that umpire."

"Then do this. Next time you feel your temperature rising?" I pause for dramatic effect. "Just tell yourself to shut the fuck up."

"Thanks, old man."

He punches me in the chest and heads to the bathroom whistling "I Wish I Was in Dixie."

As I pull off my jersey, I realize my own pain is lighter.

I get up and head toward the machine in the corner to fetch some ice for my arm.

***

"What's the player's name? I'll tell Kenzie to keep a lookout for a voicemail and direct him to me."

"Name's Randy Culbertson. And now that you mention it, here's the second thing I wanted to tell you, gossip that it is. It looks like your gal may have herself a lady friend."

I raise his eyebrows. "My gal?"

"You just mentioned her. Kenzie. She's the one who works your front desk, correct?"

"Yeah. Did you say a lady friend?"

"Yes. I was surprised, too." Then Enrique cocks his head. "Actually, maybe not so surprised."

I'm surprised, though.

"Are you sure? I've never seen her with a lady. Or a man, for that matter." *Note to self: Stop judging others based on no information. You're a counselor, for crying out loud.*

"Your Kenzie was in here last week at one of the tables with a beautiful girl and something about their body language told me they were, you know, if not a couple, trying to be."

"Huh." I'm not sure what else to say to that.

"Yes, and I know these things, Steve, trust me. I actually walked up to the table, and I think it startled Kenzie. She seemed embarrassed. But her friend was very nice. Cool customer, striking eyes. Very different than your Kenzie."

"Different in what way?"

"You know, Kenzie seems so, well, all-American, I guess you'd say. And this girl had dark eyes, short hair, piercings, tattoos. Pretty muscular, too. So, not at all like Kenzie. But then, opposites attract, right?"

"They certainly can, Enrique."

"Listen, Steve, I want to go to the office and start to close up back there. Are you going to hang out for a while? I'll stop by when I'm done. Give me twenty minutes or so. We can have a nightcap."

I think about his words once he heads to the back. Was Maya courting Kenzie? It fit in with the personality disorder family, borderline maybe, that a client might try to connect with someone close to him, if not himself. And Maya had said she was bi, so Kenzie would make sense. But given Maya's history, and his uncertainty about her after just a handful of sessions, would she pose a danger to Kenzie? Here I go, catastrophizing again. Sometimes, I'm no better than my clients.

I finish my bourbon and lay two $20 bills on the high-top. I need fresh air and a brisk walk back to the condo to think. Before I leave, I poke my head into Enrique's office.

"Hey there, friend. I'm taking off."

He looks at me quizzically. "You okay? Hope my news didn't upset you. You didn't have anything going with Kenzie yourself, did you?" He shakes his head. "No, of course not. My bad. You have a good night, Steve. Let's do this again soon. I enjoy my time with you."

I hardly hear him. I'd come to Havana Nights hoping to clear my brain. Hadn't.

***

I'd thought for hours about the right approach, even rousting Jim from retirement for a quick consult over the weekend. He had not offered a solution but did give me positive vibes just chatting. In short, he told me any fears I had for Kenzie, unless I was truly worried about her safety, were none of my damn business. Like the visit with Enrique at Havana Nights, his thoughts hadn't helped me clear my brain, either.

In the end, the issue solves itself.

Kenzie pops her head into my office first thing Monday before I even have two sips of my morning coffee. "I need to share something with you, boss."

The young woman sitting across from me is poised and confident. She looks ready to conquer the world. She tells me she has a friendship with Maya, and it is different than anything she has ever experienced.

"I had to tell you, Steve, because I know I'm not the therapist, but it's weird, and I don't want you to think I'm looking to prey on your clients, if that makes sense. I just thought you should know."

I think before I respond. She hasn't asked for my approval, which is good, since it isn't, as Jim had not-so-subtly suggested, my job to pass judgment.

"I'm glad you have shared that. It was brave of you to do that. A mature thing to do. And I'm not going to pry. Just . . ."

As I pause, Kenzie tilts her head inquisitively. She really wants to hear what I had to say. She trusts me.

". . . just know that relationships are not easy. And Maya is coming here for a reason."

She smiles. "Thank you, thank you, thank you, Steve. I knew you wouldn't be judgmental."

Now it's my turn to look inquisitive.

"You know," she continues, "judgmental about my being with a woman."

"It's not for me to pass judgment," I say, smiling inside as I parrot Jim. "But I do have a question for you, Kenzie, which I'm going to ask because it might affect working with my client. Does she know you are sharing with me about your relationship?"

"She suggested it, Steve."

"Really?"

Maya wants me to know? Who is this person?

Session Five – Discovery

ALL THE WAY TO THE OFFICE, MAYA THOUGHT ABOUT THE right greeting for Kenzie. She was scared of her growing feelings for her, given her purpose in coming back to North Carolina, but Kenzie had a combination of freshness, wonder and a kind of clean intensity that Maya couldn't get enough of. She'd found herself thinking about her at the diner, thinking about her in her apartment and grinning every time one of Kenzie's emojis popped up in a text. And she texted a lot. Maya sensed this was what love actually was supposed to be like. They'd been together twice since that first dinner and couldn't keep their hands or lips off each other. She liked waking up in Kenzie's bedroom.

But her idea of sneaking into Kenzie's nook, spinning her around and grabbing a deep kiss evaporated when she opened the door. An overweight guy was invading Kenzie's space, leaning through the open glass divider using a voice that reeked of trying too hard. Maya ducked into a wood chair that shielded her from the office so Kenzie couldn't see her. She didn't have to strain to listen to Mr. Obnoxious.

"C'mon, gorgeous. You and me. I'm a free man. Told Steve just a while ago. I'm done chasing my wife. *She walked out on me?* I'm going to live the right way. And there's no better way than with a beautiful, smart lady like you."

"Thank you, Mr. Jones, but . . ."

"Now, don't say no. You don't want to disappoint your boss's client, do you? You think about it. We'll take it easy. Just a drink to begin with. I like Farley's myself. Good Irish bar. We hit it off, we walk into the dining room, a nice Irish stew or some fish and chips? Let me tell you, honey, I've got some clout in this city. You know that, right? I know you get the newspaper. You read my stuff, you know me. I help right wrongs."

"As I was saying, Mr. Jones, you're sweet, but I really can't."

"I'm not going to believe that. I know you won't leave me hanging. I might just have to keep showing up here, or maybe in Southpoint, right?"

"You know where I live?"

"I'm a journalist, honey, I find things out. Think about us, right? Tonight at Farley's. But now I have to go, work to do. You know, keep Durham safe from the evil of corrupt politicians. Ta-ta!"

Maya couldn't see Kenzie's face, but she heard her sigh as she watched the guy swagger out. He took obnoxious to a level worse than any guy she'd ever robbed. Plus, he used Axe body spray to excess. She rose and peeked into her lover's work area just in time to see her spraying Glade, which made her laugh out loud.

"Maya! Oh my God, come here, you."

They kissed sweetly, and Kenzie kept her arm around Maya's waist, glancing into the room to make sure no one else was there. "Did you hear that guy?"

"Yeah, I did."

"He is so awful. I can't imagine what he can get out of therapy because he's so full of himself. Oh shit."

"It sounded to me like he went a bit more than obnoxious, Kenzie. He was threatening you. And what was the 'oh shit' about?"

I don't know about threatening."

"Well I do. I've been around and I've seen, Kenzie. Trust me on that."

"Okay, I'll be careful. And the 'oh shit' is that I'm not supposed to say anything that could possibly acknowledge someone is even a client. Privacy rules, you know."

"Whatever. Whether he was making an appointment or paying a bill, even I know he didn't need to be hanging over the desk slobbering over you. Only I get to do that."

Kenzie glanced at her desk and Maya's eyes went with her. They both saw the light on. "Steve's ready for you. You're working tonight, right?"

"Yeah, late, too."

"I can text you."

"If you can stay awake."

Kenzie leaned in for a final kiss. Maya let it linger before finally turning for Steve's door.

***

Maya has come in distracted, Steve thought. What caught his attention, though, wasn't her initial lack of focus. It was her look. Maya was wearing her usual blue jeans and t-shirt, but she had a new pair of sneakers rather than her old Converse. These were black, too, but they had Day-Glo lime green elements. What caught Steve's eye most was Maya's nails. She'd done them in black and matching lime green, with what looked like a spider web design.

"Nice kicks. Nails, too."

She nodded ever so slightly, a look he struggled to discern as defiant or apologetic. She waited, not willing to open the session herself, but clearly aware that he knew about her relationship with Kenzie. He decided to get it out of the way first, and reminded himself not to be judgmental. Or fatherly.

"Kenzie told me that you guys were, uh, together."

She waited again. Steve plunged forward.

"Kenzie's a young woman who can make her own choices, and I don't consider it appropriate for me to comment. And the same goes with regard to you, Maya. I'm not upset, and I hope you will each treat the other right. I will admit I'm surprised."

This time Maya shrugged at him. Again, he tried to engage, using what he hoped would be taken as an amused tone.

"So what's with the nails? Kenzie's influence, I'm assuming?"

"She's cool, Steve. She's got a lot of things I haven't. I don't think about colors. She does. She wanted to do something for me."

"Do you like fancy nails?"

"Maybe. Kind of. They're acrylic, and it takes some getting used to. But I do look at them. A lot."

"Good, good. Any other shockers for me, today?"

"Not that I can think of."

He paused to take a couple of what he hoped were subtle breaths to collect himself.

"You surprise me, Maya. I hope I'm not offending you, but I am worried for Kenzie; I don't want her to get hurt. You've led a very different life than her."

"Thought it wasn't appropriate for you to comment."

"Not a comment. More of an observation."

"Well, for what it's worth to you," she said, her voice growing more measured and defiant, "I wouldn't want her to get hurt. And I'm not sure why you wouldn't recognize that by now."

Steve considered her words, which rang true and stung him.

"You're right. I apologize. Won't bring it up again. You two are adults."

She nodded, casting her eyes downward.

"Okay, then, Maya. You know what I'd really like today? Last time you told me about your dad's death and its impact on your life. Wondering if you would like to turn to your mom's suicide?"

She was shaking her head before he even finished.

"No. Not ready to go there. Sorry. Don't wanna talk about it."

He was about to back off completely when he suddenly remembered the "Dear Old Man" essay he'd been ready to talk about, but never did, during their first session.

"You know, Maya, I'm not going to push on that. I will share something I have said to some of my other clients with parent issues. I know you're angry with your mother, and perhaps there's some anger at your father for not being there for you. And perhaps you still carry guilt over not being a 'good' daughter, whatever that is. But as an adult, I think it's important to understand that you owe your parents nothing. Parents have a contract, of sorts, to provide food, clothing and safe shelter to their kids until they leave the household. And I know yours fell down on the latter, Maya. In return, though? You owe them nothing. It's great when parent–child relationships work well into the adult years. But it's not a requirement."

She was silent through his little spiel, and he could tell she was fighting to hold back her emotion. He wanted to know more about the trauma in her life. He might have been inclined to work her trauma through a type of therapy called Eye Movement Desensitization and Reprocessing (EMDR), but she had previously told him she was familiar with it and didn't need it or want it. He didn't ask for details. Sometimes, he believed, if you have faith in your client, you go with what they want because it's their journey.

Maya closed her eyes. Steve heard her sniffle. Then he heard her breathing softly—breath in, hold, breath out, hold. He waited.

***

Her voice was petulant, with a hint of the anger Steve recognized in her current self. But her expression was softer and more pained than present day. Her eyes narrowed and darkened. She was 15.

"Joey and Anna," she said quietly, with evident distaste. "They were 15 and 16, the oldest of the five kids in the house. Anna was a brunette with a short butch haircut. My height. She made me feel good about myself again. It was only a couple months after the first asshole raped me. I could still feel him. Still sore."

Maya winced at the memory. She spoke with her head down and appeared even more pale than usual, almost shrinking into herself. Steve strained to hear her when she continued, but he didn't want to disturb her narrative.

***

"You're so cute. And so quiet. You don't say boo. This place isn't that bad. The Fosters are a great couple. They make sure to feed us decent,

and stay out of our business. My brother says this is the safest home we've been in yet. And this is our fourth foster. Besides, how can you be bad foster parents if your name is Foster?"

She giggled at that, and I smiled. Maybe this place wouldn't be so bad. The next few weeks, the last part of the school year, went fine. Anna was right; the Fosters were "hands off" as foster parents go. Ed was a computer techie and retreated to sports at night, while Joan made the dinners, offered the kids help with their homework and spent her night hours on the couch next to her husband, ignoring the TV as she read Gothic romance novels. I was a good student, so I got little attention, and I had no clue if Ed and Joan were aware of what had happened at my first foster.

I shared a bedroom with Anna and 12-year-old Caitlyn, a cute, shy blonde whose parents had died in a wreck and who hadn't had any relatives willing to take her in. Like his older sister, Joey had dark hair and eyes. He seemed okay, and I could tell he was checking me out; every time I looked toward him in the dining room, he'd immediately look away. Anna told me Joey was a perv, but she said it in such a matter-of-fact way that I figured she meant he liked to jack off. Anna told me the Fosters got me to replace Mary, a 17-year-old who'd graduated early and been accepted into Wesleyan University in Connecticut. The Fosters needed four of us "to make the numbers work." When I gave her a quizzical expression, Anna exasperatedly told me, "You know, so they don't have to work. We're all part of the Fosters' meal ticket."

None of this meant anything until a couple of months later. It was a Friday night in early August, and the Fosters were having a movie night out, with Anna in charge of the crew. She seemed very up. "First outing for them in ages! I'm so happy." She gave me one of her tie-dye sweatshirts. "Put this on; you'll look cute in it." They were hanging out in the movie room, watching one of the Avengers flicks; I didn't know them. Mom had never taken me and didn't let me go out with friends. Not that I had any, anyway. And this new foster was clear across town. When I graduated middle school, it was my third school in three years.

The movie ended at nine and Anna ordered me to take Caitlyn upstairs and put her to bed. "Then come on back down. We can hang out; the Fosters won't be back 'til late. They always get a late meal on date night."

When I came back down, Anna had taken her sweatshirt off and was wearing a midriff shirt, which looked like a sports bra. Joey was lounging with a bag of popcorn. He spoke to me for the first time all night. "Hey, why don't you take your sweatshirt off like Anna? It's fucking hot in here." He took off his t-shirt. I watched Anna glance at Joey. It was a weird expression and got my guard up a bit. He spoke to his sister next. "Should I go get it?" She nodded and turned to me as he ran up the stairs.

"The Fosters keep a big old bottle of wine in their bar. Joey knows where they hide the key, and they never miss it. We're just gonna do some. You into that? Mary sure was. She told me about it. Apparently been a tradition here. Tonight's your initiation, girl. We're gonna party!"

I didn't know what to make of that. I hated alcohol because of my parents and hadn't ever touched it. But I was curious and didn't want to be seen as a loser. Anna had already told me she'd look after me when \I got to high school in a couple of weeks. That meant a lot; truth be told, I was feeling a little intimidated heading to a new high school with no friends.

Joey had gotten paper cups to conceal the evidence and we toasted together. "To hell with everyone else but us. Cheers!" Anna toasted. Joey smiled at me, the first time he had really looked me in the eye. But it was creepy, like he was looking through me.

Anna put her arm around my shoulder. "You okay, girl? It's just wine. Not like it's gonna kill ya. Have another sip or three." So I did. Joey poured another cup and we toasted again. Anna sat next to me on the floor, our backs against the ratty faux-leather sofa. Her arm was around my shoulder again. "Wine opens you up. Mellows you, ya know?" I was feeling more relaxed. Anna stroked my hair, which was shoulder length, letting it slip through her fingers. "Your hair is so fine."

I felt nervous but also curious. I liked Anna's touch. Then I glanced away and saw Joey watching me and shuddered. Anna turned my head with her forefinger back to her. "Don't worry about him. Just focus on me. I know you want to know what this is like. I can tell."

Before I knew it, Anna's face loomed large in front of me, and her lips brushed mine. They were warm and scented by the wine. I could feel my body responding, and it wasn't like being raped in any way. I wanted more, but I was conscious of Joey watching. I began shaking my head, but again Anna placed her finger under my chin and looked at me. "Trust me. Go with it. Give me your tongue."

Without even realizing, my lips parted and Anna began exploring my mouth, and slipped her hand under my sweatshirt. I was small enough to not need a bra all the time. Anna's hand was warm on my body. I gave myself over to it.

Until I felt Joey's hands on my legs, and Anna kissing me harder and whispering "It's okay," and my will slipping away, and him pushing in down there, and tears coming down and me whispering the word "no" over and over again, but not feeling as violated because I was wet from Anna's touch, and I disappeared into the ceiling until it was over.

Joey immediately scrammed upstairs after declaring "Good stuff," and Anna began stroking my head, soothing me, bringing me back from the ceiling.

"You did great," Anna said. "We all need this. To learn, to help each other. It's our secret times when we get a night alone. And it's fine. I'll be here for you as long as you're part of the team, lovey little girl. We'll protect you at school, here, everywhere. You can count on us."

In bed later, I curled up in a ball. I thought of the cat I'd brought home and Mother had allowed me to keep her four days when I was 10 before she took it back to the shelter saying we couldn't afford it and she was allergic. My body position was imitating that cat. The pain down there was dull, not horrible as it was when I was raped the first time. I focused on Anna's kisses, her tongue, her aroma. It took me to sleep.

***

Steve gave her space to collect herself after she finished the story of the initial rape. She told him it continued whenever the Fosters had their nights out. And then it grew more violent one day when Joey caught her alone after school and she didn't have Anna to protect her in some way and he kept his hand tightly on her throat throughout the sex to keep her from screaming. It finally ended nearly two years later, she said, when she saw Joey talking with a no-longer-pubescent Caitlyn one day in the kitchen. Anna was next to him and creepily running her fingers down her brother's neck as he talked. Steve asked her if she thought Caitlyn was being groomed. Maya didn't know the word so Steve explained it, and she nodded miserably.

"But that is what made me stop them. I wrote a letter to Social Services telling them what was going on, saying it was too late for me. I stuck it in the mail and headed to the bus depot."

Maya looked at him through wet eyes and spoke in her normal voice, with anguish.

"Why did these things happen? Why me? *I'm such a fucking loser.*"

This was the first time she'd expressed a negative belief about herself as a result of her trauma. It was a breakthrough moment, and Steve knew what he said next might determine whether she'd have a shot at a future not tormented by her past.

"Maya, I'm sorry for the awful things you've had happen to you in your life. It's more than one person, any child, should ever have to live. There's a concept called 'generational trauma.' Have you heard of it?"

She shook her head, so he continued.

"Generational trauma means the effects of trauma are passed through generations. So these horrible things you've experienced in life also are the result of trauma in your family of origin."

"You trying to tell me my mom is responsible for my shit? Not exactly news, Steve."

"That's not quite it, Maya. I'm saying it's likely that your mom's own traumatic experiences—and I think her alcohol and drug use speak to that damage—created anxiety and depression in her life, something you can't escape easily, even if you won the lottery today."

"Well *that's* encouraging."

Steve didn't worry about her sarcasm. This was a teaching moment, and he could see she was engaged in learning more.

"I'd like to ask you a question. From the murder of your father to your being raped to your being raped again, did you ever feel like you had any control?"

She looked up with hate in her eyes. "Of course not. That might be the stupidest fucking thing a therapist has ever said to me." That's the reaction he wanted. He needed her focused, with all her 25-year-old anger and glory.

"You never had control."

"No."

"No control."

She shook her head. He could see her blinking back tears again, and he forged ahead.

"None at all."

"Why are you doing this, Steve?"

He watched her move to the edge of the sofa. He worried if she jumped for the door he wouldn't be able to reach her to stop her, so he ever-so-gently edged himself up to the front of his chair just in case.

"Because trauma, Maya, represents a loss of power. You're part of a generational trauma, and you had your own individual traumatic experiences. Multiple ones. You don't get to go back in time, but you can restore power if you work in the present day."

He could sense her curiosity, especially when he rose and walked to a closet where he kept various pieces of equipment. He picked out the red boxing gloves and black mitts.

"Now, I know this probably seems weird," he said, affixing his hand inside the strap of the right mitt, and handing her the gloves, "but hear me out. What if you could envision Anna's face on the inside of the left mitt and Joey's on the right?"

Maya was shaking her head slightly.

"Are you okay with this?"

She nodded almost imperceptibly, then took the gloves. Ever so deliberately, she slipped her left hand inside. She flexed it, staring with rapt attention, almost love. It was what he'd hoped to see—Maya using her fitness and athleticism as a strength in fighting trauma. He held up his hands and put one leg back, bracing for what he expected to be a good bit of force. He had one fit, angry woman in his office.

"You don't have to hold back."

Her focus was becoming steely and she began taking small, measured breaths. Steve watched her study the two mitts as she naturally drifted to her right in a boxing stance. He drifted with her. Suddenly, Maya exploded with a one-two combo, and Steve grunted at the give. She did it again. And again. Then she let loose with a good 10-shot round. And another one-two. She was breathing hard and had a wild look in those intense eyes.

"Again, Maya. Don't hold back. I can take it. See them. Your tormentors. Your attackers. Get 'em."

She began again, not saying a word. Just breathing hard, but rhythmically, and she poured her anger into the mitts. Steve's palms were feeling it, but he forced himself to not show his pain and potentially disrupt her focus. When she finally paused five minutes later, he looked in her eyes. "You ready to stop?"

She nodded.

He had one more question for her. "What are you?"

"I'm fucking tough."

"Uh-huh. I'll say." Steve pulled his right hand out of the mitt, then his left, and held them up to her. They were red.

He was thrilled to hear her state a present-day, positive self-cognition.

"So, are you really *a fucking loser?*"

She sighed deeply. "No. *They* were the fucking losers."

"That's right. At the time, you were . . ." he paused, waiting for her.

"Powerless." She said it with a bit of wonder. "You're smarter than you look."

"I'm not that smart, Maya. What we know about trauma, though, is when it happens we develop negative beliefs about ourselves that get locked in because of the trauma. If we can open up our minds, and there are many ways to do that, we can find paths to restore power. Today, Maya, you're a person of physical strength, you're self-aware and you have the control. Trauma represents a loss of power, of connection, of control. That was then. Your negative self-cognition from back then, which you've carried with you for so long, doesn't apply any more, Maya. You just said so yourself."

"I'm fucking tough." She said it like a woman discovering the truth she might have known all along but didn't have the means to access.

"Exactly."

Steve knew their time was up. "Remember the light stream technique. Or anything to soothe yourself if you feel anxiety as a result of recalling these old memories."

"Yes, Dad."

He smiled at her sarcasm. It was a sign of her being back on her game, returning to normalcy. "Next week, same time?"

Then she threw him a curveball as she passed him on her way to the door.

"There's worse than you've heard so far, you know."

Post-session: Steve

I ALL BUT RUN TO OUR BREAK ROOM TO GRAB THE GIUSEPPE'S I'd ordered that Kenzie had put in the fridge for me. As I peel back the wax paper from my Italian sub, my thoughts turn back to Maya, who surprised me with her honesty and openness today, so much so that I hadn't even gotten around to asking, or figuring out whether to ask, about what I've learned about her back story. So many questions.

Does she know that Deena is dead? I can't imagine she doesn't, which means she's leaving out some of her story.

Why doesn't she have a criminal record in North Carolina? Once again, she's leaving out information with me.

Does she have any connection with the California Maya Andino? Me, I don't believe in coincidences.

Why is she dating Kenzie? I wonder if she has an ulterior motive. And what did she mean by the parting remark?

I'm not sure I want to know the answers, recognizing I've yet to confront her about anything. On my second bite into the hoagie, I jump back a foot as oil, vinegar and a piece of ripe tomato spring loose, aiming straight for my shirt and lap. I act with the cat-like reflexes of the former pitcher I am, dodging a liner back up the box. The dripping falls on the floor. As I wipe it up with extra napkins, I get back to the problem at hand. Maya is sharing some truths with me. But she's also still concealing parts of her narrative, and I'm running out of time. Three more sessions and she'll be someone else's problem. I don't want her to be Kenzie's problem.

I pick up the phone. I hope Jim is free.

Post-session: Maya

I'M ON THE BAR WHEN BILLIE PASSES ME THE ORDER. Her look is half apology, half amusement. "Have fun, hon. But don't take too long. They're gonna be my big table of the night. And you get a share."

Two drafts, a glass of merlot, a chardonnay, a gin and tonic, a Manhattan, a Long Island iced tea, a kamikaze, a Jager bomb and an old-fashioned. "Are you kidding me?" My mind is going a mile a minute, but the order is the easy part.

Barely half an hour later, the same table is ordering a second round. "Watch for the switch-ups, love," Billie calls as she passes me the printout, blowing me a kiss. I smack her ass on as she passes by.

Billie and the diner are also taking away from the craziness of today's session. If it wasn't busy, or if it was a pre-Kenzie night, I'd be stewing over the session. I don't have time, though. I was honest today and that's both different and not nearly as upsetting as I imagined it would be.

Not as upsetting as that fucking reporter giving Kenzie a hard time.

***

The bar at Farley's was jamming for late on a weeknight, but the short-end seats were open, as were two on the other side of Jones. The other dozen stools were taken by collegians and young professionals enjoying a late night. Jones nursed his Yuengling, contemplating whether he could get away with asking for another shot from bartender Mike before last call in fifteen minutes, which would give him that extra boost. He didn't trust Mike, though, so he sulked over the Yuengling without risking incurring a cutoff. A cold blast hit him and he looked up to see a short, butch chick come in, case the room and walk his direction, grabbing a spot a couple seats down from him. No one was between them. He shifted slightly to open his body toward her. No harm trying if the opportunity arose.

Not five minutes later, it did.

As Mike came over on a pre-last-call glance, she ordered a shot of Crown Vanilla and a Modelo. Weird combo, seemed to Jones, but hey, to each his own. Then she spoke to him. "What kind of shots did you do?" she asked, bobbing her head at the two empties that Mike hadn't bothered to clear away.

"Straight Crown."

She nodded. "Yeah, I can see that. Seems like your kind of drink."

She said it while looking him over from head to toe. He regretted wearing an old t-shirt under his tweed jacket, because he'd removed the jacket after the third shot (and fourth beer) an hour and a half ago. Which meant his growing gut was on full display. He did his best to suck it in as Mike brought her drink and shot. She gestured to bartender Mike, and Jones blinked when he heard what she said: "Buy my friend here a shot of his straight Crown. He looks like he's had a hard day."

It had been so long since anyone had bought him a round that Jones didn't know what to say. He coughed out a "Thanks" before adding, "Name's Mike. You?"

"Deena."

***

An hour and a half later, Jones was feeling fine after another shot and a beer with his new pal. They'd just gotten inside his small downtown apartment when Deena pushed him into the worn, plush couch, and he was okay with that, even if he had caught a look of disgust on her face as she saw old socks on the floor next to an empty bottle of Bud. Now she was straddling him, her strong legs directly on top of his, pinning him down.

He reached to her breasts, pulling at her t-shirt, but she easily kept him at bay.

"Not yet, cowboy," she said.

Okay, so she wanted to be in control. He wondered where this would go. He wasn't as experienced as he liked to pretend. He saw her reach with one arm behind her to the bag she'd dropped on his coffee table and before he could even react, the air went out of his lungs. In one motion she'd swung the butt end of some type of baton directly into his stomach without warning. He pitched forward off the couch onto his knees, gasping for air, and scrambled to rise, wondering what the fuck was happening. He heard himself whimper "Not again. Please," and turned his head up in time to see her smile.

"Not in the gut this time, Mike Jones." She swung with both hands on the baton, bringing it in a short powerful arc from the floor between his legs, the contact with his privates through his jeans making a discernible thump.

"Take, take whatever you want," he managed to whisper as she lightly touched the baton to his head, which made him shudder.

She was just nodding. "Look at me," she commanded.

He did.

"The women you try to force your macho-ass bullshit on? Me, women at your newspaper, the women you encounter in offices, in restaurants? Off-limits, dickhead. If I were you? I'd crawl back to my wife if she'd have your sorry ass. Just keep your mouth, your hands and your ugly self away from us."

He had a sudden insight unique to journalists who still have observational skills. This was somehow related to the chick in Prescott's office. He vaguely recalled a shadowy figure wearing a baseball cap in the waiting room when he turned away from the secretary to leave. She'd made a clear effort to avoid being seen. *Was this the same woman?* Before he could finish the thought, Deena raised the baton again. Jones squeezed his eyes tightly closed and cowered.

Session Six: Truths

HE'D READ THE EMAIL TEN TIMES AND IT STILL DIDN'T MAKE any sense to him.

Hey Steve, Mike Jones here. Just wanted to let you know I'm not going to be back to see you. So please cancel my appointment for next week. I know you probably heard by now I came by to prove you wrong about me and your hot secretary when I made the appointment. And I think she really wanted me. But I had a reckoning over the past few days. You see some crazy fucking people in this world but I'm not one of them. I need to get back to my wife and stop chasing these skirts. It's dangerous out there. Cheers.

Steve punched his phone and asked Kenzie to come in.

She was wearing a deep red blouse that was, for Kenzie, quite daring. It went with her light hair and the red lipstick. Funny how that might appeal to Maya, who was such her opposite.

"You look quite beautiful, Kenzie. I'd say you were aglow, but you'd probably think that's corny."

"Aw, thank you, boss. I'm glad you like it. I wore it for Maya, though, not for you."

"I know. She's at 11. But I didn't call you in for that, Kenzie. Would you come over here to my computer and read this email I have up? It's from Mike Jones."

She walked around and Steve caught a whiff of her vanilla-tinged perfume. He was struck again by the difference between her and Maya and made a mental note to talk to her or maybe even them both, about how opposites can attract but have to work harder at it. But that would be another time and place.

"Hmmm."

"That was my reaction, too, Kenzie. He clearly mentioned you in this. Do you have any clue? Did he come in and did something happen?"

She hesitated, but then shared how Jones had been obnoxiously pushy in front of her.

"You sure you didn't do or say anything to him that would result in this kind of response?"

"No."

He noticed another hesitation and how Kenzie could not keep her face from turning red. There was more to this story. He felt like Maya's personality trait of caution toward others might already be rubbing off on his trusted admin. He didn't like it.

***

Maya almost sashayed in, flashing a charming smile that Steve hadn't seen before. He, on the other hand, was pensive, uncertain of whether and how to challenge her on some of the vagaries of her story, her very identity.

Jim had advised that if Steve felt uncomfortable with the amount of information he did not have about a client, it was up to him to be curious. "You know the old saying, Steve, 'The antidote to anxiety is curiosity.'" Of course, Steve knew it. Beyond the years Jim had preached it, he used it himself with clients all the time. He decided to be curious in a safe way.

"You seem in a cheery mood this morning, Maya. What's going on?"

"I've been thinking about that a lot. Things are coming together. It's Kenzie; she's new and I don't usually like new. But I've just been going with it."

"What are your fears? And do you feel them physically inside?"

"If I give in to them, sure. It gets me right in the gut, Steve. I go on, I guess you'd call it hyperdrive, right? Getting my guard up. Worrying what's gonna go wrong or who's gonna take this away."

"But for today you've managed to squash that part of yourself.

"I guess so. I was feeling good when I came in. I got to see Kenzie. I got to touch her face and see her love. Just how she looks at me. That doesn't ever happen for me, Steve."

He watched as her eyes became watery and her face turned red in her effort to suppress the tears.

"I'm happy for you for that. I really am. Can I ask you something, though, about what you just said?"

She nodded, looking at him cautiously.

Steve plunged on. "You previously talked about your relationship with Deena being very special, particularly in those early months. Which means this has happened for you, Maya."

She didn't get mad, which to Steve represented progress. She was using her thinking brain, not going to her reptilian brain when challenged.

"I did love Deena. That's true. But it was different. Not like this. She was like a mentor, a teacher. And I loved her for that early on. I guess I thought that was love. But Kenzie is like, well, a peer. We're the same age just about. I'm more life experienced, I guess, but she's got things that I don't have. And I love her showing me that, just in the way she lives. So fucking normal. I'm less scared of it seeing how she handles life, if that makes sense."

Steve smiled at her. "It does make sense, Maya. I'm curious about something else. Do you have any contact with people from California, or have you been in touch with any of your old friends? Deena?"

It was a little test, and he could see her body stiffen. She began breathing in a regulated fashion and took her time before answering.

"Something I did not tell you, Steve, is that Deena is dead. She was found murdered in her apartment. That's what led me to leaving California more than anything else."

"Why? Tell me more."

"I guess they found her body late in the morning. It was nine months ago now. March 14. I think six different people came up to tell me the news when I got to the bar that afternoon."

She paused and Steve was about to ask one of the dozens of questions in his mind. But he channeled Jim and held his tongue. "*Let them talk, Steve. Once you have a person sharing, let them go all the way. You'll have your chance. Use a pad to write down questions if need be. I do.*"

Steve regretted he'd never been one to use a pad. Now he had to hold the questions he had in his head while also focusing on Maya.

"The cops came by the bar that night. I told them the truth. I didn't know anything. But I didn't like the tone of the questioning. They knew we'd been together. They also knew we'd had a bad breakup. Someone told them how I said I'd kill her. But, of course, the story got warped. The cops heard that she stole $5K from me 'cause I'd bitched about it to everyone. I wanted people to know her true self. But now in their minds I fucking killed her.

"They didn't hear that what I said was I'd kill her if she ever came into my bar again without bringing back my money. The cops cost me an hour on the clock that night. And the only reason they went away is that I'd been working the night before until 2 a.m. and I was able to show them the time stamp from logging off the bar's register.

"The prick detective said to me, I mean he actually said this right? 'Don't leave town.' Fucking asshole."

"So why *did* you leave?"

"Well, I mean, it took me a couple of weeks to decide. The cops never stopped by again, but I was worried. Deena had a lot more friends than I did, and if they'd already fed the cops about the breakup, what else might they tell 'em? What I thought, and I'm pretty sure of it, is that some dude she swindled figured out who she was and came for her. And then I was worried I'd be collateral damage if the cops started looking into her. I did participate, you know. Cops always screw up the real story. I mean, look at my dad's death. And my rapes. Cops, Social Services, school principals, *counselors, too*, Steve. You just don't ever get the story right."

Oh, those defiant eyes staring him down. Daring him to challenge her. She was heading into fight or flight. Steve needed to pull her back. He walked over to the closet and held up the red boxing gloves. "You want these?"

"No, I'm good." She took a deep breath. He watched as her tension passed and she straightened her spine, shifting to a more upright position on the sofa. "You've gotten a lot of the true story. More than my other counselors. Really."

"Glad to hear that. I'd like more, Maya. You alluded to there being worse at the end of our last session. Care to go there?"

Steve was willing to set aside further talk about Deena, though he wasn't totally convinced he had the whole truth from Maya. That remark about him getting "a lot of the true story" was like a warning bell.

"Okay, so Anna and Joey. The fuck twins. Did I tell you I call them that?"

Steve shook his head.

"Yeah, that's what I began calling them after I ended it."

"When you sent the letter to Social Services, right?"

"Yeah, but there's more."

Again, Steve waited.

***

One day, not long after I turned 17, Joey came after me from behind in the laundry room, grabbing me around the waist and sneaking his hand up to my left breast. He'd been doing shit like this for two years, with or without his sister. Pawing me, molesting me. Three times on his own raping me. I'd always been frozen, unable to act. This time, perhaps without even thinking or perhaps because I decided I was too old for this shit, I put all of my 110 pounds into back-kicking him in the nuts as my leg came up directly between his. He fell to the floor in agony. Seeing him crumble empowered me for what seemed like the first time in my life. All the fear that always froze me around them dissipated seeing Joey doubled over and weak. I could almost see a lightbulb form above my own head. "Awww. Sorry, Joey. You just startled me. Do you need me to heal it? C'mon, take it out and I'll make it up to you." He groaned, which emboldened me further. I yanked down his sweats and underpants to expose his shriveled-up little thing, switched my cell phone to camera mode and began clicking. I wasn't sure if he was aware, but I grabbed a broomstick next to the dryer and clocked him in the nuts again anyway. Before leaving him lying there, I whispered in his ear. "I guess I didn't want to play today. And guess what? You aren't going to do a thing about it. You or Anna. Not to me, not to Caitlyn. No one. No more. Got it?"

He opened his eyes, looking at me with hatred. I wielded the broomstick over his penis as he quickly covered it, trying to protect, clearly terrified. "I said, got it?" This time, he nodded.

Upstairs, I downloaded the photos to my iPad and worked the rest of the night making my vision a reality.

***

"My only regret is I didn't save any of those damn flyers. I really should have."

Steve couldn't help but smile. It was a helluva revenge, plastering her tormentor's tortured manhood and image across the high school.

"And you just left town that day?"

"Yeah, I'd worked all night to create the flyer, write the letter to Social Services and pack the stuff I could fit in my purse and school bag. The next morning, I went to a copy store and spent my own money, $27 as I recall, to get 500 copies of it. I had to stand there doing it myself because, ya know, it's not like you can ask them to make copies of a dick pic.

"I got to school really early and started just flinging out the flyers down main hallways, the cafeteria, the gym. It actually was easy enough to do without being seen. I was kind of faceless around that school anyway. I stuck around long enough to begin to see the reactions. Then I ditched my cell phone and took off for the bus depot."

Steve paused before responding, wanting to share his insight into Maya's trauma response until she raised her eyebrows at him.

"Okay, you're probably going to be surprised, Maya, but I think you acted appropriately with Joey from a trauma point of view."

"You're not shitting me?"

"No, hear me out. You recall our discussion of the triune brain and fight-flight-freeze?"

She shook her head. "Duh."

"Well your response to Joey, Maya, by attacking him, was a straight instinctive 'fight' response. That's exactly what your primitive brain is trained to do. You protected 'self.'

"Then, think about what you did next. Once he was disabled you took images and then spent hours creating that flyer. The crisis was over, and although you were still wanted to fight, you devised a creative solution to put him in his place for good."

Maya looked at Steve, ducked her head and smiled. He thought he saw her face redden. She wasn't used to getting compliments. He wanted to reinforce the message.

"Maya, your response to Joey was not dysfunctional. It was classic reptilian brain switching to thinking brain. It actually was a pretty ingenious, protective response."

"I guess so. I just kind of snapped. I'd had enough."

"Tell me, Maya, have you ever done that at other times in your life? Just snapped?"

She frowned. "You trying to trap me, Mr. Counselor?"

"Not intentionally, no."

"Well I didn't snap with Deena, if that's what you were implying. God, you're just like the cops."

Steve didn't immediately respond. He was assessing her tone.

"That was a joke, Steve." She smiled tentatively at him, and Steve breathed a little easier.

"Okay, I get it. But you can be hard to read."

"So they say."

"Who is they?"

"Got you again! Do I have the famous counselor Steve Prescott rattled?"

"You might at that, Maya. Do you mind if I ask you a question?"

She splayed out her hands in a "go ahead" gesture.

"The first couple of sessions, you asked me about my worst case and you seemed seriously interested in that. Lately not so much. I'm just curious."

"I've been too busy revealing the story of my life, Steve. Do you have more you want to share about that suicidal client?"

"Well, to be honest, Maya, your questions and presentation at the time made me worry about you potentially being suicidal. And then some of what you have shared made me worry about you being homicidal."

"Hence your questions about Deena?"

"Possibly."

She arched an eyebrow at him.

"Okay, probably."

"I'm neither, Steve. Not this instant, anyway. Chalk it up to love?"

"I'll do that. Sometimes I think I see clients growing before my eyes. I hope you're one of them, Maya. I really do."

Post-session: Steve

I'D FELT MY CELL PHONE VIBRATE DURING THE SESSION with Maya, and I glance at it: Jane. I debate whether to read it through. My mind is still on the many threads of Maya. Capturing her personality is *so* elusive. She's the tough girl, but she falls for, seemingly, a girly girl in Kenzie. She masks parts of herself, but at times she shares so much as to shock. And enjoys the shocking. And she also is being okay with showing her emotions now that we've had a chance to establish a therapeutic bond.

I wonder if the fact I still haven't read Jane's text is indicative of my own reticence. She's smart, attractive and bold. Significantly younger. And yet even with fine sex, I'm ambivalent. I need to analyze myself. I finally peek at the text.

***

We're at a Mexican joint near Southpoint Mall after a nice day of walking and talking. Jane is sipping a pineapple margarita, frozen, while I have a traditional, on the rocks. I'd ordered queso fundido, and with the chips and salsa, we might snack our way out of staying for dinner.

"Steve, can I ask you something?"

I take that as a warning sign. It is a question I often heard the last year of my marriage.

"Of course."

"I feel like I've told you a lot about me and my life, my hopes and dreams, what I want to do after law school. I still feel after, what is it, three weeks we've been getting together, that I hardly know you other than you once played ball and now you're a counselor. I mean, you're a nice guy. The sex is good. But aren't you supposed to be tuned in to relationships? Do you think this is developing nicely?"

My face reddens. I know she's right. I reach behind her neck, caressing it softly and giving her a light kiss. I can smell the tangerine of her shampoo in her red hair. I should be feeling and caring more.

"You're right, Jane. I don't know what to say."

"You could start by telling me why you're so ambivalent."

"A-ha! You want to play the counselor."

It was a stall and we both knew it.

"Honestly, Jane, you're great fun. We've had a good time and as you point out, I'm the counselor. I often tell people having relationship issues that it usually starts with the physical and if it's meant to develop, both people have to work at the emotional and spiritual

connection."

"And you think you're working at that?"

The way her brow furrows when she asks is both worrisome and sexy. I wonder if I 'm simply attracted to the physical because it has been so long. I'd been thinking about sex from the time we'd ordered our margaritas.

I reach for her hands. Her fingers are long and strong; she has beautifully done nails, an emerald green that accents her hair. I run my thumbs along her palms.

"I don't think I've done well at all, Jane. Part of it may have been my assumption at the start that you would not see a long-term relationship in me, someone a dozen years older than you. And I don't mean that as an excuse. I'm just saying maybe I haven't gotten beyond that in my head yet."

"You know, Steve, I'm not saying I was looking to get married. Just that a relationship means opening your soul a little to the other."

"No argument."

"Where do we go now?"

"I'm hoping we can go back to your place, make love, stay the night and then I'll head back to my place and make you a lovely Sunday brunch omelet."

"You want to connect to me through food?"

"Tell you what, bring Astro and we'll make it a foursome!"

She considers. "Okay, counselor, I will accept that offer. But I would like you to promise me more 'you' in our conversations."

"I'll do my best, Jane."

***

She's being fair; I know she is. *Stop feeling guilty. Stop feeling like you can't.* If I want to have a relationship, I have to try. That's all she's suggesting. I stare at the text again. She's free again Saturday and wants to do something fun. I text Enrique. There's live salsa music at Havana Nights starting at 10 p.m. And I've never been disappointed there. Maybe she won't be either.

Post-session: Maya

I STEP OUTSIDE STEVE'S OFFICE AND THEN SNEAK BACK around to the front office, hoping to steal a kiss from my girl. But she comes from her desk into the sitting area with fury on her face.

"You did something to Mike Jones. I know you did."

She's beet red, standing with her hands on her hips. I move toward her for a hug and she halts me with her arm.

"Tell me the truth!"

"Whoa. Whoa. Slow down, Kenzie. I'd never do anything to hurt you. I did this to help you."

"Help me? Help me, really? Just tell me what you did. Did you get physical with him?"

My alarm bells go off. If I really want to be with this dynamo in front of me, I have to consider my words. I don't think Kenzie, strait-laced perfectionist that she is, can imagine someone who lives, or has lived, anyway, my kind of life. I hadn't really told her much at all about me. Not like I'd spilled to Steve, anyway.

"I didn't really do anything to him, lover. I did go to see him that night at his bar. You know, the one he mentioned when he came to you in the office that day?"

"When? You were working that night. Or was that a lie, too?"

Too? I feel rage. Have to breathe. Slow in, slow out. *FOCUS, Maya!*

"Lover, I am not sure where this is coming from but . . ."

"Dammit, Maya, stop it! Don't try to sweet-talk me. That was what that asshole reporter was doing."

My hands are clammy. I'm about to blow this relationship before it's even really begun. *I'm a fucking loser.* The thought startles me, and I feel the tears forming. Then I hear the positive alternative in my head. *I'm fucking tough.*

Before I open my mouth, Kenzie has embraced me, squeezing tight, so tight I can't move my arms beneath her grip. Who's supposed to be the tough one here? "I'm sorry, Maya. I didn't mean to upset you. You're crying. Stop, stop, stop. I trust you. I really do."

I nod my head into hers and kiss into the side of her face. "Look, I did something wrong. I shouldn't have gotten involved. It was my instinct. It's who I am, Kenzie. And you don't know who I really am. I mean, I'm here, right? Your boss is my counselor? I'm sorry."

"So you did do something?"

I look directly into Kenzie's brown eyes. "Isn't it enough to know he won't be bothering you anymore? And to know I didn't *really* hurt him?"

Kenzie pushes back from me and for an instant, I'm sure I've blown it. Then she looks at me and says, "Not even a little bit?"

Relief floods over me and I smile as she laughs and grabs me by the waist. I've never felt this kind of connection before.

"Yeah, well, maybe a little bit."

"I have to get back to work, you. But we need to talk and I want you to come clean. I want to know who you are, Maya Andino. I'm not letting you get away this easy."

I nod and feel tears forming again and turn quickly for the door. In my car, I text her. "Will you wait up for me tonight? I can come to your place after my shift ends."

***

"Can I call you Red?"

"Only if you want me to beat your ass."

We were lying naked, twisted amid the no-longer-crisp blue sheets of Kenzie's bed. Her tabby, Paddy, is back now that our thrashing is over with. The cat surprises me by jumping onto the bed right between us, as close to me as he has been since we started our thing. Kenzie instinctively reaches out to stroke him, and I put my hand on Paddy's head as she strokes his body.

"He likes you, Maya."

"I don't know."

"Well, I do. I've had cats my whole life. He never would have jumped up here if he didn't feel safe with you in the house."

He is pretty. I keep scratching his head lightly. He turns and gently bites me.

"Hey!"

Kenzie giggles. Such a girly, high-pitched thing. I can't imagine why it's not annoying to me. But it's not.

"Ha-ha. You must have hit a sensitive spot. There's only so much he'll do before he'll turn and bite when that happens. But he still likes you or he would have jumped down."

"Thanks for the cat psychology lesson."

"So can I ask you something?"

I reach over and kiss her, lingering and brushing my tongue across her bottom lip. "I'd rather we just do it again." I twist my body across her, easily using my strength to place myself on top so our breasts are touching. As she reaches down to touch my hip with her left hand, Paddy decides he's reached his limit.

"See, you scared him that time. He doesn't like sudden movements."

"What about you?"

"I like your sudden movements." I think I'm beginning to rub off on Kenzie. She's way more daring than I ever imagined she'd be. "Well, you know, as long as Paddy's scrammed, why not take advantage?"

I reach for her again, and I feel her breath draw in as she responds.

***

"Hey, Maya. I'm serious about this, but why did you go black?"

I ponder this. It's a fair question 'and maybe it's time for me to come clean with Kenzie a little.

"Kenz, have you ever felt like a loser in life? You know I'm seeing Steve, so you know I've had some heavy shit happen to me."

"Like your drug arrest?"

Uh-oh. Her gaze is clear, but her voice belies a slight

skepticism. I just want to kiss her again and not deal with this. I know it's not fair to want a connection and not be honest. Deena sucked me in by not telling me the truth about the life she led. Should I really do that, too?

I still haven't answered, and I can tell by that forehead furrow that Kenzie's not happy. But she's not furious like she was earlier, either. She pulls the sheet up to the top of her chest as she sits up, and I turn to my right and lean on an elbow to face her.

"Yeah, about that . . ."

Ten minutes later, she is not yelling at me, but I know by the twitch and how she's biting her lower lip that she's angry. I shared some of the story, the part about Deena and coming to North Carolina to get away. I need to tell her I didn't have a drug arrest, that it was all a ruse. I need to be more honest. But it's so fucking hard.

I can feel my lips quavering as I tell her about faking the drug arrest. I end with a plea. "But you can't tell Steve. When the time is right, I will. I promise."

She kisses me deeply, her tongue reaching gently for mine.

"I won't say a word, Maya. But . . ."

I sense her questions, her doubt, despite the kiss. And I can't look her in those blue eyes. I focus on the furrow above her eyes.

"You're upset. I know you are, Kenz. Before you say anything, before you tell me to leave, I need to share one more thing. Please hear me out."

I breathe in, hold it two seconds and slowly exhale through my mouth. She's waiting expectantly, lips still pursed.

"I'm crazy for you. You changed my equation in coming back to North Carolina. I started off thinking I'd just flirt with you because I needed you. I never imagined, I mean, I've not been . . ."

"Not been what?

"In love." I can't stop myself from qualifying it. "I think."

"You think, huh?"

I feel my eyes tearing. "It's the best I can do, Kenz. Can we just hold each other for a while?"

I feel her nod. We stay locked in place for what seems an eternity. It's a foreign feeling. Home.

***

Kenzie's staring into my eyes. She's the first person since I've returned who I've taken out the dark lenses for.

She kisses my eyelids and gazes deeply into my green eyes. "So beautiful," she murmurs. "You are crazy to disguise these."

"I dyed my hair black and got the dark contact lenses because I needed to change, different place, different look. North Carolina represented failure, trauma, rape. That was the redheaded me."

"But you said you didn't dye it until you were leaving California to come back."

Boy, Kenzie didn't miss a beat. "Yeah, that's true. I guess I was more interested in making myself different and coming back on the down low, ya know?"

"I'm still not sure I understand why you would make up a drug arrest story to be able to see a therapist. And to fake a court order besides?"

"Hellooooo. Trauma." I'm hoping my sarcasm will slow her questions. When I admitted to making up the drug arrest, I'd left out the reason why I needed to see Steve in particular. Strangely, she hasn't picked up on that.

"Any more questions?"

"No, Maya. But can I share something with you?"

I nod.

"I'm glad you didn't dye your puss."

I burst out laughing. This girl kills me.

"I had to hold onto some piece of me, Kenz."

"That makes sense."

She asks about my family, and I share how both of my parents are dead.

"And you don't have grandparents, aunts, uncles, cousins?"

"My mom was an alcoholic and she was estranged from her family, and my dad's parents died in a car accident when I was a baby. I think that's one of the reasons he drank so much. I never knew family, Kenz. I mean, no happy Thanksgiving gatherings, no Christmas Eves. Nothing. Just me and my parents, until my father died. Then me and my mom. She once yelled at me for watching the Thanksgiving parade."

"What? Why?"

"You really want to know what she said?"

Kenzie nods. I do my best imitation of the hardened voice my mom used to make a point.

Just a bunch of phony people smiling and laughing. It's all fake. Stop trying to live a fantasy.

Kenzie looks thoughtful. She gives me a quick squeeze, puts her forehead on mine, whispering, "I'm so sorry for you." Then she reaches down to her work bag and pulls out her laptop.

"I want to show you something, Maya. It's the Ancestry website. Don't know if you ever heard of it, but I was able to find relatives of generations before me, and also found modern-day relatives. I have a couple of cousins I never knew about growing up. You might find something like that, Maya."

I study her hands and the screen as she works.

After she finishes showing me some of her family tree, she snuggles in. "I can do stuff like that for you, Maya. Everyone has family. You don't have to feel so alone."

"I'm not alone, Kenz." I kiss her, but she's undeterred.

"You know what I mean."

"I do, but trust me, I do not want to know more about my twisted family. Even if, say, there are 'normal' people somewhere in my family line, they never tried to find me, Kenz. And after all this time, and all the shit I've been through, I'm just not interested. Please accept that."

She frowns. Then she closes her laptop.

"Thank you. No qualifiers. I love you, Kenzie Aguilera."

I pull her back down to me.

Session Seven – Like Mother, Like Daughter

STEVE PONDERED THE SIMPLE MANILA FOLDER BEFORE HIM. He'd asked Kenzie to bring it to him after hanging up with Social Services and confirming with a live department body there was no record of a Maya Andino in the North Carolina system for any recent drug arrest. Each client had two folders: one that Kenzie kept, the manila one, containing all relevant "official" paperwork on clients, including the forms clients sign before starting treatment and any forms clients bring with them; and one that he kept (color-coded by client last name—Maya's was red for A–G) with his progress notes written after each session, as well as the client treatment plans and any other relevant therapy-related notes. Only when clients terminate do the two folders get merged and put into a locked storage cabinet in Steve's office.

He hadn't said anything to Kenzie about what he wanted when he asked her to bring him Maya's admin folder, and she didn't ask. He didn't want to create any possible rifts, and it wasn't that unusual for him to ask for a client's admin folder. But he did sense a raised eyebrow when Kenzie handed over the folder.

Steve opened it and looked at the Social Services form referring Maya for treatment. It was a standard printed PDF with the Social Services department logo and the relevant added detail in fresh ink. There was an "8" filled out on the line for "number of sessions" and Maya's scrawled signature, which consisted of a capital letter that might be an "M" and a long straight flourished line. That was it. He took out Maya's "consent to treat" form, a standard protocol for any health visit, physical or mental, in which a person consents to be seen by the provider. Her signature was, once again, a scrawl. He looked at the first letter of the two signatures. He guessed they were the same.

He closed the folder and put it next to her red folder of progress notes. Then he had a sudden thought and reopened the admin folder, thumbing through until he found the copy of Maya's driver's license. The signature was different. It still had the scrawled "M" at the start, but on this one, the "A" of Andino was pronounced; it clearly had separate first and last names. He studied the "M" of all three documents. He was not enough of an expert to judge if they all matched. But his bullshit meter was running high. His time with Maya was potentially nearing a conclusion and he still wasn't sure who the hell she actually was.

Steve opened Facebook and searched for Maya Andino in California, quickly locating her again. He thought briefly about the counselor ethical mandate to "do no harm," which typically meant limiting non-office contact or snooping. But he'd been at this long enough to be aware that not having information about a client can be just as harmful, a lesson he'd learned long ago with Kiely.

Hesitating only a second, he opened Facebook Messenger, typed out a one-sentence question and hit send.

***

Steve only had ten minutes before the session with Maya and he wanted to compose himself. He tried box breathing and then grounding, but he couldn't keep his thoughts from running away. His ethics told him that, by backgrounding a client without her permission or knowledge, he was breaking a trust. But he also felt worried yet again that he had Maya pegged incorrectly. As much as he liked her at times, she had a hidden side that could be anything from antisocial to borderline. Or she could simply be a troubled young woman with a traumatic past trying to find her way. She clearly had secrets. He worried whether Kenzie would be able to handle herself with Maya, and then immediately felt guilt for his thoughts intruding into his client's private life, much less his admin's.

He forced himself to change subjects and his mind landed on another problem—his date with Jane over the weekend. It hadn't ended well. They enjoyed the food, the drink and even Enrique's company when he stopped by to chat for a few minutes. But Steve still wasn't connecting with her on an emotional level, holding her at a distance. He could tell she was cautious with him, almost testing him to see if he would engage with her. Their conversation was banal throughout the night, even when they took to the floor for several salsa dances. He simply couldn't find the space to inquire about her life and world. When he brought her home, she stopped him from kissing her good night.

***

"I don't think this is going to work, Steve, do you?"

I apologize, telling her I am not sure where my head is, and that she is a good person who deserves a chance to make a connection with someone more engaged. It is an easy way to back out, to not have to work harder. She isn't having it.

"You know, Steve, I don't give myself to people easily. I work hard, study hard, play hard. I thought I saw that same quality in you. It's what turned me on initially. You're clearly a good guy, passionate about his work, his dog. I just can't figure out why I can't even get a smidge of that from you."

"I understand. I'm sorry."

"Really? You said that a few days ago and made a date for tonight. And now I'm standing here thinking I should have just opened a book and studied with a nice glass of pinot."

I look at her face, its scowl making her red cascades of curls seem darker. For a second I see Kiely's face, and it startles me. I get so lost in the thought, even if it's just a couple of seconds, that she pushes past me.

"I'll see you in the dog park sometime, Steve. I hope you figure yourself out."

***

He pictured Jane now as he considered her parting words. She did resemble Kiely beyond the hair; they were about the same 5-foot-6, same thin, yet physically fit build. There wasn't much similarity in their personalities or life outlook. Perhaps he'd seem himself as a savior to Kiely; clearly, Jane was someone on the move who didn't need saving. Was he not attracted to a secure woman? What did that say about him?

And he was startled by another intrusive thought. Did he think Maya needed saving? Is that why he was so fixated on her true story? Just then, Maya opened the door.

"Hey."

***

Maya sensed that Steve's mind was not on their session. He hadn't given his usual cheery greeting and invitation, nor had he asked her what was on her mind. She crossed her legs on the sofa Indian-style and arched her back while rolling her neck in a slow, stretching circle. It felt good after a hard night at the diner and then being with Kenzie. She wondered if Steve was envious of her and Kenzie. Could he have a thing for Kenzie? She'd seen so many older dudes eyeballing her and the other waitresses at the bar in Venice and now at the diner. She looked up and Steve was looking right at her.

"Done stretching?"

"Yeah, I guess."

"I know I normally throw this to you to get us started, but today I'd like to ask you a question to provide the thread for our session, if that's okay with you."

"Sure thing." Maya wondered what he had up his sleeve, but she was quite sure it had to do with the fact she had only one more session after this. He was totally hung up on the number of sessions and time running out. If he only knew, right?

"You're not in the system, Maya."

Steve held her eyes and Maya held her tongue. Kenzie had betrayed her confidence. *Goddamnit!* She wasn't ready to deal with it or let Steve know how angry she was right now. So she decided to go in another direction.

"I've been thinking a lot about the shit in my life, Steve. You've helped me confront it. And I think I'm ready to share about my mother's death. If you want to hear it."

She pulled her legs up to her chest and wrapped her arms around them, looking to him for approval. She sensed he'd drop the questions about billing.

He nodded. "Well, that was going to be the thread I wanted us to explore. Let's talk about the system question at the end. Go ahead."

Maya smiled inwardly. She knew him, and she could play him. She also had a sudden, odd insight. She'd come back to North Carolina intending to hurt Steve Prescott. Now she had affection for him. It was Kenzie she was furious with.

***

I'd spent half an hour getting this just right. Mom had shown me how to butter the outside of the bread to make the best grilled cheese sandwich, and she'd been so cruel lately and drinking so much I didn't want to forget a single thing. I brush a bead of sweat from my forehead before it drips into the frying pan. My ponytail feels like a lead weight on my neck. It is really hot in here, and Mom will be home any minute. I gently turn over the sandwiches, with one finger on the outside to hold it in place so it doesn't come apart, just like she taught me. The flip side is nicely browned and the cheese already looks gooey. This is gonna be soooo good. Mom is going to love it. She'll especially like it when I thank her for teaching me. The only thing making her tolerable lately is the cooking class she's taking. I take the sandwiches out and plate them, and because I don't want the cheese to ooze out, I use sone of the big, new knives she got when she joined the class. Next, I move to the fridge and find the applesauce jar and set it on the small wooden table—except, shit, my homework is still there—so I quickly throw my notebook and text onto the living room sofa. I turn off the burner, then grab my homework and walk it down the hallway, tossing it on the bed. Last thing I need is to set her off for making a mess. Between the class and her afternoon shift at the bar, she's going to be on edge. Just as I head back into the kitchen, I hear the lock turn and call to her when she steps inside.

"Hi, Mom, I made us some dinner. Figured you'd be hungry."

She doesn't say a word, pushing me in the hallway to get to the bathroom. She hates day shifts at the bar, bitching every time she has one that "none of the day drunks tip" and then complaining that they won't let her work nights because "they're all jealous of me." It's clear from her flushed face she's been sampling between customer pours at the bar. I walk to the kitchen, getting out some glasses. I pour two waters, though I'm sure she's going to get more vodka. She suddenly screams for me from my room.

"I knew you were a slut, and now I have the proof!"

"Mom, what's wrong?"

I ready myself for a wave. I'm so sick of this. I swear I'm not going to take it anymore. I'm 13 years old and a lot more responsible than she is.

"Two assholes from that crew doing the school expansion stopped by, and all they talked about was getting some from the girls. One of 'em said he loves that young freshman pussy."

"Mom, I am not in any way interested in those gross workmen."

Her face is as red as her hair as she triumphantly holds up her right hand, which she'd been hiding behind her back since I walked into my room.

"Then what are these, you little slut?"

She's holding a box of condoms, and shit, I realize my pal Annie had pleaded with me two weeks ago to hang onto them for her because her mom was on the warpath about her boyfriend. She'd told her mom they weren't sleeping together, but her mom was inspecting her room, and it was only a matter of time 'til she found the condoms.

Before I can stammer an answer, she cracks me hard across the face and I feel blood on my lips before my knees hit the ground. Next thing I know, she's on me from behind, grabbing two handfuls of my hair and bobbing my head hard up and down.

"Do. You. Think. I'm. Stupid?" Each word comes out in cadence to her pushes on my head. She smacks me hard across the back of my skull, and I see stars. I can hear her breathing heavily herself, the exertion and the booze driving her over the edge. "Get up and talk to me, you dumbass. What pathetic excuse do you have for these?"

I scramble away to the door side of the room. My head is pounding, half from her smack and half from anger.

"What difference does it make, since you won't believe me anyway?" I'm trying not to, but the words come out as a sob. A pathetic sob. I use my legs to slide up on the doorframe, driving to my feet and stumbling through the living room and into the kitchen. My head pounds as I sniffle.

"Don't you run away from me. Get back here."

She grabs my arm and I yank it free.

"If you think you're gonna get pregnant and walk out on me . . ."

The venom in her voice is scary, but I can't resist fighting back against her warped logic.

"Mom, the idea of condoms is you don't get pregnant. But—"

I don't get to finish the sentence ("But I told you these aren't mine, and I'm not sleeping with anyone.") because she grabs my arm, hard, around the wrist and yanks it up and back at an awkward angle.

I howl. "Ow! Mom, that hurts. Stop it!"

"Doesn't seem so good now, does it? And what's my knife doing out?"

Between her grip on my arm and my sudden fear at how carelessly she's holding the knife, and her drunkenness, I have a sudden, urgent voice screaming in my head, "Run!"

I yank free, and she goes spinning right into me. Her head hits my chin and I'm seeing stars again as I hear the clatter of the knife to the ground. I go to pick it up, and she looks at me with a crazed expression, not seeing me at all. Her face is almost inhuman; her mouth is open like she's saying something, but no words are coming out. She charges me, and I instinctively put up my arms and she runs into me again.

I hear the squishing sound of the knife making contact, jump back, shriek and run for the bedroom. It's the same sound I heard three years ago. On the way, a sickening thud pierces the otherwise deadly quiet. I close my door and jump under the covers, curling into a fetal position. I don't move. Nothing moves.

***

"Remember last session when you asked how I didn't seem curious any more about that patient that you lost to suicide?"

Steve was caught by surprise when Maya jumped so suddenly from the intensity of the story of her mother's death to this disconnected question. When a client did that, it usually meant either they were uncomfortable with the topic or they were searching for sudden connection and meaning. He peered into her face and could see only curiosity, not fear or anger.

"Yes, of course. But we didn't dwell on it last time."

"Well, I do have another question about it. Maybe telling my story just now jolted me."

"Okay, you know as before I can't go into much detail about other clients, even after they're dead. So, I'll do the best I can with your question."

"Why did that woman come to therapy to begin with?"

"I think I mentioned she came in with depression."

"Yeah, but what prompted her to come in? Like, you know, I came in because of the drug thing."

Steve saw an opening.

"Yes, the drug thing. I'll get to your question in a minute, but about your 'drug thing.' You know what? There is no drug arrest record for you in the North Carolina criminal records database. In fact, there is hardly any 'you' in North Carolina. I actually Googled your name, which normally a therapist isn't supposed to do, by the way. I'm telling you because I've been concerned about you, Maya. I'm not sure you are who you say you are."

"You didn't answer my question."

Steve felt like he'd pulled the handle of a garage door and it had slammed down fast. But he didn't want to give in to her.

"I'll answer your question if you answer mine."

She was pouting and jumped off the couch.

"That's not fair. I asked first."

"Maya, all I'm asking for is honesty. Why did you make up drug charges to come here?"

Her voice suddenly raised in pitch to that of a teenager, or maybe younger.

"How do you know I made up the drug charges?"

The desperate tone of her question gave Steve pause.

Then, as if scared she had shown a side of herself she didn't intend to, her voice dropped to its normal tone. But she spoke so quietly Steve strained to hear her.

"You're right. There was no drug arrest." She was shaking her head, and she swiped at the corner of her eye. She spoke more directly, without fear.

"I'm sorry, Steve. I was very angry when I came to you. I knew I needed to see someone. A lot more than when all the other shit happened to me."

"So you're saying that you made yourself the perpetrator of a serious crime so you could see a therapist?"

She shrugged, and her lips curled up in half-apologetic smile. "I guess I felt like I needed to have a reason to come to therapy, and I didn't have one."

"A reason to come to therapy." Steve let his words hang. This part of her answer actually sounded sincere.

"Yeah, you know. Every time I came to therapy before it was because something awful had happened. So what was I just going to come in and say 'I need to talk'?"

Steve wanted to reach out and give her a hug. For someone very sharp and worldly, she had just exposed a vulnerability about herself. All he had was words.

"That's exactly what people do every day, Maya. You don't need to have had something bad happen to come to therapy. The traumas you've had in your life will trigger you throughout your life, I'm sorry to say. And talk therapy is one way you can begin to address those, whether you're in an immediate crisis or just want to process things that happened earlier. I know, or I can now see, you didn't understand that. But it's okay just to want to talk. Any time.

"You remember how at one of our first sessions I mentioned maybe you'd like to extend therapy? I knew you were not prepared or even thinking in those terms then. But I raised it at the time because the kind of stuff that's happened to you in life often takes a long time to process."

Her anger flashed.

"How would you know about trauma, Steve? I mean you study it, but did you ever have shit happen in your life like I've had in mine?"

Steve had to tread carefully here. He didn't want to lose her.

"No, Maya. Your trauma has been horrible, and it's unique to you. There are big T traumas like you've had and little t traumas, the smaller kinds of things—like having a horrible boss, say—and even though there are huge differences, research shows they can affect the human brain in the same way.

"So if you'll indulge me, in our first session, you asked me about my background, and I told you the generic part about being a ballplayer. What I didn't tell you was about some of the "little t" trauma I dealt with as a teen, when my future on the high school ball team played out in public. Over the course of two years—and that's a long time in trauma terms, big T or little t—I had a bad coach and a bullheaded father and it created a tough situation that I had to figure out, where some of my teammates despised me and others championed me. And here's the thing about it: I didn't have anything to do with causing this trauma. I think you know exactly what I'm talking about.

"What I'm trying to say is our brains always have that instinct to go into fight-or-flight mode when trauma comes up. Learning to recognize the signals your body sends, then finding the tools to soothe yourself in the moment, is a huge part of overcoming trauma.

"I've given you some tools, Maya. And I have a lot of confidence in you. You can hate what's happened to you. You also can use what's happened to you. And I mean in a good way. I think you're doing that in this relationship with Kenzie . . ."

She still seemed on edge, and Steve wasn't sure why. She started pacing.

"You must think I'm stupid, though."

"I thought we'd been through that, Maya. Why are you going back to a negative self-cognition?"

"I can't help it, Steve. It's who I am." Her voice rose alarmingly. "I don't see things. I never know who's got my back. Even today."

Now he was confused. After his big speech, did she not realize he had her back?

They sat in silence for a minute, Maya not looking at him and he glancing at her face and posture for any signal, trying hard not to be caught studying her too closely. He decided to break the silence by returning to direct questions about a piece of the story he didn't have yet.

"Hey, Maya, one thing I'm curious about with the referral. Did you steal a referral form from somewhere and fill it out?"

She responded right away, but in a more detached manner. This wasn't what she wanted him to ask about.

"Actually, I asked a cop who's a regular at the diner what they do if they arrest someone who needs a referral for counseling because of drugs and he told me there's a form, and I told him I had a friend who'd gotten in trouble and lost their form. He brought one the next day. I think he thought my 'friend' was me."

"And it was, right?" He wanted to give her a soft landing. Instead, she pitched a curve.

"Now you know why I asked about your patient, the one who committed suicide. I didn't realize she could just walk into therapy because she was depressed. I figured maybe she did something."

Steve could picture Kiely's sweet face, the eyes that held so much pain and depression that the things she was doing—drinking, mistreating her daughter—were wrong. He thought back to when she first came in. He decided to share a truth; he didn't know if he was belying his ethics, but he was quite certain that for some reason Maya needed to hear this.

"My client came in because her drinking was out of control. She knew it, and she was powerless over it. It was making her a bad person. I saw good in her. Perhaps I didn't realize the depth of the pain. I was more focused on treating her depression, helping her solve problems, than in simply being present and truly understanding. I honestly didn't see her as suicidal."

Steve realized he'd been looking down as he spoke, not making eye contact with Maya. He did not like acknowledging flaws in his own work, even though he knew his flaws made him human. He was struck by the thought of how much he was not a savior. He hadn't been with Kiely nor in relationships with any of the women in his life, most recently Jane. Maya's sniffles brought his gaze up to her, and he saw tears in both of her eyes. He pushed the Kleenex box toward her.

"You didn't really know her," she said, quietly.

"No."

"You don't really know me, either."

"No. But I want to know more, Maya. I think we've made good progress so far."

"You don't even know why I'm crying."

He waited for her.

"It's about betrayal, Steve. And not by you, so don't worry."

"Your mom?"

She shook her head, got up and walked to the door. "Time's up."

"Let's talk more about betrayal next time, Maya. We have another session, right? Maybe more?"

She opened the door and left without responding.

Post-session: Maya

Two months with Steve and he still can't figure it out. Even when I all but give him the final piece of the puzzle. I'm exhausted. Exhausted in retelling the story. Exhausted with therapy. Exhausted with betrayal. How could I have been so foolish as to believe Kenzie, such a good girl, wouldn't report what I told her to her boss.

Once again, a person I love letting me down. How many fucking times does this have to happen?

***

I wake up in a ball on my bed and it's dark outside and quiet inside. My cell phone says it's 12:43 a.m. I remember the sound of the knife and shudder. So cold. I finally get the courage to open the door and I tiptoe to the living room, which is illuminated by the kitchen light that was left on. I see her crumpled body in front of me. And a lot of blood. I call 911 and think about how to explain this. Only one thing comes to me.

It takes the police eight minutes to arrive. I've composed myself, but as soon as the first officer steps inside, I surprise myself by bursting into tears. He walks me down the hall while three other officers kneel by mom.

"What happened here, miss?"

I tell him I honestly don't know. She came home and had been drinking. She got mad at me and sent me to my room. Without dinner. I fell asleep. I woke up a little while ago and found her on the floor.

He stays with me until a woman from Social Services arrives. She smells like coffee and cigarettes. She introduces herself as Mrs. Hammond.

"Honey, this is a terrible thing. Do you have any grandparents or aunts or uncles we can call together?"

"I don't have any relatives. It was just my mom and me. My father died three years ago."

She asks me about my mother, and I tell her we got along except for when she drank.

"How often did she drink?"

"Every day."

I lay down, and despite everything going on outside, I doze off. Next thing I know, the Social Services lady, Mrs. Hammond, is back with the officer from before.

"Honey, Officer Drake and I are going to take you to a hotel nearby, and I'm going to stay with you for the night. Can you take some clothing and maybe your school bag with you? I'm not sure what's going to happen later today, but you have to leave here for now. And don't worry, we'll get you into a good foster home."

I throw a couple days' clothes in a paper shopping bag and pile my school stuff into my knapsack. This is so crazy. No one's blaming me. No one's yelling at me. Foster home?

***

Thinking back on that awful night reminds me of the tasks ahead, like quitting the diner and having to tell Billie. But moving on sure is a familiar feeling. What was it that I told Dan the trucker that night? Traveler? Wanderer? I wound up settling for thief that night. Thinking about it now, I'm pretty sure wanderer was a good word. I may have Steve to thank after all. He did help me talk out some of this shit. My traumas.

Part of me wants to see Steve again. I had it wrong about him, way wrong. But the reason why I'm thinking about him is the part of me that wants to give it to Kenzie. I want to tell her to her face and let her know just how she cut me no different than if I were doing it myself.

A thought occurs. *I first tried cutting after Mom killed Daddy. Then after I killed her. Then after the first foster rape. And after the fuck twins. And during and after Deena.*

But I didn't cut myself after today's session. Even though this hurts so much. Does this mean I really do love her? Did love her?
I feel the tears and start breathing slowly and steadily.
FOCUS, Maya!
No, fuck that!
FOCUS, Suzie!

***

Billie wouldn't take me up on my offer to go out after the shift, but she agreed to talk after hours, so I draw up her rum and Coke and I spritz some water into a glass with ice and cranberry to flavor it. I grab a lemon slice and throw that on, too. I'm still behind the bar and she's sitting on one of the four stools on the other side, normally used by people waiting for a table in the dinner rush. I slide her drink to her and rest my elbows on the bar.

"You're not gonna like me, boss."

"Oh shit. Don't say it."

So I don't. Instead, I use my best sexy voice. "How come you didn't want to go out? I thought you were a *young* 40."

She smiled wanly. But then played the game.

"For you, I almost would, dear. You're pretty hot. I never told you that, did I?"

I shake my head as she reaches out and touches the side of my cheek with her calloused palm.

"Don't think I haven't been tempted ever since you arrived, dear. But I'm in a committed relationship. And you know that. Besides, what about that cute girlfriend you've been bragging on the past couple of weeks?"

I feel the tear ducts getting ready, and I will myself to stop it, doing a box breathing without being obvious before I answer. Billie has it figured out anyway; her face creases with warmth.

"Okay, I get it. Come here, you."

She reaches over the bar, grabbing me by the shoulders for a long, stretched embrace.

"I may have gotten some snot on your shirt," I say when she finally lets go.

"You want to talk about it?"

"Not a lot to say. She betrayed my trust."

"Been there. Do you know who she cheated on you with?"

"Oh, no. Not that way."

Billie waits for me. This is one of the things that made her a great boss; she doesn't impose herself on others, whether on the job or, as I've come to learn, in simple conversation. It reminds me a little of Steve. I sigh.

"I told Kenzie something in confidence, and then I learned she told someone else."

"That must hurt."

"It means the end."

Billie looks at me with pursed lips.

"You know, Maya, just because you were burned doesn't mean you have to run. I know why you wanted to talk with me. I can tell. You're quitting. And something tells me you're going to run away and leave here."

"Billie, I'm not like you. I don't have a girlfriend. Don't have family here. This is what my life is. I'm a wanderer."

"Wandering can get old, hon. I've done that, too, earlier in life. But you're smart, the customers love you and you've kicked butt in this job. It hurts me to see you go. And things aren't always as they seem. I've learned that the hard way over the years."

I come out from behind the counter and grab her, an embrace with more conviction than I've ever hugged anyone in my life. I smell her sweat from a full shift of work, I smell the frying oil from the kitchen that's made its way through the bun she's tied her brown hair into. I feel the hard muscles of her shoulders from the years of waiting she's put in. And I think, *Why couldn't this woman have been my mother?*

***

The talk with Billie provides me the closure and strength I need to do two things before I crash.

Kenzie had texted me a couple of times during my shift and I'd replied, "Busy, more tomorrow" to put her off. I know she turns her cell phone off when she goes to bed, so I'm hoping she doesn't get this one until the morning, when I'll be on the road.

"It was never going to work out, Kenzie. We're two very different people."

I'm proud of myself for not whining about betrayal. She is who she is, loyal and a person who does the right thing. It's what attracted me to her to begin with. No need to burden her with my anger. That would be what Mom used to do to me.

I go to my browser and call up the site I need to begin working on my second task. A destination.

Post-session: Steve

WHEN MAYA LEAVES, I HAVE THE FEELING I'VE HAD AT times with certain past clients: *I'll never see this person again.* I'm not sure why I get the feeling, but more often than not, my intuition is correct. I feel so close to a true connection with Maya, yet I also feel I was being tested and missed something.

My thoughts turn to Kenzie and whether, if I'm correct about Maya, that she isn't coming back, that means Kenzie will also run. Although I want to talk with her about what just happened and its implications, I can't divulge the contents of a therapy session. But I do need to update Kenzie on Maya's false referral and get the paperwork going to write off her visits. I could charge Maya my full fee for the sessions she's had, but I'm not an idiot. It's a lot easier to let go of the financial part than of the emotional withdrawal of a departing client, planned or unplanned.

My time with Maya has been fulfilling in its own way. As I wake up my computer, I think about that sense of gain from my work. The sacred place of connecting with a client, of knowing or seeing growth—even when it's incomplete—may not fill my financial coffer, but it fills my human coffer. That's the feeling that keeps me going year after year, and I have to take stock of that once in a while. I can thank Maya for this latest surge, even if my spider-sense about her ghosting therapy is correct.

I buzz Kenzie, asking her to stop in when she gets free, and then see the red "1" of a new note on Facebook Messenger.

I don't know who you are, Steve Prescott, but yes, my driver's license was stolen about a year ago. Did you find it?

Thinking again to not directly divulge client information, I craft a careful reply.

Maya, I can't really say a lot because of ethics laws in my profession, but I'm hoping you'll humor me by answering one other question. Did you ever room with a woman named Deena Fuller? Please know that I am not an identity thief nor the police. I think again, and as a sign of good faith, I tell her she can call me if she likes. I type out my cell and hit send just as Kenzie walks in.

"You rang, boss?"

"Hi Kenzie. Hey, have a seat."

I lay out the relevant news, telling Kenzie that we need to drop our paperwork on Maya pertaining to reimbursement from the system, and that we can mark this down as a write-off moving forward.

"She lied about the drug arrest, her reason for being here."

Kenzie wears a frown.

"How do you know, Steve?"

"I've just been doing some checking on her through searches on different sites. I mention it because . . ."

"Wait, Steve, did you tell her that in session, how you knew?"

The rising pitch of her voice belies her anxiety.

"I'm sorry, Kenzie. You know I can't reveal things said in session."

Kenzie's face reddens, and she's nodding, but I sense her unraveling. She begins hyperventilating, and I reach for her elbow and guide her to the couch to sit. She's shaking to her core.

"Kenzie, can you hear me?"

She nods.

"Okay, please watch me. I want you to repeat what I'm doing. Breathe evenly, and focus on your exhale. Put your thoughts into a long slow exhale. It's not about the intake of breath, but the exhale." As she does that, I cross over to the mini-fridge I have under the shelf behind my desk and grab a bottle of water, an ice cube and a paper towel.

"Now, Kenzie, close your eyes and hold out your hand. I'm going to give you an ice cube. As you continue to focus on simply breathing in and out, I want you to feel the ice cube and put your attention on it. Feel the texture as it melts, the way the droplets run down your hand. Sense the coldness. Lick the cube if you want to feel the cold on your tongue. And just keep breathing."

She sits that way for five minutes and I can feel her coming back. She also starts to weep, gently.

"It's all right. Just keep breathing. You're in a safe place."

***

As I watch Kenzie calm herself by focusing on the ice cube, I move back to my desk, rather than my therapy chair. I want to reiterate to her that our conversation is about work, and is not anything having to do with therapy, even though I know it's really about both.

I tap on my computer and see a new message awaits in Facebook Messenger. Kenzie's eyes remain closed, so I open the message.

Look, this is kind of creepy. Yes, I knew Deena Fuller but if you don't want me to report you to Facebook for stalking, you need to tell me what this is about.

I realized I'd opened Pandora's box when I messaged her, and now the moment is here. I've been composing a way to explain this in my head since the idea occurred to me. It was put up or shut up time. I type my response just as Kenzie opens her eyes.

I hand her the paper towel and the water bottle I'd taken out before.

"Thank you." She's quiet, while also appearing angry. And scared.

"You seem more upset than I would have expected. You and I both were aware of the problems we were having tracking down this referral."

"I know, Steve. I'm not mad at you. But I'm worried about how you shared this with her because she shared this with me— at least the part about her lying. And I'm afraid she now thinks I ratted her out to you. If she doesn't trust me . . ."

She didn't finish her thought. She didn't have to. It isn't my place to console Kenzie, and I hate myself for thinking this, but I do wonder if she'll be better off—and me, too—if Maya is gone for good. Maya. Wait a minute. I look back at my screen and call up the latest message from California Maya.

Thank you for sharing your credentials and that you are backgrounding some criminal profiles. As I recall, the women in the apartment were Jenna, Michelle, Suzie, Deena and me. Deena and Suzie were together. Deena was a bitch, btw.

I only feel a little bit of guilt for fibbing to California Maya.

"I'm better now, Steve. I'm heading back out front."

"Hold on, Kenzie. I just want to warn you about something. I'm not sure the person you are dating is the person you believe she is. By that I mean . . ."

Kenzie holds her hand up and sighs.

"She's not, Steve. And it hurts."

I hear a swallowed cry and she runs out.

***

The world is spinning a little as I sip from my third Kolsch at the bar of Havana Nights. This was a day.

I arrived two hours ago after a couple of bourbons at home and a trip with Sam to the dog park, where I promptly ran into Jane, who greeted me breezily and didn't want to engage at all. Yeah, good day all around. I've barely touched my pork nachos, and my head is already beginning to pound. I'm glad the bar crowd has thinned out and the volume is down. I signal to the bartender and ask for water.

"Hey, my friend, are you all right?"

Enrique has come up behind me, clapping me on the shoulder. We've caught eyes a couple of times during the night, but he's been so busy he hasn't had a chance to stop by.

"Everything's great."

"I see. Do you want to talk?"

"Enrique, I'd love to talk but it's work business. Well mostly. So I can't talk. And Jim is on a fishing trip. Thus, I figured I'd drink."

"You know, you once told me about—let me think how you said it—ah, yes, 'dysfunctional' responses to bad things happening?"

I smile. At least I got through to one person. And, of course, he's spot on.

"Don't worry about me, Enrique. I'm done drinking. And I'm either walking or Ubering. I do thank you for caring. Let's do dinner soon."

He heads back to his office, and I gaze mindlessly at a college basketball game while I slowly sip my water. I let my mind consider all that happened. *Yes, it was a day.*

Session Eight: No Show

THE TWINGE HAPPENS, THE SLIGHTEST WEIRD LITTLE GRINDING IN my elbow, as I'm tossing lightly near the left field seats an hour before gametime against Charlotte with my catcher, Bobby Prudell. I don't give it a second thought other than to absentmindedly rub my left elbow, switch the ball to my right hand and underhand throw it back to him.

"Something wrong? he asks.

"Nah, must've slept on it bad. Happens sometimes."

"Tell Skip. They might not want you pitching on it."

"What are you talking about? It'll stretch out during warm-ups."

He gives me a look. At 26, he's had his cups of coffee in the bigs and is on the downside. But he loves the game and knows his future is coaching, so damned if he isn't going to talk me into doing the right thing. Young ptichers get twinges; they need to tell management.

On the fourth pitch of my warm-ups in the top of the first, it happens again.

This time the twinge is sharper and I shake my arm. Bobby stands up behind the plate and looks into the dugout, and Trevor Mayer, our pitching coach, yells out for me to stop. Blue has come out behind the plate with his arms up, which is funny because it's only warm-up anyway. He and Trevor speak at the same time.

"Something wrong, son?"

"That didn't look great, Steve. What's going on??"

The elbow doesn't hurt, but my gut tells me Blue is right. Something is wrong. I look up and the sky is gray. Probably wouldn't have gotten in more than a couple innings, anyway, given the forecast.

"I guess I should get it checked out. It's kind of a sharp twinge. Maybe something's not right?"

Bobby chimes in for good measure. "It happened during soft toss, too, Trevor. I told him to get it checked out but he wanted to see how it would be during warm-ups."

Thanks, Bobby. *I slowly walk off the field. A couple of people in the crowd clap in an appreciative "hope you're okay" way. I vaguely hear the click of the Durham paper's photographer as I cross the foul line toward the dugout.*

***

In the orthopedics office four days later, I face a dour physician. The black script on his crisp white doctor's jacket reads "Dr. Hough." It's just me and him; no one from the Bulls is here. I told my dad I'd call him afterward, after talking him out of flying in.

"It's torn, son, your medial collateral. You're going to need surgery."

"Tommy John?"

The doctor nods. "I've notified the organization. We'll have to be back in touch about scheduling it. For now, you just want to reduce any use of the arm, especially the elbow. Don't put any pressure on it, and ice it regularly. I'm giving you a set of instructions and a prescription for anti-inflammatory medication."

"Dr. Hough, I've been reading about this. I don't have a lot of swelling or bruising. That means I don't have a bad tear, right?"

"Son, it's torn. It needs surgery if you want to pitch again. There's really no other legitimate way. I'm sorry."

He rises, and that's the extent of it. A minute with a doctor to deliver the news. I look out the window of his office, and I can see our stadium downtown a couple of miles away.

***

"When's the surgery?"

My father gets right to the point as we drive from the airport to my place. He decided to come for a long weekend to cheer me up.

"They need the swelling to go down. The date's not set. Probably in a month to six weeks. Then a lot of rehab. A lot of waiting. Soft tossing. Probably won't throw for a year. They have a whole schedule."

"Everything I read about this is it's so routine now. You might even wind up throwing harder once it's done."

"I know, Dad."

"I can see you're worried."

"Actually, I'm not really worried about the surgery."

"No?"

"No. What I'm worried about is disappointing you, Mom, the team . . ."

"What are you talking about? You're not disappointing us. You can't control something like this. It's just God's will. An injury is something that tests you, but you'll do just fine. Be back out there like gangbusters."

Inside, I laugh. My parents are not particularly religious, and I find it amusing that God's will is evoked when something goes wrong. It's just my father's way, I know, to mask his own disappointment, which is something that's been troubling me since the twinge.

Is this the time to speak my truth? I decide it's not and drive on.

***

Dad's idea of cheering me up is to be positive. He wants me to come home, back to Evanston, after the surgery. "We'll hang out, it'll make your mother happy to have you home; you can still do whatever rehab you need."

I decide this is the moment.

"Dad, did you know an ulnar tear will heal itself? It's true. With rest and proper care, a little rehab, your elbow is fine."

He looks confused and brings a large hand up to his face, as if he had a beard to stroke.

"But you can't pitch for a long time if you do it that way."

"Actually, Dad, I can't pitch anymore, period, if I do it that way."

"You're saying you're quitting?" He can't keep the disappointment out of his voice, but inside I'm elated because his tone sounds like acceptance. I've been so worried he'll be crushed not to have his kid in the big leagues—bragging rights unsurpassable among his world. Perhaps something to redeem his own dreams at being more.

"It sounds like you're a little disappointed, Dad."

"Well no, Steve. I'm, I mean, I'm not. You've accomplished so much. I'm very proud of you. I know this is a setback. Maybe you just need some time to think. Surgery is scary, and it's a long, hard rehab."

I move in and hug him hard, smelling the old mix of his sweat and the menthol of Aqua Velva. I'm aware I'm also a full head taller now at 6-foot-1. I want to please him, but a metaphor from my off-season psycho major work suddenly intrudes:. If you're going down on a plane, put your own oxygen mask on first before you start taking care of others.

"Dad, I've been thinking about this for a very long time. Have you looked at my record this year? I have, and I have to be brutally honest with myself. It's been six years. I'm 24, and I'm just an average, mid-rotation guy here in Durham. I honestly don't think I have the talent or drive to get to the next level. Now I'm probably not going to pitch again until I'm 26."

I let it sit out there, and my dad, God bless him, is thoughtful rather than reactive.

"What do you want to do from here then, son?"

***

It's a cold, gray early February Tuesday as I gaze out my office window, staring without focus. I notice a sudden swirl and light snowflakes appear, tossed aimlessly among the winter wind. They dance at eye level, not bothering to land. I'm grateful for a pleasant moment of nature's power.

Maya is ten minutes late and I'm well aware she's not coming. I call her cell anyway, as I routinely do when someone is late. Her phone number is no longer in service. Not that I was unaware. Kenzie has been disconsolate for a week, reporting how she's been unable to reach Maya. Kenzie was collateral damage of Maya's therapy. But I know instinctively that my work with Maya was productive; she gained self-knowledge and showed personal growth during our time together. After that, all you can do is let go.

Still, loose ends bug me, and I did tell Kenzie I'd let her know if I heard anything from Maya before the scheduled session. I buzz her to come on back.

She takes one look at me and understands why I called her in. Her shoulders slump, and I point to the sofa. She flops down and takes a tissue from the pocket of her sweater, blowing her nose and swiping her eye at the same time. I point to the tissue box in case she needs more. Which seems obvious.

"She didn't show, as you can see. She didn't call or email. I want you to know that, Kenzie, so you're aware nothing's going on behind your back here."

"I would never think that, boss," she says, sniffling. "I just don't know why or what."

"Okay, Kenzie. I'm going to talk in general terms, because, you know, confidentiality. But I hope you'll find some comfort."

I pause to think this through. Kenzie is a smart young adult, maturing by the minute, and I want to keep her around for as long as possible before she realizes there's more for her to accomplish in the world than being an admin in a therapist's office.

"When someone has trauma—childhood trauma especially— it is almost always going to affect them as they get older. We'renever sure of how issues might manifest, but untreated, trauma is going to hurt a person physically or mentally down the line. Or both, even."

"You're saying Maya had trauma. I know that. She and I even talked about some of it, Steve."

"I'm not saying Maya had trauma. I'm just talking about trauma in general. You know Maya and I have had only seven sessions. That's hardly time to do anything in our world."

"But you told me the average person who comes to therapy stays for about six sessions, so she's at least had more than that."

I understand her logic, and the fact that I know where it comes from—her desperate sense of wanting to believe she'll still have a future with Maya—allows me to feel her pain.

"Trauma is different. And to be honest, Kenzie, in six sessions, clients can gain some insight into themselves. But research shows it typically takes six months to a year of therapy before true progress is made. And with trauma? Well, all bets are off."

She takes this in with more sniffles and a blow.

"You're a great young woman, Kenzie. I'm sorry you've been hurt in this. If there were anything I could do to change things . . ."

She holds up her hand to stop me.

"I would never change anything. Our time was incredible. I felt alive with her. I still feel alive. And I want it back."

"I can't help you there, Kenzie. But—" A thought strikes me about solving some of those lingering questions for me that my gut says would be ethically okay.

"But what?"

"You know, we still should be trying to bill her for the services, as she was not coming on a required basis. And I think it's legitimate to try to track her down in that regard before we write off the visits as 'no pay.'"

"She doesn't have a phone anymore. Or an address."

"I know. I am aware, however, that her name doesn't appear to be Maya."

"What?"

"Her first name is Suzie. I think she stole the identity of a former roommate when she lived in Southern California."

Kenzie's eyeliner has run amid her tears.

"Listen, why don't you take a few minutes. Wash up and we can talk about what help a first name is for you in going about a search. All we have to do is put out a general call for a short dark-haired woman whose name is Suzie but who goes by Maya." I laugh at the absurdity. "Oh, and we have her address here in Durham if that helps."

"Thank you, boss. You know," she says, turning back to me before she leaves, "she doesn't really have dark hair."

"Hold on, Kenzie." My wheels begin to spin. I remember having thought about Maya changing her hair color when she first came in, and I'd never followed up. "She told you her real hair color?"

Kenzie's face reddens, and when I realize why, mine does, too.

"Say no more. Other than her hair color."

"She's a redhead."

"Really?" My mind is going a mile a minute. Redhead. Maya. My brain feels like I need to take time to calculate, but I can't handle what's being thrown at me.

"And something else, boss. I showed her my Ancestry.com website and how I'd tracked down relatives? And when I got on the site yesterday, I happened to look at my search history and there was a weird name there. I never looked it up. I think maybe Kenzie figured out my login and got into it. After our last night together."

Recalling that scene sets Kenzie off in tears again. I approach and, after a second of thought—counselors rarely make physical contact with clients, but my admin is not a client—I embrace her, and she clutches me tightly.

Twenty seconds later, I ease back and she lets go, clearing her throat and wiping her eyes with the tissue she's been holding the whole time.

"You were saying she looked up stuff on Ancestry?"

"Just one name, actually. Hanrahan. Kiely Hanrahan."

My mouth drops open like the pizza oven at Giuseppe's when they're pulling out a fresh pie. Kenzie notices.

"It's a name you know, Steve?"

"It's a name I know, Kenzie."

***

I absentmindedly finger the Indian-head nickel with the hole in it. Kiely's folder is open on the desk before me. I've been staring at it for fifteen minutes. There, on the very first page of documentation she filled out so long ago, is the name of her daughter. Susanna. Age 13.

Suzie. Maya is Kiely Hanrahan's daughter.

Somehow, she knew I had been her mother's therapist. She came back to North Carolina because she wanted to learn more about me, the last person who had any connection with her mother. I might have even been a target when she arrived, but I passed muster.

All these years, I had been blaming myself for missing something, for not seeing Kiely's suicidal tendencies, but in fact, she hadn't killed herself. Suzie had done so, albeit in a defensive posture against a woman driven to a state of high rage by her alcohol use and—

Wait a minute. My mind races. Alcohol is typically a depressant, but it has been known to have an enraging effect on some people. It is a dysfunctional response to trauma. I frantically look through my notes in Kiely's file and can find almost nothing about her upbringing. She left home at 16 in a fight with her mom and no contact since. Father died sometime after she left home; she said he had alcohol issues. I hadn't diagnosed Kiely as alcoholic, hadn't gotten that far. There is the evidence, staring at me now, 12 years later, thanks to Suzie filling in some of the details of her home life. Kiely was "a double winner," in AA and Al-Anon parlance. Child of an alcoholic and an alcoholic herself. Also a child of violence who became violent herself.

And I missed the connection. *But what drove that poor girl's generational trauma that she passed down to her daughter?*

I realize my breath is shallow and inside I'm anxious; I can feel my stomach jumping and heart fluttering. I reach for my water bottle and drain it. Then I try to regulate my breathing.

It's not my fault. But I can't help feel like a relief pitcher who's blown a save. What is it that Jim says? *Everything we do in these rooms is an experiment.* I know this. I still feel jumpy.

I shut my eyes and do a mindfulness exercise. Simple grounding, paying attention to my breathing, feel my feet on the floor, my spine in my chair. *Center. Relax. Let it go*

When I finally open my eyes after a few minutes, I feel better. I am quite sure I failed Kiely, but I have to be at peace with that. It is my fault that I did not learn enough in our time together to understand the scope of her pain. I gained knowledge from that.

As for her daughter, I know our seven sessions were not enough, but something happened during that time. For her. For me. And that is the heart of a good therapeutic relationship. Client and counselor both grow.

I'm breathing easier and the jumpiness is gone as I close the folder, slide my chair over and put it back into the filing cabinet. I lock the cabinet, pocket the key, then use my right foot to pivot back to the desk.

I feel lighter.

***

"She's here, Steve."

"Thanks, Kenzie. Send her in."

The door opens and I smile at the familiar face.

"Hi, Steve. It's been a hot minute, huh?"

The smartly dressed, attractive 40-something eschews the couch and plops right into the red side chair, crossing her legs and giving me a dramatic head-down, eyes-up stare.

"You would *not* believe my life since our last session."

I manage to keep "you ain't the only one" from escaping my lips and instead go with the thinking brain response.

"Catch me up, Jill."

Epilogue: Beyond

LILAH REACHES WITH A LEATHERY HAND FOR the white teapot with the green rose on the side, faded but still visible after two decades years of use. "Oh," she squeaks softly as she touches the handle, overly hot from being too close to the gas flame of her old stove. She sets it down quickly and grabs one of her dishtowels to pour. Her morning Earl Grey.

The toast pops and she reverses course to the toaster, buttering it lightly from the container on the Formica countertop. Her kitchen is an ode to the past and Lilah is just fine with that. No need for fancy. Everything still works. She eases herself down into one of the chairs, feeling her bones creak. She can't help but pull her forefinger to crack the knuckle. Dr. Young, the lovely young woman now seeing her at Clinic on the Hill, scolds her awful, but you just can't change a habit like that overnight. Lilah blows across the top of the cup, admiring the ripple her breath makes. She sips, oh so cautiously. No need to burn even her lips, much less the roof of her mouth. And without her dentures, she needs to be sure to go slow with the tea.

Lilah is an old 60, and she knows it every time she rises in the morning. It's gotten a little better since she quit smoking five years ago on account of the lesion they removed from her lung. She didn't quit right away, mind you. She wasn't going to give that doctor the satisfaction. She took her time and about four months later crushed out her last Camel, loyal to her brand of 40 years and her late husband's employer.

She glances at the paper that Jimmy, the nice deliveryman for the *Mount Airy News*, brought inside a little earlier. She loves her news, even though the darn paper is getting thinner by the minute, a shell of what it was years ago. Might as well just call people up and read it to them, she sniffs to herself. And how can they call it a daily when there's no paper on Monday? But that's a small grievance. At least she can know who's passed and who's being arrested for silly nonsense, which is all anyone in these parts seemed to get arrested for nowadays. Last week she read that Bobby Boots, her former next-door neighbor, all grown up and living in one of the Section 8 apartments round yonder, got himself into a pickle for shooting at his neighbors on what the police called a "meth high." That's all she seemed to read about in the police blotter. *Meth this, meth that. It's madness is what it is,* Lilah thinks.

She can't focus on the paper, and her TV is playing the local morning news show too softly to hear. When Jimmy came in, he turned the volume down so they could chat, and he never fixed it. Now where did he leave that remote?

Riiiinnngggg.

The harsh chime of her front doorbell confounds her. Who the heck is ringing her bell so bright and early? She crinkles her eyes to see the hands of the clock on her stove. Crazy that old stove still works and the clock still keeps time. It's 10 minutes past nine o'clock.

"Come on in," Lilah calls in an Irish-tinged, raspy voice. "It ain't locked."

A young woman in a black baseball cap ducks through the entrance, staring with wonder at the heavenly mess that is Lilah's home, most every inch of floor space taken up with furniture, and most every table filled with knick-knacks, doodads and memorabilia. The visitor bends to avoid the gaggle of hanging plants, chimes and an assortment of colorful windcatchers.

As the visitor moves past the last windcatcher, a feather-laden brown wood with green highlights, she takes off her cap and her face comes out of the shadow. A tiny gasp escapes Lilah's lips.

A green-eyed, red-haired ghost stares back at her.

Steve

MY BASEBALL DISAPPEARS INTO THE HANDS of the gentle giant sitting across from me on the sofa. He rubs it up just as he would on the mound. Randy Culbertson is 6-foot-5. He's slouched on the sofa, his long legs splayed out on the floor between us so that if I didn't have my legs crossed, I might be touching them. I've let him hold my keepsake baseball during our time together since our first session. It soothes him.

"I'm pitching well, Steve. I'm feeling it these past three starts."

"How's it between starts?"

"The arm's great. No twinges anymore. I'm doing all the between-starts shit they throw at me. You know."

"Yeah, I do, Randy. But that's not what I meant."

I get a hang-dog face in return. Randy has a large head and this season he's grown a droopy mustache that, combined with his shaggy '80s haircut, gives him the look of a sad golden retriever. But with brown hair.

I have cut back, Steve. I'm not drinking between starts, and I've taken your advice. I'm not taking my parents' calls."

I wince inside. I don't like to be told I'm giving advice. That's not what therapy is about, so much as helping clients find insight themselves. What I'd wondered aloud to Randy was whether his daily conversations with his parents soothed him or left him more stressed. I do think it was a smart decision, though, especially because of the intrusive nature of their calls. Mom and Dad tag-teaming a 22-year-old to provide guilt (Mom) and coaching (Dad), neither of which is appropriate given their son's need to learn his craft from his own coaches and his organization.

"So what's wrong, Randy? I'm detecting something in your voice. Am I wrong?"

He won't meet my eyes. It bothers me, because I've gone to the park a couple of times to catch him. He's the real deal when he's on. Righty with a mid-90s fastball, wicked movement and a nice off-speed slider. I need to give him time to share what's on his mind.

He's rubbing his thumb into the middle of his pitching hand. Round and round. A small, tense smile turns his lips up just a bit. He finally looks up and makes eye contact.

"You ever have doubts, Steve?"

"Sure."

"No, I mean real doubts."

"I'm here, right?" I smile to break his tension, but it doesn't do a thing. If anything, it gets him more agitated.

"You got injured. You never had to have a doubt. You didn't have a choice."

"Actually, I did, Randy. But this isn't about me. What's bugging you today?"

"I don't feel confident out there. Yeah, I'm getting guys out, but I don't feel like I'm in control."

"Very common."

"You had that?" He says it with wonder.

"Of course. We all do. And the ones with all the bravado? It's bullshit, Randy. It's how they get by, convincing themselves. Everyone doubts."

"It's harder for me without drinking."

I think about that a minute. He had said a few minutes ago he wasn't drinking between starts.

"In other words, if I'm hearing you right, alcohol was your bravado."

He drops his head again and speaks so softly I lean forward to catch his words.

"I don't think I can do this without it."

We're running low on time, and I can't let it end here. My mind goes a thousand miles a minute.

"Did I ever tell you how I left the game, Randy?"

He offers the tiniest of head shakes.

"So here's how it went. I tore an elbow ligament warming up. It probably had been partially torn already and I blew it during warm-ups. Never got to throw a pitch. I was 24. Sure, I could have done the rehab and come back and kept going. But I listened to what my heart said, kind of that still small voice within. Never pitched again. And here I am. That feels to me like it's a lot different from your situation. I suspect withdrawal from alcohol has changed you. And that's okay.

"Randy, I can't tell you what to do. We've worked on some mindfulness and meditation ideas in the past few months. Perhaps you can get in touch with that still small voice within."

The big man rises, knowing time's up. He offers a fist bump and shuffles out, ducking his head to get through the doorway.

***

Among the bills, psychoeducation seminars and junk mail I poke through at lunch, I pluck out one plain white envelope with no return address and a lump inside. It doesn't match the crisp feel of the rest.

Thinking it's just more junk, I open it carelessly, making a bigger tear than I intend. A silver necklace chain slides out in a pile on my brown leather deskpad. *What the … ?*

I look inside the torn envelope and find two small pieces of white scrap paper folded over. I open the first one:

Try this with the nickel. They should be back together now.

We're amid a record heat wave, likely to set an August 10th record of 104, but I'm pretty sure my shiver isn't from the sudden blast from the AC that has kicked on. It's hearing from her after all these months. I smile at the simple "S" signature. She's aware I would have figured out her name by now. Despite the passage of time, I think of her every day; she's all but replaced Kiely as the former client most top of my mind. But this is in a better way. I'm also reminded of her thanks to the selfie Kenzie took of her and Suzie, which sits desktop right next to her computer. Kenzie says it's so she sees her constantly while working.

I slide open my middle drawer and remove the nickel. The chain is a perfect fit. I wonder if sending it was a form of closure for Suzie. I consider giving the necklace to Kenzie. She's been focused on pursuing a master's in counseling, an idea I encouraged. I think she can be a fabulous therapist; she has the empathetic nature essential to working with others in a helping profession.

She starts school in just a couple of weeks. Like many in our business who throw themselves into learning about the nature of human behavior, Kenzie has suffered a wrenching loss. She's going to keep working while she attends school, and I'm more than happy with her decision. I can't imagine not seeing her every day. She helps keep me grounded simply by her presence. Of course, she's going to have some hellacious years ahead with study, work and, eventually, internship.

I think I'll hold off on giving her the nickel necklace. It's a distraction. I unfold the second piece of paper:

"I probably need to say more. My father gave the nickel chain to me, not my mom. He told me a Buffalo head nickel is something special, just like me. And she just took it away. She said it was because I was too young to wear jewelry. But fuck her. She took it because she was jealous of my relationship with him. He actually loved me. She was a user. Of people. When a cop told me she'd been seeing you, I sent you the nickel in anger. Sorry. But I was 13! I'm okay now, btw. Not gonna pull stupid shit anymore. Tks 2 you. See ya around."

I fold the two slips of paper and get my filing cabinet key out, pulling the "Maya Andino/Suzie Hanrahan" chart. Way back then, she sent me the nickel and kept the chain. Not quite willing to give up on a connection with her father. What a smart, instinctive girl. I had no idea why that nickel arrived in the mail after Kiely's suicide. Check that: after Kiely's death. In any event, I didn't even give the fact that the nickel suddenly showed up a thought. Which reminds me how young a therapist I was and how emotionally jolted I was by the death. I wonder how Suzie might have turned out if I had simply taken the time back then to write her a heartfelt note. Maybe it would have helped her to know she had a friend, someone who cared about her.

But you can't go backward in time. You can only use the past to inform the present and your own future decisions. I pick up a paper clip, then reach underneath the desk to my recycling bin and grab the envelope the notes came in. I fold the notes back up, and drop the reunited nickel and chain necklace inside, and use the paper clip to keep the thing together. As I slip the package back into the Maya/Suzie folder, I notice the postmark on the envelope.

***

On my way out, I go through the front office and find Kenzie buried in paperwork. Her eyes dart from computer to file folders and back. Her slim fingers fly.

Although I've hesitated to engage Kenzie in conversation about Suzie, I did give her the name of a colleague I trust. I like to think her idea of going to school for counseling came as a result of her own therapy, though she hasn't mentioned it and I haven't asked.

She is so focused on her work I'm not sure she notices me, so I clear my throat.

"I knew you were there, Steve. I just needed to get to a stopping point."

I'm not sure if it's simple maturity or her grief at the loss of the relationship—a person doesn't have to die for survivors to experience the same emotions as if they did—but she doesn't have a problem being direct anymore. I notice she's following her new fashion trend of wearing more black than her old bright colors; her outfit today is black pants with a gray-and-black blouse. Professional. But somber.

"Say, Kenzie, your grandparents live in Mount Airy, right?"

"Uh-huh. Mayberry country. What brought that up?"

"No particular reason. Had a client was talking about being raised in King. That's right near Mount Airy, I think."

"Yeah, maybe twenty-minute drive."

I stand there, not knowing what to add, not knowing how to handle the next question I anticipate she'll ask. But "why do you ask" doesn't come.

181

"Okay, boss. I have to get back to work if I'm going to finish the counseling theories book you gave me before school starts."

"Right." I turn back to the office but sneak a peek. Her Mona Lisa smile is punctuated by a small shake of her head. It looks like her lips are moving and she's talking to the image of her and Suzie on her desk and not the computer screen next to it.

Suzie

MY EYES ARE DARTING ALL OVER THE place, this tiny crazy quilt home. I realize I haven't been listening to the old lady. She said something about her daughter, Mom, just up and leaving and never hearing a word since. Said she figured she had a right to, but it still hurts not knowing whatever became of her *or her daughter.*

"Look at you," Lilah says in wonder for about the seventh time in the half hour since I rang that whacked-out crank-style door buzzer. "Spitting image of your mother. Red hair. Green eyes. Spitting image, like I say."

I bite into a stale Oreo from the plate of cookies she'd put out on my behalf. Breakfast of champions. I pass on her offer of tea.

Lilah clutches my hand on the table, and I willingly accept it, studying the lines and the sharp blue veins along the tops of her hands and feeling the strength and intensity of her grip. A thought slams into me. *FOCUS, Suzie!*

"Wait a minute. Did you say you didn't hear a word from my mother since she left home at 16?"

"That's correct. Never a word."

My head is spinning. I have to ask, but even as I mouth the question, I'm feeling unnerved.

"Then how did you know she had a daughter?"

I watch Lilah carefully as she appraises me. She seems less mean than Mom, and shrewder. Not impulsive at all.

"You want to hear a story and I'd like to tell it, young Suzie. But it's gonna take time. You got a place to stay nearby? Maybe you come visit me in the mornings when I'm still sharp and I'll share it."

Time is on my side, I think to myself.

"Yeah, I got a place."

"That's good, 'cause as you can see, this ain't exactly the Hilton." Lilah throws back her head and cackles.

I smile at her. "Aw, it's not that bad."

"You know, Suzie, I'm not stupid. It's a dump. But it's my dump."

I walk over to the fridge, but she has no water bottles.

"Do you have ice? I could use a drink of water. And what would you like me to call you?"

She points to the freezer.

"You'll have to crack some out of the ice tray. And call me Lilah. Don't have to be getting all sentimental with Grandma or—God forbid—Memaw."

***

After visiting every day for two weeks, I've come to a realization. I kind of like Lilah's stories. It's a strange new world for me about my Irish heritage and family—Patrick Hanrahan, Kevin and Hannah Flynn—warped as they are. Or were. I also realize now there's some sense to Mom's mood swings and all the sense in the world to her drinking. I'd been hearing that alcoholism could be an inherited disease from every therapist I'd ever seen.

Lilah always watches me when I wander around her place, inspecting all the trinkets.

"Someday, this will all be yours, young Suzie."

That sets her off cackling, and I crack a smile watching her go.

I ask Lilah how she came to own the house.

"We rented this little place when we first moved here, then your grandfather had a bender and we had to leave for a while. But I persuaded the owner to give us a second chance when the tenant he had after us got arrested for running a whorehouse, I mean, a house of prostitution here."

"Really? Here? It's only got the two bedrooms, right?"

"I guess it was a small whorehouse, dear."

I giggle. Looking at the place now, it's obvious anyone doing anything in this house would be heard throughout. Two tiny bedrooms down a short hallway behind the living room with the bath accessible to both. I realize Lilah has paused and I look over. She's fallen asleep mid-story. She dozes with her head still up, eyes closed, her hand still gripping her teacup.

I drink from the water bottle I've taken to bringing with me. The ice cubes in Lilah's freezer give water a stale flavor. I still need to understand why Mom left this place and Lilah and Patrick behind. And how Lilah knew about me. It's been on my mind a week, and the possible answer is scaring the shit out of me.

***

Lilah didn't think twice when Kiely didn't come from school that Thursday afternoon. She was upset. Might even be trying to find a doctor to solve her problem. Couldn't blame her. It was when she didn't come home Friday that Lilah became curious. But Kiely didn't show up over the weekend, either. Asshole hadn't even noticed, or if he had, he hadn't said anything.

It was only after she opened the closet and saw Kiely's stash gone— the money Lilah let her keep, the money she knew her daughter would need at some point—that she realized Kiely had pulled on her what she'd done to her mother a generation ago. Disappear.

Lilah figured she wouldn't ever hear from her again. Unless she needed something. But Kiely wasn't the needy type. She just hoped she'd be smart in her choices. Smarter than her.

Patrick didn't blink when Lilah told him their daughter had taken off.

"Gone? Just up and gone?"

"Appears to be that way."

He took a couple of steps toward her, and she knew he was going to hit her. She decided he'd at least get something from her first.

"Don't be getting on my case. It was you that sent her away."

He cracked her good across the face, backhanded, and she couldn't keep her feet.

"You don't know shit, Lilah. Say another word and I'll give it to you harder."

"Speaking of hard, how'd you manage that, anyway?"

At that, he yanked her up by her hair and she screamed in frustration. He punched her in the gut, which took all her wind out, then walloped her in the eye. It wasn't going to look good. She didn't mind. She deserved it. She'd failed to protect Kiely. All those years she knew what was going to happen, and she'd even gotten her job and saved her money for the chance to leave before Kiely came of age. She just hadn't had the guts.

Patrick stomped out, slamming the door. He'd be gone for hours and passed out on the front step by morning. She locked the door. Her phone rang and it was her nosy neighbor, Erma Livengood, who lived to hear the sounds of violence and express sympathy and offer help, words that to Lilah rang as phony as a menthol cigarette.

"You want I should call the sheriff, Lilah?"

"No, Erma. Please don't. I'll be fine."

Her planning for the demise of Patrick Hanrahan began that night while he was getting sloshed at the Triple Aces bar.

***

In the end, it happened easily enough. Took four months, but Lilah became a regular at the shooting range, gaining enough experience with Patrick's rifle to be able to defend herself.

One early Sunday morning when she'd locked him out and her eyes were still black from the latest beating, he began pounding on the door and bellowing her name like he was Stanley Kowalski and she was Stella.

"Go sleep it off elsewhere, fuckhead."

"You're gonna pay for that, Lilah."

Patrick Hanrahan used his elbow to break a pane of glass in the door, reached in and unlocked it. When he stepped through, he faced square to his own rifle.

"You gonna put that down before you hurt yourself, Lilah. And . . ." The comical look on his face as she blasted him in the chest was worth whatever she might face.

***

"So what happened, Lilah?"

"Nothing, child. The sheriff was glad to be rid of Patrick Hanrahan. Self-defense. End of story."

"But it wasn't, right? I mean, did you get arrested, get a trial?"

"Nothing, honey. In these parts, what I did was righteous."

I know it's time to ask the million-dollar question. I can feel the blood red blob in my stomach. It's made of lead. Same exact feeling as when Mom threw the Subway sandwich in front of me and Dad. Same as when she accused me of being a slut. Same as that horrible moment more recently when I thought Kenzie had betrayed me. Steve Prescott's face and voice suddenly pop into my thoughts. *Physical sensations are a sign of being triggered, Maya. What color do you think of when you of healing?*

I close my eyes and begin box breathing, letting my purple light soothe the blob inside my stomach. I'm not sure how long I pause, but when I feel the blob recede and open my eyes, Lilah is waiting patiently. Curiously. I'm dead sure she knows what I'm about to ask.

"You said you told Patrick, my grandfather, that it was he who sent my mother away."

Lilah looks at me sadly. And kindly.

"I didn't use those exact words, Suzie. What I said to him was 'it was your dick that sent her away.'"

Lilah comes from her side of the table to mine and grips my shoulder blade intensely.

"I'm so sorry, child."

I have nothing to say. And I'm powerless to stop the tears.

***

I stumble from the house and roam in my Mazda through back roads in King and eventually north. It's noon, and I stop at a 7-Eleven and fill up, thinking *I'll just drive and drive and drive.* Instead, my numbness keeps me glued in my seat for two hours, doing nothing but sipping water and zoning out, a local rock station blaring. The store clerk comes out at one point, walking to my car with intent. But something about my look scares him right back inside. Good thing for him. Definitely would have been recipient of "fight-or-flight." And it wouldn't have been flight.

Ultimately, I decide to simply drive back to where I'm staying. The candy red Kia Sportage in the driveway brings me to tears again. She's early.

Kenzie bursts through the front door of her grandmother's house upon hearing my car and grabs me for a fierce hug, pinning my arms at my sides. Her gym work is paying off. She notices I'm not responding and finally looks in my face.

"What's wrong, love?"

All I can do is hang on.

***

Kenzie's grandfather, John Clodfelter, is as old school North Carolina as it gets, a tobacco farmer turned tobacco exec whose buyout amid the shrinking of the industry allowed him to get out early and live more comfortably than he ever imagined. He stayed home for a full year figuring out what he wanted to do with his life before settling on creating a non-profit to raise money for early childhood education and parenting support programs. He left the business end to the experts and focused on fundraising, using his 40 years of tobacco connections.

An angular 6-foot-3 giant with a shock of white hair, he is beloved in his community and a fixture at town landmarks such as Snappy Lunch and the Mount Airy Museum of Regional History, the latter at which he serves as a weekly volunteer. If there's a word townspeople use to describe him, it's "kindly."

When Kenzie reached out to him about putting up a friend of hers in need, he didn't hesitate. At least not once he cleared it with Kenzie's grandmother, Anna, his wife of 41 years. Suzie had been at the house for three weeks the afternoon she came inside a teary mess, Kenzie protectively holding her. When Kenzie finally let her go, to get her some ice water, John guided her to his study, a paneled room filled with shelves of books. He got her into his cushy recliner and gathered a wrap usually used by Anna when they sat in the room to simply be present with each other. Suzie took it, showing her gratitude with her eyes and wrapping it tightly around.

Kenzie returned with the water, but John touched her shoulder to stop her when she began to go inside. He spoke in a whisper, so that Suzie couldn't hear.

"Do me this favor, Kenzie. Your friend knows you're here. She knows how much you support her. She knows how much you love her."

Kenzie started to answer but John held up his hand.

"Hush, Kenzie. Let me just sit with her a while. Sometimes, a person needs new perspective, a safe older person. Whatever she's going through, you're not going to lose her over this. You'll have to trust me."

Kenzie did trust her grandpa, but she so wanted to hold Suzie. Something very bad had happened to her today and she wanted to find out. To be there for her.

"You'll call me in? When she's ready."

"Of course I will, honey. Go help your grandma. Help her whip up a batch of her brownies. I don't know a person who's grieving who's ever turned down your grandma's warm cherry brownies."

Kenzie nodded.

"And tell your grandmother I'm doing some horse whispering."

"What?"

"Don't worry about it. Just an expression that shows hold old I am. Relax. Things are going to be fine."

***

I appreciate the chance to simply chill. I can't help it but I find myself rocking in the blanket, and I know John is watching me, but he's not pushing it. And I'm glad he made Kenzie wait outside. I'll always love her for how she wouldn't let us go. Tracking down Billie was genius. I hadn't told her that much about my job or Billie, but she instinctively knew. And then getting Billie to contact me and be the intermediary. I was wrong about Kenzie. Why would I think she would hurt me?

I feel the tears coming again.

I'm too used to being hurt. *"Too used to being hurt."* My mutter catches John's ear.

"It's not fun to hurt."

"No."

"Anna and I have enjoyed having you here, young lady."

"I appreciate you taking me in."

"Do you mind if I show you my age?"

"What do you mean?"

"It seems to me you're in deep pain right now. I don't know what about, and it's not for me to know. I suspect it's something traumatic to you."

I'm frozen listening to him. He is such a nice person. I already love him and Anna. I know how much they love Kenzie. It's something so foreign to me. I take a deep breath before I start to rock again. John notices. He's intensely present. Reminds me of Steve.

"Suzie, I'd like to share something. When I was a boy here, I lost my twin brother at age 9. Andrew. We were climbing over yonder in the mountains, off trail, just having fun. We were athletic and it was what kids did. No one thought twice. He missed a step. I heard a snap and a cry, then a scream. And just like that he was gone. I couldn't do a thing."

"It's not anything like that for me, John. I appreciate your sharing, and I'm sorry about your brother, but…"

John holds up his big hand asking me to wait. He sits next to me.

"We don't get to go back in time, young lady. I'm 74 and have lived with my brother's death for 65 years. I couldn't change what it meant. I watched over the next few years as my parents blamed each other. The house seemed to be either completely silent or filled with bitter accusations. They wound up divorcing when I was 12. I couldn't do anything about that, either.

"What I decided, in time, as I got confronted my own grief, was to focus on me. Being a better person, rising above. Wasn't easy. But Andrew is part of me, the part that wanted me to rise above. I know you're an amazing person, Suzie. I know it deep in these old bones. You know why?"

I shake my head. A tear comes loose and drips down my cheek and I swipe at it.

"Because my Kenzie is an amazing person, too. And I can see how in love she is with you. Now, I know you haven't said anything, and if you're worried neither has she. It was as plain as day when she walked in with you an hour ago. I trust Kenzie. And Kenzie clearly trusts you. That's enough for me."

The tears are coming fast but I'm feeling better.

"John, can I share what I learned today? I want to trust someone."

"Thank you, honey. Of course you may share."

"My grandfather raped my mother. I'm the product. What am I supposed to do with that?"

John doesn't even take a second to think about it before responding.

"Be the best person you can be, Suzie. Be the woman who lives a righteous life with Kenzie. That's what you can do. That's a person I'd be proud to call my granddaughter-in-law."

For the second time in an hour, I bury my head in a shoulder and just let it stay there. A thought occurs amid sniffles. Steve told me it isn't always about the trauma, but *what comes next.*

My head is still on John's shoulder when Kenzie and Anna walk in carrying a plate of the most tantalizing aroma I've ever smelled.

They put the plate down on a coffee table, and we share a tight group hug. Then John asks us to step back and we reach out and simply hold hands. John puts his head down. We all follow his lead. I'm dazzled with a thought born of love. This is what family is supposed to be.

***

The wind whips from behind, causing me to shiver. I hold Lilah's hand as we walk the grassy edge of a tree line in search of the gravestone she is looking for in one of the last, remote rows of King Memorial Park cemetery. With her free hand, she suddenly points.

"Over there, three stones in."

We walk over, Lilah a little unsteady and me a little cautious. It's a damp late April day and that's how I feel after a weekend of emotional turmoil. Reconciling who I am, an inbred, born of trauma, victim of trauma, and, unfortunately I know, perpetrator of trauma. My head's been pounding all weekend, right through Kenzie's departure back to Durham. She wanted me to come with her, to see Steve again ("I know he'd see you for free, Suzie. He's got an aid fund for that."). She doesn't know about my cash stash or my past yet, and the fact that I have to tell her weighs on me. She knows about my pain; she doesn't know what I've done in my life. Other than to that stupid journalist dude.

Lilah is leaning over the gravestone, picking out some weeds that have grown in at the base. It's a really simply stone. Just his name and the years he lived.

"It wasn't like I was going to give him some great tribute. He made my life hell. Drove away your mother."

"Why'd you stay, Lilah?"

For two full minutes, all I can hear is the wind rustling the leaves above us. I feel a shiver along my neck and it runs right down to my spine. I should have taken a jacket at this higher altitude. But the shiver wasn't about cold.

"I've wondered that very often myself, child. I guess what it comes down to was I didn't have the strength, the guts, to leave."

I nod to her. I get it. I so wanted to leave with Dad. Just the thought rips me apart again. *He wasn't my biological father.* I hate being a fountain of fucking tears. The image of John Clodfelter's warm face and soothing words suddenly pops into my head, and in that instant I realize something profound about Tony Marino. *You always were and always will be Dad.*

Lilah is watching me and waiting, giving me space. She's a decent person.

She looks at me and nods, then reaches into her shopping bag, one of the re-usable kinds they give out. Lilah must have had three dozen of them lying around her house. Holding the bag over one arm, she uses a hand to grab my arm while removing an envelope inside the bag with her other hand.

"Come, let's do a service."

"Uh, Lilah, I'm not feeling in the service mode here."

"Please trust me."

With that, we stand at the foot of his stone, both looking at it. The sky above us is still gray, the wind still whipping. Not a soul is in site, and even though it's midday, no sounds reach us from Old Highway 52 a quarter mile away or the access road we took to get to this area of the cemetery.

Lilah begins.

"Forgive me father, for I have sinned. I took this man on my timeline and not yours. I know that. And I don't expect to gain any just reward for doing it. My granddaughter is with me, and it so happens she is also my and … oh, dammit, I have no idea how to say this … my late husband was both her grandfather and her father, and he sinned in that way and he sinned in many more ways, hurting those who were his kin. Causing a lot of pain to others."

"Amen." I mutter loud enough for Lilah to hear, but she doesn't turn her gaze from the stone.

"I'm here to begin making things right, and I'm grateful, father, that maybe you have allowed me to stand witness to your creative powers with this beautiful young woman with me today who's had so much grief, who only now knows her past.

"Amen again, Lilah."

She squeezes my hand. With intensity.

"Patrick Hanrahan, you did not succeed in completely ruining those around you, try as you might. Although I have not ever tried to profit off of what I done, I want you to be witness to this act of cleansing you from the pain you've given out in life and even in death."

With that she unclasps the 8-by-11 manila envelope and pulls out a single sheet of paper. It's some kind of document.

"Twenty two years ago, Patrick, I took out a decent size life insurance policy. When you died, I collected on that policy."

Lilah turns to me holding the paper and looks me in the eye.

"Well, Suzie, with the blessings of the sheriff and his nephew—he's a financial advisor, and, you know, he invested it —I now pass this account to you. I've only ever taken from it what I needed to survive. Which you know seeing my place isn't much."

She thrusts it into my hand and I can't help but peek at the number at the bottom.

$923,478.

My mouth must have been hanging open, because Lilah leans over and gets on her tiptoes to whisper in my ear.

"Interest, honey."

"This can't be mine, Lilah."

"Oh, but it is, Suzie. I ain't lying. I always prayed one day God would let me find you or let you find me. Look at what it says there."

I follow her leathery forefinger to the name on the account: *Lilah Hanrahan, in trust for child of Kiely Hanrahan.*

"Now help me to the car and let's get back to the house, child. It's freezing out here!"

Steve and Suzie

I WALK INTO HAVANA NIGHTS AND IT'S GOT A buzz about it on this first Tuesday of November, opening night of the World Series. The Tampa Bay Rays have made the series against the Atlanta Braves, pitting the Bulls' major league affiliate against the team many have adopted as their own in North Carolina. Randy Culbertson is on the Rays roster. He was called up in late August as a reliever and became a key set-up man in the pen. He'd occasionally called in the months since our work together, and earlier today I'd gotten an email from him, thanking me for listening, being a sounding board and never criticizing him for poor choices.

I'm not drinking at all, and I'm finding I never needed it in the first place, Steve. I'm sorry you never got this opportunity, but know that your wisdom allows me to be who I am today and I will forever be grateful to you for that.

As I move into the restaurant, I see some familiar faces from the Bulls organization, including players who stick around Durham in the off-season. Not only is the restaurant jamming at 7:30, but the bar and the high-top tables are full, as are the six booths behind them.

In one of the far booths, I notice the familiar face of Enrique, elegantly coiffed, his black hair showing more than a hint of gray at the sideburns. The gray reminds me of me. I acknowledge his wave and make my way over.

"Great idea, Enrique. This should be fun."

"Bunch of folks from the Bulls here for the game."

"Don't blame them. You know some of them, don't you?"

"Sure, sure. They are grateful for the discount I offer to the organization."

"And maybe they're also happy for a member of the family, Enrique?"

"Perhaps, Steve."

My eyes wander around the room, and I'm again struck by the diversity of the crowd at Havana Nights. I'm proud of Enrique for establishing this as such a melting pot gathering place. I see a couple of young athletic guys who I recognize as Bulls at the bar, happily engaging with a strawberry blonde at the next stool. Enrique calls over a server to order us some a couple of beers. He's been wanting to get together to try a new Mexican lager by one of the city's microbreweries, Ponysaurus.

"Two Inauthenticos, please, Raven. And please say hello to my good friend Steve Prescott. He's a former Bull, too."

Raven was a multi-pierced brunette with a beautiful smile and warm way about her, evident even before she spoke.

"Great to meet you. Enrique has been talking about you ever since I started here months ago. Let me go get you those beers."

I look at Enrique and see a twinkle in his eye.

"Okay, I'll bite, my friend. Why do you think she needs therapy?"

"Actually, Steve, she doesn't need therapy. But I wanted you to know her for a different reason."

I raise an eyebrow.

"And that is?"

"I had the opportunity to meet her mother, who came in with her the day she applied. Raven is a wonderful young woman. She and her mom lost Raven's father to cancer some years ago, and her mother has had some poor, violent relationships since then."

"I see. Grief counseling, anxiety?"

"Not exactly."

We're interrupted as Raven returns with our Inauthenticos. She waits as I take a sip.

"Wow. This is perfect. Good call, Enrique. And thanks, Raven."

She winks at Enrique and turns back toward the bar, only to have her arm yanked by a man at a high-top. Enrique stiffens, but Raven gracefully turns toward the man, leans down to speak to him and briefly puts her hand on his shoulder to acknowledge his request.

"That's what I mean, Steve, Raven is the best."

"It's not easy finding good servers."

"I'm grateful for anyone I can find. I was starting to tell you I don't think Raven needs counseling. Nor her mother. But her mom is a delightful woman, and Raven and I were talking and . . ."

"You want to set me up?"

Enrique shrugs. "Maybe. Chat with Raven tonight. She's crazy about her mom."

A shadow crosses the table and suddenly Kenzie is standing next to us.

"Hello, guys! Can I join you?"

She slides in next to Enrique without waiting.

I can't help but notice her old glow is back. She's happy. School is going well for her, and she's taken to popping into my office during my lunch hour quizzing me about principals of counseling theories while I gobble a Giuseppe's sub.

"I didn't know you were interested in the World Series, Kenzie. Caught up on schoolwork?"

"I am, boss. And, like you say, self care, right?"

Enrique is grinning widely.

"What is it you, two? What am I missing here?"

Kenzie takes a small envelope out of her purse and pushes it across the table to me.

"This is for you, Steve. I wanted to hand-deliver it because it's not work-related. Go ahead and open it. I see a friend at the bar. Be right back."

She jumps up so quickly that she catches the underside of the table with her knee, simultaneously saying "ow" and putting her hand out to steady her water, which was precariously near the edge of the table and tipping from the impact. Harm avoided, she ducks out with a quick "sorry."

"If I didn't know her better, Enrique, I'd worry about that one's energy."

He smiles and nods at the envelope.

I slip my finger under the seal, pop it open and remove the card:

KENZIE AGUILERA AND SUZIE MARINO
ARE PLEASED TO ANNOUNCE
THEIR ENGAGEMENT ON
OCT. 18, 2022

I grin aimlessly—the kind of wide-mouthed gaping look that would earn a sucker punch from my old teammates just because—and stand up to look around the room to search for Kenzie. Enrique gets up next to me, puts his arm around my shoulder and points me toward the bar, where Kenzie's back is to me. She's standing behind, her arm draped over and laughing with, the strawberry blonde next to the two Durham Bulls.

"Suzie." I say it softly, and Enrique pulls me into a hug and whispers in my ear.

"I knew those two had it for each other the first time I saw them in here."

As if on cue, Kenzie looks over and spots the two of us in embrace, taps Suzie and they both look at us. Suzie catches my eye, then ducks her head. Shyly. She grabs her beer and they make their way to us.

***

After the hugs and congratulations, I find myself surreptitiously staring at Suzie.

Which of course she immediately picks up on.

"What are you staring at?"

"I guess the 'undisguised' version of yourself."

"Yeah, well, this is me."

Kenzie squeezes her tightly. They're already all but sitting in each other's laps.

"How did you find each other again after you left, Suzie?"

"That was all Kenzie. She tracked me down within a couple of days and then wouldn't let go."

Kenzie picked up the thread.

"Remember, Steve, how you once told me it's hard for people to let go of something, especially when they know they're right?"

I nod.

"In this case, I knew I'd done nothing wrong, but Suzie didn't know that. I had to let her know."

"It seems to me that I also noted in that conversation, Kenzie, the saying 'Do you want to be right or do you want to be happy?'"

"Exactly! Well, I was right and I wanted us to be happy."

I can't argue with logic like that, even if wasn't the point of the saying.

Suzie speaks up. "Here's the thing, Steve. I've been wrong too much in life. I'm fucking tired of being wrong. Kenzie was one thing I knew was right in my life, yet I chose to believe the worst. Until I didn't. Had to rid myself of the old negative thoughts. I think one of my counselors taught me that."

I smile at her playfulness and confidence.

"Is that why you changed your last name?"

"Yes, I decided it was time to have a name of someone I honestly loved, the only person I could ever call Father. It turns out Tony wasn't my biological father, Steve. I had to work that out. Still working that out, actually. But thanks to Kenzie—and her family—I'm okay for now." Kenzie squeezes her shoulder and kisses her check. "I may even come back for some more sessions, Steve."

I nod to her as I feel my emotions welling. Once in a great while, counselors get to visibly see and audibly hear growth. "I'd be honored to see you again. And by the way, I have a certain piece of jewelry you might like back."

Suzie smiles. "Kenzie told me you got my envelope. But you know what, Steve? I think I want to let that Buffalo nickel necklace stay with you."

She taps her heart. "He's in here. That's what I know."

"Fine by me, Maya . . . I mean, Suzie. Sorry. Habit. And you ever decide you want it back, just give me a buzz."

Enrique orders champagne for the table, Raven pours it and we clink glasses. The bar is even louder as the game gets started, but we tune it out.

"Oh, hey, Enrique, I brought this for you."

Suzie removes a jar of salsa from her bag.

Enrique holds it up, smiling. "Is she willing?"

"She is. But she says you have to do right with any profits."

I'm confused. "What's this about?" I ask.

Kenzie jumps in. "Suzie's grandmother makes all kinds of homegrown stuff. She'd given me some and when I came to ask for Enrique's help, I gave him the jar and he loved it."

"Wait a minute, you've known about these two, Enrique? For how long?"

He shrugs.

"*Lo siento, mi amigo.* I was bound to secrecy."

"So what, now you're going to be in business with Suzie's grandmom?"

"No, she is sharing her recipe, I'm going to use it as a product and, as Suzie says, we're going to do some good with this. What do you think about proceeds going to domestic violence shelters, young lady?"

"My grandmother would like that."

***

Two hours later, I'm in a state of pleasant exhaustion. Kenzie and Suzie have tag-teamed in telling the story of Suzie's past, her discovery that she had a grandmother in King and the proximity to Mount Airy. Which just happens to be one of those *noncoincidence* coincidences. It turns out my admin had found Suzie long before I'd tried to give her a clue in the office that day—and persuaded her to stay with her grandparents, a connection that allowed Suzie to, for the first time in her life, discover that family sometimes could be loving.

Seeing my admin and my client—my former client, I remind myself—in such obvious and overwhelming love is a remarkable after-the-fact reward for hope. In this state, I lean over to Enrique and whisper, "I'd be happy to meet Raven's mom."

He smiles in return, then speaks up.

"By the way, everyone, if you haven't figured it out yet, this whole night is on me."

Kenzie gets up, reaches over the table and plants a kiss on Enrique's lips.

"Thank you so much for everything, Enrique. I just knew you were the right person to arrange this tonight. But now Suzie and I are going to head out. I have class at 9 a.m."

I ask Suzie what she's planning to do next.

"You know I once dreamed of owning a bar. But Kenzie has convinced me of a better path to being there to talk to people. I'm going to college, Steve. Then grad school. I want to catch up with Kenzie. We're going to open a therapy practice together. Trauma focus. Might give you a run for your money."

"That would be awesome. There's no such thing as too many counselors in this crazy world. And hey, when the time comes, let me know if you need any financial tips or assistance. I can probably . . ."

Suzie interrupts me.

"Don't think that's gonna be needed, Steve. Not that we don't appreciate it."

Kenzie giggles. Suzie and Enrique join in.

I turn my eyebrows up at them in a "now what gives" look.

"Should we tell him?" Kenzie says to Suzie.

"Story for another day."

They both giggle again.

They exit with their arms around each other's waist. I hear their laughter and watch them kiss going through the doors. I'm struck by how different Suzie looks in her natural redheaded state and with green eyes instead of the dark. A part of me misses the intense jet-black "Maya."

Enrique breaks into my thoughts.

"One more round to take us through the end of the game?"

"Sure."

He catches Raven's eye.

"You're going to like her mother, Steve. As you can see, I know my stuff."

"Yes, you do, Enrique. And thank you. Thank you for being a true friend."

He nods and offers a fist bump. We sip our beers and turn to the game. The Rays are down a run coming up bottom of the ninth. They still have a chance.

Acknowledgments

As the author, I am indebted to and appreciate many people along the way who helped shape me—from my earliest days as a writer to my recent years as a counselor.

First, I will mention a few writing mentors who inspired me in school, journalism and beyond. Two of those figures are now gone, but I owe them deeply. My ninth grade World Literature teacher, Lawrence Dorson—"Mr. Dorson"—was the first person who ever taught me the importance of structure in writing. Osborn Elliott, my magazine writing instructor at Columbia University Graduate School of Journalism, helped me to understand the nuances of longer-form writing.

At *The Hartford Courant,* writing coach Bruce DeSilva inspired me on the subjects of voice and narrative, and the Poynter Institute and its many faculty provided depth and insight into the craft of writing. As a longtime journalist, I'd be remiss if I didn't credit my first publisher, George Riggs, with allowing me to grow on the job at the *Fontana Herald-News* and for supporting our tiny newsroom.

My decision to become a clinical mental health counselor late in life brought a wave of new mentors. These include: my former boss at the National Board for Certified Counselors, Sherry Allen; the late Sam Gladding, an inspirational force during my schooling in Wake Forest University's Department of Counseling; my internship and initial supervisor at CareNet Counseling, Ron Wachs; my former site supervisors, Deborah Morton and Jeremy Fox; CareNet's former Piedmont Triad regional manager, Barbara Saulpaugh; CareNet's former president, Bryan Hatcher, who also has written the Foreword to *Unwrapping*; Gary Gunderson, former vice president of the Division of FaithHealth at Atrium Health Wake Forest Baptist, who helped me make the transition and paved the way for the start of my counseling career; and communications guru Tom Peterson, whom I collaborated with during Division of FaithHealth work for more than a decade and whose sage marketing advice and early, enthusiastic review of *Unwrapping* gave me hope.

In writing this novel, I relied upon the assistance of several people who deserve special mention. The first and most im-portant of those is my wife, Terrie, who encouraged me from the beginning to write—and then put up with the hours I would spend tinkering, which usually meant delays in whatever plans we had for the day or evening. My former colleague at the National Board for Certified Counselors, Catherine Clifton, is one of the best line editors I know, and she offered a thorough and detailed edit of my first draft. Russell Siler Jones, director of CareNet's two-year residency program in psychotherapy and spirituality (which I completed in 2021), has been a mentor for four years. He helped me validate and navigate trauma scenes, much as his thoughtful leadership has long taught me about empathy, empowerment and spirituality for clients.

Two other people from my past I depended upon are Richard Boyd and Lou Davis. In the late aughts, Richard and I helped lead the *Winston-Salem Journal* newsroom, he on the design side and me on the news side. Richard is the kind of creative talent who can do graphic design by day, lead a country band, the bo-stevens, in the evenings and on weekends, and still be true to his love of art. He brought Maya to life on the cover. I was fortunate to work with Lou, a terrific photographer, in the Creative Communications department at Atrium Health Wake Forest Baptist for several years before he retired. He captured a sharp portrait of me on the inside cover. In addition, my friend, John Murph, took my shell of a website and has brought lesliegura.

com to life.

I am, of course, indebted to Micki Cabaniss, founder of Grateful Steps Publishing, who took a chance on this first-time author from a simple email query, and went on to help me "hear" my own story in a new way, via oral editing. Grateful Steps' copy editor, Cathy Mitchell, provided valuable insights into the story that finalized the shape of *Unwrapping*.

Finally, I humbly thank my late parents, Pete and Muriel Gura, who encouraged me to pursue and want more throughout childhood, but who also instilled the value of compassion and the concept of social justice that I've tried to live throughout my life. My father, a dry cleaner, was constantly reading—newpapers, novels, magazines. Long after his death, we discovered letters he'd written to his parents from overseas during World War II, and those letters clearly showed he had a storytelling gift. I'm grateful to have inherited that part of him.

About the Author

Unwrapping is the debut novel of Leslie Gura, who, as a journalist for newspapers in California, Connecticut and North Carolina, specialized in narrative storytelling and criminal investigations. Along the way, Gura won numerous awards, including the inaugural Taylor Family Fairness Award from the Nieman Foundation at Harvard University for his *Northeast* magazine story about a Yale instructor wrongfully accused of murder by New Haven police.

After eight years in marketing and communications, Gura went back to school, earning his degree from Wake Forest University in clinical mental health counseling, where he has made trauma a specialty. In his work as a writer and therapist, he has used narrative techniques, first to tell and most recently to discern stories.

He lives with his wife, Terrie, in Winston-Salem, North Carolina, where they enjoy cooking and shooting 9-ball, having met in a billiards hall. Their home is ruled by their calico, Taz.

www.ingramcontent.com/pod-product-compliance
Lightning Source LLC
Chambersburg PA
CBHW041311120726
48005CB00014B/1957